Thug's Passion

By

Tracy Gray

This book is a work of fiction. Names, characters, place and incidents are results of the author's imagination or are used fictitiously. Any resemblance to locations, actual events or persons, living or dead is entirely coincidental.

Precioustymes Entertainment
229 Governors Place, #138
Bear, DE 19701
www.precioustymes.com

Library of Congress Control Number: 2007924291
ISBN# 0-9776507-6-6
        978-0-9776507-6-7
Partial Editor: Laketa Lewis
Proofreader: Crystal Gamble-Nolden
Cover Design/Graphics: OCJgraphix

First Trade Paperback Edition Printing July 2007
Printed in United States

Dedication

This book is dedicated to my husband, Michael G. Caruthers and my daughter, Kacie B. Caruthers.

It is also dedicated to the memory of two very important men in my life.

Rickie B. Gray (1952 ~ 2001): No man ever created by God had a more gentle spirit than you did, Uncle Rickie. I miss your smile...your dimples. I miss your presence...your essence.

Paul Q. Caruthers (1977~ 2003): You were the first person to accept me into your family. You weren't my baby brother-in-law; you were **always** my baby brother. Marriage didn't make us family; you were blood. I miss you so much. *Nothing is the same without you*!

Acknowledgements

El Shaddai: Thank you for your many blessings, your patience and your love for me. Thank you for the revelation that my gifts are not for me, but for others. Thank you for your peace, your joy, your favor and most importantly your faithfulness. There is none like you in all the earth.

Mike: Thank you for eleven wonderful years of marriage. Thank you for your patience, and your perseverance. Thank you for the three years you hustled hard and let me live life as a stay-at-home mom. That was the time during which Thug's Passion was conceived, written, re-written, edited, submitted and accepted. It was all you, Baby. Thank you for your love, and for your dedication as a provider. Thank you for being an awesome man of God. I love you.

Kacie: Thank you for your patience. I know it's been hard sharing mommy with the computer. I know there's been a gang of times that you wanted to talk to me, hang out with me, and just have my undivided attention. Yet, that darn computer was always stealing your shine. Thank you for being mature beyond your years, and trying to understand the bigger picture. I love you, and I'm all yours now…at least for a little while (wink).

To my family: **Mom**, thank you for your constant love and support. Thank you for your hustle and for your spirit. Thank you for raising my brother and me to have our own minds and be independent people. Thank you for being my mom and my dad. Thank you for being my mom and my "girl". Thank you for laying down the law and keeping my feet on the right path. Thank you for reading in front of me. Your love of reading inspired my love of reading. Most of all, thank you for introducing me to God. I love you. **Grandmother** (Gammy), thank you for encouraging my love of reading. I'll never forget the day you surprised me with the book "Justice and Her Brothers". That book took my mind to incredible places. Thank you for all of the Judy Blume books that was given as Christmas presents. Thank you for our long talks about your life as a young woman, a young wife, and a young mother. Thank you for teaching me my family's history, so I know where I came from. I promise to pass it along. **Aunt Gloria**, thank you for being one of the few trusted people to read Thug's Passion for me and offer feedback. Thank you for your encouragement and your support. Thank you for being a confidante. I thank God for our relationship and our closeness.

To my friends: **Jackie Nichols**, thank you for your support. Girl, eight hours at your house trying to figure out how to reformat the book after pulling it off of email was a trip. Not to mention the whole "scanning episode" or the disk that wouldn't open situation. The two of us should never be left alone, we're just counter-productive. I appreciate your dedication to me and my dreams. I know we've had our ups and downs in 23 years of friendship, but I can honestly say that after it all, you are the epitome of a true friend. **Shwanda (Riley) Cross**, thank you for always talking me off the ledge. You have to be the most logical, reasonably sound friend that I have. I can always count on you to put the emotions to the side and just deal with the facts. I love that about you! Thank you for never hesitating when I told you about the book. Thank you for offering your sorority sisters (the lovely ladies of Zeta Phi Beta) as hostesses for my first book signing. You've never wavered and I appreciate that so much. **Chez Parker**, thank you for being friend enough to tell me the hard truth. I know it wasn't easy to suggest that I give up my dream of being an educator, but your words were ordained by God. I had to let go of one dream in order to pursue another. I thank you for your obedience to the Father and I thank you for your friendship. **Barbara (Hilton) Johnson, Angela David, Alma (Myers) Friar, Kimberly Cole and Darnesha Evans**, thank you guys for your excitement, support, and encouragement. Thank you all for loving me enough to celebrate me. I realize that everybody won't/can't do that.

To my lawyers: **Jeff Dillard and Brandy Brown**, thank you both so much. I know that you all were sent from God to assist me. Thank you both for working to put me in the best position possible in a business that I knew nothing about. I won't get amnesia. I won't forget.

To my "team": **LaShann (Rochelle) Bailey**, what can I say? You're my cousin, my friend, my silhouette – the other side of me. No one has worked harder with me on Thug's Passion than you. You've been there since the inception. You read every page as it was written. You advised, suggested, encouraged, directed and corrected. You believed when NOBODY else did. You're as raw as they come, and I respect that to the utmost. You didn't care about my whining, my tears, hurt feelings, bruised pride or anything. You told me what you thought and let the chips fall. You've made me better and you know you've made me stronger. When I called you for sympathy you weren't having it. You would be like, "I guess you're not hungry. Did somebody feed you? Because you used to be hungry." Thank you for the hard criticisms, the ugly truths, the bluntness, the realness, and your "take it how you wanna take it" attitude. Of course it wasn't all tough-love. Thank you for loving certain scenes. Thank you for understanding and knowing the characters in your heart the same way I do. Thank you for reading and rereading. Thank you for going with me to the Aurora bookfest where we met Kimberla Roby-Lawson (LOVE HER!). Thank you for giving up your time, and making my dream a priority in your life. You didn't have to do it. Thanks for the love, the support, and the loyalty. Thank you for seeing it through to the end. You know the deal. When I hit, you hit, Shonnie.

To my publisher: **KaShamba Williams (Precioustymes Entertainment)**, thank you for taking a chance on me and on Thug's Passion. Thank you for your guidance, your patience, your correction and your ability to pull the talent out of young writers. Thank you for your vision, and for "paying it forward" (wink). I'll do everything I can to make it worth it.

Look at what God can do with a little girl from the south side of Chicago. Watch out world, here I come!

Tracy Gray-Caruthers

Thug's Passion

by

Tracy Gray

"A Thug + Romance = Thug's Passion! What a beautiful thing. Every page was worth me turning I loved this book."
KaShamba Williams, Essence Best Selling Author of Mind Games

CHAPTER ONE

It was a busy Saturday morning at *Platinum Plus Hair and Nail Salon*. The smell of chemicals, sweet shampoo, and frying hair blended together to create the scent that was uniquely the smell of a hair salon. I bobbed my head to the sounds of the soul station as it softly filled the upscale space. I sighed to myself as I signed the check for my booth rent. I was tired of renting a chair in somebody else's place of business. I wanted a hair salon of my own as I let my eyes glance around *Platinum Plus*. It was a beautiful shop. The walls were painted a soothing color that fell between mauve and dusty rose and they were lined with oil paintings that featured outrageous hairstyles. Chrome chairs, workstations, light fixtures and accents gave the space a modern feel. The ambience made clients feel like they were coming for more than just a hair-do hook up. They were coming for a relaxing, high-end experience. It had the same feel and look that I wanted my own hair salon to have.

I tore the check from my checkbook, and walked to the office of the salon owner, Taffi Booker.

Taffi looked up as I sat the check on her desk.

"Hey Miss Hill, how are you doing today?"

"I'm fine. Thanks. How are you?"

"Blessed and highly favored."

I smiled at her religious response. My grandmother always said the exact same thing.

"Have a good day," I said, and started to leave her office.

"Miss Hill?"

I turned around as she asked, "Is something wrong?"

I briefly considered whether or not to confide in her. My first inclination was not to. Talking about your personal life in a hair salon was like calling an open forum. Anything and everything said inside the walls of the shop was open for discussion. Nothing was sacred. Taffi drummed one of her perfectly manicured nails on top of her desk as she waited for my answer. I looked her over. She was older, maybe about thirty-eight or thirty-nine, tall and slim. She had creamy, mocha colored skin. She was the type of woman who always looked dressed and prepared for a photo shoot.

She had loot to afford a luxurious lifestyle, as she should. That much was obvious. She owned three *Platinum Plus Hair and Nail Salons* in Chicago. One on the West Side, one on the far South Side, and the one I worked at, in South Shore. Taffi wasn't flamboyant and outrageous with it though. She was classy, with a capital "C".

I was just about to respond to her, confide in her with my list of troubles, when my name was called.

"Passion, are you goin' to lunch with us or what?" I heard Keena Price, another stylist, standing with Jainelle who was also a stylist there as well, blab out impatiently.

I gave Taffi a shallow smile and waved goodbye. "See you later, Taffi. My check is good."

10

"It better be," she warned, leaning back in her oversized black leather chair.

I met Keena and Jainelle by the reception area of the salon.

"What were you doin' in there with Taffi for so long?" Keena pried, with her nosy self.

"Nothin'. I was payin' my booth rent."

"So, are you goin' to lunch with us?" Jainelle waited for my answer, while removing the mauve colored smock that protected her clothing.

"Nah, I can't go. I got some errands to run."

"You ain't been to lunch with us in three days." Keena reminded me with her hands on her hips. "What's up, hoochie? We piss you off or something?"

"Nah. I just have some other things to do."

Keena looked like she wanted to discuss what my "other things to do" were. Jainelle on the other hand, was ready to leave. I could tell when she grabbed Keena by the sleeve.

"See you later, Passion. We've got clients lined up. We don't have time to waste on you if you're not coming."

I waved at them then, walked out to my car. I tried to get away from the salon expediently, before I broke down in tears. I had been doing that a lot lately. And I had my reasons. The first anniversary of the death of my boyfriend, Lorenzo was coming up. He was gunned down on a busy corner, in the middle of the day, standing beside his truck. The murderer literally blew his head off his shoulders.

Lorenzo Murdock was a man that I never wanted to love. He was a hustler, and my life had been full of tragedies concerning hustlers. My daddy was a hustler once upon a time. He was a top dog, too. A real dangerous type cat. So much so, that a lot of people felt my daddy was better off dead. Unfortunately, for my daddy and me, when these individuals couldn't accomplish their goal of killing him, they took the second best from us, my momma. They laid her to rest, just like Lorenzo, except her head wasn't blown off. Momma was sitting at a red light, minding her own business, when BOOM, in the blink of an eye a bullet took her life. I was nine years old when it happened. My daddy stopped hustling right after that. He was fearful that I would be the next victim, so he moved us down to Dallas, Texas. We stayed there for five years, but the call of Chi-town drew him back.

I met Lorenzo when I was a freshman in high school and he was a senior. Initially, Lorenzo was different to me than other guys. I would see him in the hallways at school, and he was...cocky, off the chain. Him and his boys were always doing some wild stuff, like pulling fire alarms, or setting off the sprinkler system. It was his wild and crazy behavior that drew me, except I wanted it to stay away from me. That didn't happen. That would've been too much like right. I pulled back from him, but my disinterest seemed to intrigue him more. The harder I tried to stay away from him, the harder he pursued me. I stood my ground at first, refusing to holla at him if he couldn't stop wilding out so much. I came up with every excuse not to be with him, but of course, like any good thug, Lorenzo was persistent. He decided that he was gonna have me, and he wasn't gonna stop until I was his. To win me over, he showed me another side of himself when we were together. The calm side; the side that occasionally chilled, and I decided to become his girl... The hustler's wife.

In spite of what I wanted, he brought me into his world real quick, not realizing that the life of a hustler wasn't something new to me. In actuality, I was all too familiar with how hustlers got down. The game knew me by name. Balling, the paper chase, everything about that world came back to me real fast. The game wasn't that different from when my daddy was in it.

At first, Lorenzo thought I was just a quick-study. But when he found out that my daddy was the legend he had been hearing about for years, he acted like he hit the lotto.

"Your pops? Hell yeah! That's what's up!" He was all excited when he learned my father's identity.

I hated being back in that life. I didn't want any parts of the drug culture. Everything about it was a painful memory to me. Everything about it reminded me of my mother and of her death. I would try to explain it to Lorenzo, but he wasn't trying to understand. He was too caught up. Besides, his father was a dope fiend, who died in the game, too. In his mind, death was death. He felt like if he could get over his father's death and hustle the same thing that killed him, I could surely get over my mother's death and move on.

It wasn't that easy for me.

One of the hardest things about Lorenzo's death for me was that I was pissed off at him when he died. I tried for months to get him to leave the game. I begged and pleaded with him to move us down to Dallas, so we could make a new life for ourselves. But no, he was adamant about staying in Chicago.

After high school, I went to beauty school and got my license. I told him I could open a salon in Texas, my own salon, and he could manage it. But that was a no-go. He wasn't interested. To him, money in a legitimate business couldn't compare to the money he made on the block. The warning signs were evident: he was on the fast track. Old heads were comparing him to my daddy. No way was he blowing the spot when he was at the top of his game.

The morning Lorenzo died, I wouldn't answer my cell phone and he was blowing me up. I was pissed off at him and didn't feel like arguing with him, because arguments were all our conversations amounted to. It was at the point where all we did was screamed at each other. I was sick of the madness and I was sick of fighting with him. It wasn't like he was trying to change, because he wasn't. He was still bringing guns and work into our home. He was still rolling in at 6:00 and 7:00 in the morning, letting the sun beat him to the crib. We were still going for days without really talking to each other, unless we were arguing. I felt like he was choosing the hustle over me.

I knew that not answering my cell phone would make Lorenzo angry. Hustlers have a thing about not being able to get in touch with their women. It drives them crazy. And that was Lorenzo. If he couldn't get in touch with me, he assumed that I was out hoe-hopping. I knew he was gonna act an ass when he caught up with me, but I didn't care. I kept letting his calls go straight to voicemail.

When I heard yelling, and somebody started ringing my doorbell like they were crazy, I didn't know what was going on. I swung the door open, and got ready to go to battle. However, there was no drama at my door; it was Lorenzo's guy, Jinx Waters. Jinx was a muscular, attractive go-getting guy that helped Lorenzo control the streets. I knew something had to be

14

wrong, because first of all, Jinx's skin was flushed. I'd never seen him look like that. Secondly, he was out of breath, like he was having an asthma attack, or short-winded. My stomach tightened, and my body stiffened. I knew he was about to deliver bad news. I could sense it. I held up my hand to stop him. I wasn't ready to hear whatever he was about to say. What I really wanted to do was take a sip of Hennessey or smoke some green to calm my nerves. I needed to mellow the hell out, but Jinx wouldn't let me do things my way. Nah, he just had to go running off at the mouth.

"We gotta slide. Somebody just shot Lay-Law."

Lay-Law was what everybody, except for me, called Lorenzo.

I looked into Jinx's bloodshot eyes. "Is he dead?" From my experience, that was really the only question I needed to have answered.

"Yo, get your shoes, purse, whatever the hell you need," he said, more forcefully, evading my question. "We gotta blow. I don't know who the hell shot him. They could be on their way over here. You wanna be next?" He was pacing back and forth from the front door to the window.

I did what Jinx told me to. I slipped on my Nine West mules, grabbed my Gucci shades and my Coach bag and left the apartment. He practically shoved me into the passenger's seat of his Ford Expedition.

"Where we goin'?" I called myself trying to remain calm.

"I'm takin' you to your father's spot. That's where Lay-Law would want you to chill until everything goes down."

We were stopped at a red light, and even

though Jinx's windows were tinted, I didn't feel safe. I wanted to hurry up and get to my daddy's house. I wanted to feel the reassurance of his strong arms wrapped around me, protecting me, and comforting me. The same way he did when he had to give me the news that my mother was in heaven.

"Is Lorenzo dead?" I asked, even though I felt in my heart that he was from the silence of that question.

"Baby Girl, I hate to be the one to tell you this, but they peeled his cap. Lorenzo is gone. Closed casket on this one, baby."

I didn't say anything for a minute; didn't even cry. I sat emotionless.

Finally I spoke. "Where is he?"

Jinx shrugged his broad shoulders, "Probably at the hospital or the morgue, one."

"You think they'll let me see him?" The reality was I needed to see him to believe he was gone.

"I don't think you wanna see him. It was ill how they left him."

That was when he told me that Lorenzo's head was basically blown off. The thought of my man being left dead and headless in the street made me nauseous. My stomach started to churn.

"I need to get out," I murmured, ready to vomit.

"What?" Jinx watched me, puzzled.

"I need to get out. You gotta pull over. I need to get out." I stressed.

"I'll let you out as soon as we get there."

"Nah, I need to get out now. I gotta throw up."

I don't remember anything else about that day. I don't remember anything after getting out of Jinx's truck and puking my brains out on the shoulder of I-57 while traffic whizzed by me.

I do remember the funeral, though, as if it were yesterday. I remember sitting on the second pew, next to Jinx and crying until my eyes literally burned. I remember blowing my nose so much that it bled. I remember feeling numb when I packed up all of Lorenzo's belongings. I remember wishing that whoever murdered him had killed me, too. I was a street widow at the age of 22! Instead of being the hustler's wife I was now a hustler's widow.

The only good thing to come out of Lorenzo's death was my friendship with Jinx. He stepped up and looked out for me after Lorenzo was murdered. Jinx made sure that I had everything I needed. It was Jinx who went to the car dealership with me and negotiated the deal on my BMW. It was Jinx who helped me find my condo. And it was Jinx who hooked me up with Taffi when I needed a job. Taffi's husband was his uncle, so he put in a good word for me. Jinx became the older brother I never had.

I reached into the glove compartment of my car, and pulled out some tissue. I wiped my eyes and blew my nose. I glanced over at my clock. It was almost time for me to get back to the salon. I closed my eyes for a minute and tried to put my mind on more pleasant thoughts. If I went back into the salon with a tear-stained face, everybody would have a question. Everybody would be all up in my business, and I couldn't handle that. Not today. I needed to keep Passion's business to Passion.

CHAPTER TWO

The salon was still buzzing when I finished with my last client around 8:30 that night. Music from the soul station was coming through the wall speakers, and customers were still discussing the latest gossip with their stylist. I looked over at Jainelle's work station. She was sitting in her styling chair, leafing through *Black Hair Now* magazine, waiting on me to give her a ride home. She didn't have her own car, and she lived about three bus lines away from the salon. I swept up the loose hair from around my work station, and put the broom away. I walked over to her station, as she put the magazine down and stood up.

"I wanna get my hair cut," she said, looking at herself critically in the mirror.

"No, you don't."

"You gonna come in early tomorrow and cut it for me?" She ignored my comment.

I lifted a few strands of her long, soft hair. "Jai, I don't wanna cut your hair. I like it this length. It frames your face perfectly."

She placed her hands on her slim hips. "Are you

gonna cut it or not, Heifer?"

"Let me think about it." I knew that if I didn't agree to cut it, she would just get another stylist to do it. I didn't want to see her hair jacked up. "You ready? I'm try'na bounce."

"I'm ready," she said, and grabbed her bag.

Both of us waved at Kimberly, the receptionist, as we exited the salon.

"So, what's up with Keena? Why she ain't wait on me?" I asked as we walked to my whip.

Jainelle shrugged her shoulders. "Girl, she messin' with some new cat, and he wanted to see her tonight."

"I thought she was serious with what's his name, 'Psychotic'."

Jainelle laughed. "You're stupid. His name is Lunatic."

"Whatever." I shrugged, and hit the remote to unlock my car.

"She *is* messin' with Lunatic. She's messin' with this new guy, too."

"He a baller?" I knew he was. Keena only messed with ballers.

"You know he is," Jainelle admitted, sliding into the delicate lushness of my leather interior.

I slid into the driver's seat. "One of those ballers is gonna end up killin' her. She better cool out cheatin' on them."

Jainelle closed her eyes, and moaned. "Girl, I love your car."

"Thanks."

"You are so lucky," she said, not knowing all of the bullshit I'd been through. "I wish a brotha *would* hit me off with a fly ass whip like this."

19

She didn't know how I got the oxford green metallic BMW 330xi. She assumed Lorenzo bought it for me, but that wasn't the truth.

The truth of the matter was after Lorenzo's funeral, his family swarmed down on our apartment like vultures. His momma was the co-signer on all of his bank accounts. She took all the money, and bounced. I haven't seen her since the funeral. Other members of his family took the furniture; his clothes; and his whips. They didn't leave me with nothing.

Nothing but the stuff that they didn't know about and the only thing that his greedy ass momma didn't know about was the safe in our bedroom. It contained $105,000.00 in small bills.

Even though Lorenzo and I weren't legally married, I was recognized around the way as his wife. As his wife, I should've been looked out for after his death. Since he didn't take the necessary measures to see to it that I was; I took care of it myself.

Jainelle knew very little about my life with Lorenzo. She had no idea that he wouldn't let me have a car while we were together. That was his way of keeping me dependent on him. After he died, the first thing I bought for myself was a car. The second thing I bought was my condo. Once those two purchases were made, the $105,000.00 was gone. Two weeks after I closed on my condo, I rented a styling chair at *Platinum Plus*.

"I don't feel like goin' home yet. You wanna hang out? Get a drink or something?" Jainelle suggested.

I was tired. All I really wanted to do was go home, sit on my couch, and try not to think about Lorenzo. But, when I looked over at Jainelle, she had a really hopeful look on her face.

"Okay," I agreed. "But I'm not tryin' to be out here all night, Jai. I have a 9:00 appointment in the morning."

"So, what you sayin'? I have a 9:30 appointment. We won't be out long. One drink, that's all."

"One drink, Jai? Whatever."

She grinned at me. "I got you."

"Where you wanna go?"

"Ripple's Red Room."

* * * * *

Ripple's Red Room was on the other side of town. It was a neighborhood lounge where everybody was a regular. The name of the spot fit the décor perfectly. Almost everything in Ripple's was red. The walls, the bar stools, almost everything. A lot of hustlers hung out there, so I wasn't surprised that was where she wanted to go. She had just broken up with her last guy, and was looking for somebody to help her with her come up. The two of us sat down at the bar.

"There's some cuties in here, tonight," she said, looking around.

I didn't care how cute a dude was, if hustling was how he made his living, I wasn't interested. I was looking for a white-collar guy. Somebody who wore suits and ties to work and smelled like Clinique's Happy For Men. A man that worked in an office, and got a paycheck. Ballers had given me enough pain and heartache. There wasn't a material possession in the world that could make me go that route again.

The bartender walked over to us. "What can I get you?"

"Pineapple juice and Malibu rum," I requested.

"Amaretto sour," Jainelle ordered.

I reached into my purse to get my wallet. When I looked up, a dude was approaching us. He was a hustler. I could tell by the way he was dressed, and by the way he carried himself.

"What the deal?" He asked us.

He was tall, the color of chocolate, bald headed with gold fronts.

"What's up?" Jainelle replied, reaching for her drink from the bartender.

I didn't say anything.

"I ain't never seen you in here. You from around this way?" He shamelessly questioned Jainelle.

"Nah, I don't stay out this way."

Again, I didn't respond to dude's question.

"So, what's your name?" He was looking at me when he asked, but then he turned his attention to Jainelle when I didn't answer.

She kept talking to him. I was paying major attention to my drink, minding my own business.

"Jainelle," she answered too eagerly, which caused him to turn back to me.

"What's your name, baby? Damn, you all into that drink. Slow down, I'll buy you another one," he offered, like I was a busted chick or something.

"No thanks." I didn't want or need his attention.

"Ay, I already asked you twice what your name is. You keep ignoring me. What's your name, ma?"

"Passion," I said, and waited for the stupid remark that I knew was coming.

My parents were really wrong for sticking me with the name Passion. I couldn't go anywhere without somebody commenting on it. Not to mention that being named "Passion" seemed to automatically make men think I was some kind of regular hoe.

I downed my drink as he watched my every move.

"So Passion, do you taste like fruit?"

I knew he thought he was being clever, with his whack ass. "You know what? I've never licked myself, so I can't answer that question."

"What's your name?" Jainelle interjected, taking his attention off of me and putting it back on her.

"Busy. Everybody calls me Busy."

I looked down at my watch. It was after 10:00. I glanced over at the clown. He was grinning in Jainelle's face, and getting comfortable on the barstool next to hers. He wasn't going away any time soon. I pretended to hold back a yawn.

"Uh, Jainelle, you ready to ride? Girl, I'm exhausted."

She nodded then, gave the clown a bright smile. "It was nice meetin' you, Busy."

"Word. Maybe I'll see you around sometime," he responded happily.

"Maybe you will," Jainelle winked, flirting with him.

"Later Passion."

"Later," I barely mumbled.

When we got out to the car, I looked over at her. "Why were you flirtin' with dude?"

"Why not? He was...cute."

I put my car in gear. "No, he wasn't." I shook my head, "Especially with those teeth."

"What's wrong with gold teeth? Mack has gold teeth." Mack was her ex-boyfriend.

"Jai, I hate to be the one to tell you this, but Mack wasn't cute either."

Her mouth fell open.

I laughed. "Close your mouth, girl."

She shut it.

"Are you serious? You never thought Mack was cute?"

Now, how in the hell could I think somebody with acne, gold fronts, and crossed eyes was cute? What was wrong with her?

"Did you really think Mack was cute?"

She thought about it for a minute. "Well, the more dough he spent on me, the cuter he got."

"Gold digger," I joked.

"Whatever," she said waving me off. "What's been wrong with you lately? How come you ain't been goin' to lunch with me and Keena? You know she been doggin' you."

"You know my last boyfriend, the one I told you about?"

"The one who got shot?"

"Yeah," I said nodding. "He died around this time last year. It'll be a year this Sunday."

"Word? I am so sorry. I didn't know."

"Sometimes, I need to be alone. You know, to think."

She sucked her teeth. "I'ma tell Keena to shut her hatin' self up the next time she starts talkin' garbage about you."

Jainelle and Keena were both cool with me. I met them the first day that I started working at *Platinum Plus*. For whatever reason, I just clicked better with Jainelle. Maybe deep down inside I knew Keena was a shit-starter.

"What'd she say?"

She looked over at me. I could tell that she didn't wanna tell me. Jainelle didn't wanna be

24

responsible for starting a beef between me and Keena.

"What did she say?" I asked again.

"She thinks you're gettin' too close to Taffi."

"Too close to Taffi? What does that mean? I don't really even talk to Taffi. I don't even really know her. All I know is that she makes sure to cash my booth check two days after I give it to her."

She sucked her teeth. "Man."

"What's wrong with you?"

"I shoulda given old boy my telephone number, that's what."

"For what? Dude was a loser. You better step your game up."

"You don't know that. You're only sayin' it because you got something against ballers." She cut her eyes at me. "I don't know how you do it, Passion. You've been single for a year. I ain't cut like that. I need a man. Girl, how do you go without sex?"

I chuckled. "Girl, I keep my mind on runnin' my business. Plus, I'm still tryin' to get over Lorenzo."

"It's been a year, and you still ain't over him?"

"Nope, not yet. It's not that easy to get over somebody you were with for three years."

"That must have been some serious love."

"It was what it was," I mumbled.

I didn't tell her that I was never head over heels in love with Lorenzo; death just affected me really deeply. Loss was something I had a hard time dealing with. And with Lorenzo, there were so many things that I never got to say to him. There were so many problems that we never worked out. That was probably the biggest reason why it was so hard for me to move on. I didn't have closure.

We were both quiet.

I dropped her off in front of her house, and made my way home. As I walked into my condo, my cell phone started ringing.

"Hello?"

"What's up, Baby Girl?" It was Jinx.

"Hey Jinx. What's up?"

"Nothin'. Where have you been? I called your crib like three times. You ain't been there."

"Why didn't you call my cell?"

"I don't know. Where were you?"

"I went out after work with Jainelle. We went to Ripple's Red Room."

"What are you doin' at Ripple's? You know that place ain't for you."

"I know. That was some of Jainelle's stuff. You know she's single now. She's lookin' for a brotha to help her get back on top."

Jainelle had a crush on Jinx. She had asked me a time or two about him when he came into the salon. I didn't blame her, though. Jinx was a handsome guy. He had the cutest baby face, and warmest dark brown eyes with the longest eyelashes. When he smiled, you could see dimples deep enough to skinny dip in. And he was built. The boy had mad body. He had broad shoulders, big arms, and thick legs. He was smart and self sufficient, too. He wasn't just street smart; he was book smart. He owned his own business. After Lorenzo died, he got out of the game. He took his drug money, and invested in an auto body shop. The body shop was very successful. But the most important thing in my book was that he wasn't a baller anymore. He definitely would've been a step-up from anybody Jainelle ever dated.

"Jinx, what do you think about Jainelle? You

think she's pretty?"

He chuckled.

I could picture him shaking his head, even though I couldn't see him.

"Yeah, she gotta pretty face, but she ain't my type. And I ain't a hustler, so I ain't her type."

"I don't know. She's always askin' about you."

"Word? What does she wanna know?"

"If you're messin' with somebody. She thinks you're cute and whatnot. If you wanna holla, you know I can hook somethin' up."

"Nah, no thanks." He shut me down. "I ain't interested. All I could really do with somebody like Jainelle, is sex her. That would put you in an awkward situation. Yo, anyway, I wasn't callin' to get hooked up on no ass. I called because I'm goin' to the cemetery to see Lay-Law on Saturday. I'm tryin' to find out if you wanna roll with me.

I sighed, because the last thing I ever wanted to do was go to a cemetery. As far as I was concerned, if I never went to another cemetery in my life, it would've been too soon. But it was the anniversary of Lorenzo's death. I had to go see him to pay my respects.

"You know Saturday is my busiest day at the salon. Can we go on Sunday or Monday?"

"We'll do it Monday. I'll scoop you up at 9:30 in the morning. Be ready."

"Okay," I responded, unhappily. Just the thought of having to go the graveyard was enough to send me into a depression.

CHAPTER THREE

The next day, I got to the salon at 8:30am. I was expecting my favorite client at 9:00, and she was always prompt. Just like I knew she would, Summer Weddington walked into *Platinum Plus* at exactly 8:57. She smiled, and her pretty face lit up.

I couldn't help smiling back at her. My father used to live next door to her years ago. The two of us became cool over our backyard fences as teenagers. We weren't exactly friends, but we were cool. Summer was sort of wild and fast. She ran with a different crowd than I did. Not only did she get high, she stayed out late, and skipped school. My daddy wasn't having that. But we were cool. I liked her.

I took in her pink Burberry shirtdress and white Burberry strappy thong sandals. I shook my head. Females did not play when it came to going to the salon. Most women would floss their cutest, most eye catching outfits.

She sat her Burberry snap tote on top of my work counter. I picked it up, and put it in the drawer with my bag.

28

"So, what's really good?" she asked, as I took her hair down, and combed it out.

"Nothin', girl. What's really good with you?"

"I just came back from Miami. Have you ever been there?" she asked, admiring her pink fingernails.

"Yeah. Where you stay?"

She waved her hand dismissively. "The Best Western, but I did the damn thang."

I didn't say anything, but I was thinking that it was sad to go all the way to Miami and stay in the Best Western. There were too many upscale hotels in the Miami Beach area to go out like that. Plus, the girl was wearing a $200.00 dress, and carrying a $400.00 purse. Why would she stay at the Best Western?

"Rico took me to the Source Awards down there," she continued.

"Word? Who's Rico?"

"My newest sponsor," she joked.

She liked to call the cats that spent dough on her "sponsors". I figured that sounded better to her, than calling them her pimps.

I wasn't impressed with her trip to the Source Awards, but since I could tell that she wanted to brag about it, I played along.

"Girl, did you see anybody famous?" I coaxed, while applying relaxer to a small section of her hair.

"Girl, I saw some of everybody. I was walking through the lobby of one of the hotels, and that guy from the Diplomats grabbed my hand. You know he was trying to holla. With his fine self. What's his name?"

The only hip hop cats that I cared about were Nas and Common. I wasn't even really sure who all the Diplomats were. "I don't know. Cam'Ron?" She had me on that one. Cam'Ron was the only one I knew, and I knew him because he rolled with Mase at one time and Mase was alright in my book.

"Not him, the other guy." She waved her hands around. "Anyway girl, most of the dudes were trying to holla. I saw the group 112 down there. One of them was all in my grill. But you know Rico was blockin'. He ain't tryin' to lose all this." She gestured to her slim frame.

I smiled to myself, and kept applying relaxer.

"I'm tryin' to hook up a 'ladies only' trip back down there. Leave Rico at the crib this time. You wanna go?"

I thought about it for a few seconds. Going out of town with somebody like Summer would be a challenge. She was kind of slutty. I figured that she would probably get down to Miami and get really loose.

"When?" I asked to buy myself some time.

"I'm not sure, but soon. Probably within the next few weeks or so."

"Well, let me know once you work out the details."

We were both quiet for a minute.

"So, are you datin' yet or are you still in mourning?" she blurted out, unsympathetically.

I stopped smoothing the relaxer into her hair for a second. She caught me off guard with that question.

"You know, I think I'm still in mourning," I admitted, and continued with the relaxer.

"It's been a year since Lay-Law died."

"Yep. It'll be a year tomorrow."

"Don't you think it's time that you try to move on, girl?" she asked, turning to face me.

I didn't respond. Time was subjective.

"Well, just so you know Rico got some single friends. A couple of 'em are real live cuties."

"How do they make their money, Summer?" Whenever a, "helpful" person in my life offered to hook me up with somebody, that was always the first question I asked.

"Well, Rico don't ball no more."

"I'm happy for Rico. But, these cutie pie friends he has, do they still ball?"

"Some do, some don't."

"Well, which ones don't? Because I don't mess with hustlers, Summer. You know this."

"Well, Alcatraz is straight. He don't ball."

About then, I almost dropped relaxer in her face.

"What kind of job does somebody named Alcatraz have?"

She laughed at herself. After a second, I started laughing, too.

"You're right. I'ma stop tryin' to hook you up. I know you'll date when you get ready."

"Yeah, I will. Let this sit for 10 minutes and meet me at the washbowl." I tapped her leg, then, adjusted her cape.

* * * * *

After Summer's hair had been rinsed, deep conditioned, blow dried and flat ironed, I teased it a little to get the height and fullness that I wanted. While I was putting the finishing touches on her hair, I heard the unmistakable sound of glass breaking outside of the salon. Everybody else heard it, too. We all stopped what we were doing and looked up.

Daniel, one of the barbers, ran outside to see what had happened. When he came back inside, he walked right up to my station. My heart sank. I knew something happened to my car. That car was one of the few things I had left over from my life with Lorenzo.

"What happened? Please don't tell me that somebody hit my whip."

"Some cat knocked your driver side mirror off." Daniel sadly informed me.

I let out a sigh of relief. It was only the side mirror. I could easily have that replaced at Jinx's body shop. Plus, I knew he would do it for free.

"Dude's comin' inside," Daniel pointed.

"Yo, I hit somebody's whip out front." Dude walked into the salon, and with no hesitation let everybody know what was up.

I looked to the front of the salon where he was standing. He was tall, about 6'4 or 6'5. His skin was caramel colored, just the way I liked my men. He had deep set eyes, a small nose, and a lush mouth. And even though he was wearing an unimpressive polo, and blue jean shorts, I could tell he had chips.

The watch he was wearing was iced-out. It looked like Cartier from where I was standing. The bezel was encrusted in diamonds. His earlobes were catching frostbite from the big ass diamond studs he was rocking. And the chain around his neck was sick as hell. Platinum with a phat diamond and platinum cross dangling from it. Could he be some unmistaken pro player? Nope! He was a baller. I could tell just by looking at him. To me, he had the look of hustle all over him. Plus, he was related to Summer. That alone was enough to confirm it: he was in, "the life." She didn't come from a family that was on the up and up.

As much as I screamed that I was through messing with ballers, I had to admit that dude was fine. He was fine enough to make me break my *own* rules.

"Damn." I heard Summer mumble.

That snapped me back to attention. I waved my hand to get his attention. "Uhm, the green BMW 330xi?"

He looked over at me. I could tell he was checking me out. He let his eyes search my body and face.

"Yeah. That's the one."

"That's my car. Come back to my station, so we can straighten this out."

As he walked through the salon, everything got quiet. It was like Alicia Keys' vocals weren't coming through the speakers anymore. All of the conversations stopped. All eyes were on dude.

Instead of speaking to me, he addressed his first comment to Summer. That surprised me. I briefly wondered if he was Rico.

"See, this never woulda happened if you wouldn't have asked me to pick your stupid ass up from here," he yelled at her.

"The hell with you, Solly. It wouldn't have happened if you could drive. You done tore up my girl's whip." Summer looked over at me. "Passion, this is my cousin, Solomon. We call him Solly. Solly this is Passion."

"Passion," he repeated.

I held my breath and waited for the inevitable stupid remark. But he didn't make one. That impressed me.

"Yo, it's crazy. I can't believe I messed up your mirror, man," he explained. "My cell was ringin' at the same time I was pullin' up. I got distracted."

I smiled at him. I didn't mean to, but I couldn't help it. He was too damn fine.

He smiled back.

"Quit flirtin'!" Summer hissed. "I told you, Passion is my girl. I don't want crazy ass Isis comin' up here wildin' out."

I assumed that Isis was his girlfriend, and changed my whole demeanor.

"So, how you wanna take care of this?" I asked, in a no nonsense tone. "Uhm, do you have insurance?" I knew he wasn't trying to go through his insurance company. Why would he want to go through legal channels? Ballers had their own set of rules.

"Hold up, hold up. We ain't gotta go bringin' my insurance into this. You think you can estimate how much it'll cost you to fix it?" He reached into his pocket and pulled out a wad of money.

Some of the women in the salon actually gasped.

"Well damn! It's like that?" I thought to myself. Then, stopped myself from smiling. Hustlers were so predictable. They always wanted to buy their way out of trouble.

"I'll hit you off with whatever you need," he continued, "and a little extra for your trouble." He showed me his pearly whites, that didn't have so much as a *drop* of gold on them.

I placed my hands on my hips. "Now Solomon, it is Solomon, right?" I asked, playing him like I didn't remember his name.

He knew I was fronting. I could tell, because he chuckled. "Yeah, it's Solomon."

"Now Solomon, I'm not a car expert. Plus, I've never had anything like this happen to me before. So, I have no idea how much it would cost me to get that fixed."

"Well, you want me to estimate for you?"

I cocked my head to the side, and looked at him like he was crazy. "No, I do not."

"I won't do you dirty, Shorty. Straight up," he promised.

"It's not that I don't trust you. My brother owns a body shop. I can have him come out and assess the damage. He'll give me the estimate, and I'll let you know."

"How long is it gonna take?"

"I'm about to call him right now. You wanna wait?"

He looked down at his ice-encrusted watch. "I ain't really got time. I gotta get in the wind. There's money out there to make."

"That's fine. Give me your number. I'll holla back as soon as my brother tells me what's up."

"Is your brother gonna jack up the price? Cuz I gotta boy that'll fix your whip for free."

"I'm not interested in your 'homeboy hook-ups'. My brother's a professional. He'll make it happen."

Solomon rattled off his phone number and I entered it into my cell phone, as the other stylist, barbers and clients pretended not to be watching and listening.

"I'll call you as soon as I know somethin'." I told him.

"Cool," he said, then, he turned to Summer. "You almost done? I got places to be."

I was finished with her hair and ready to send her on her way.

"I just need to pay Passion and then I'll meet

you outside."

Once Solomon was out of earshot, all of the females in the salon started cackling like hens. Talking about how fine he was and about how he pulled out that pocket full of money. And, about the expensive watch and chain he was sporting.

"Let me hurry up, because he's real impatient," she informed me. "Mmm. Mmm. Girl, I know my cousin and I could tell by the way he was lookin' at you, that he's diggin' you. You always say that you don't mess with ballers. Well, Solly is the biggest baller I know. You don't wanna mess with him, Passion. He ain't right for you."

She was tripping.

"Summer, I'm not interested in your cousin at all."

"Good, keep it that way. You're my girl. I don't wanna see you get dogged out by him. That's Solly's number one skill...doggin' women out."

"You don't have to worry about that. You just need to pay me." I joked, reaching into my drawer to retrieve her purse.

"How much do I owe you, the usual?"

"Yeah, $60.00 and you're good with me."

"Let me ask you something, when you said you were calling your brother, you meant Jinx, right?"

"Yeah."

"Tell Jinx not to overcharge Solly. Dude is crazy. Tell Jinx to be straight up on his price," she warned.

"Girl, you know Jinx ain't like that. He's an honest dude."

"I hope so. See ya," she said, then left the salon to catch up with Solomon.

36

* * * * *

Jinx made a major deal of coming to get my car later that night. He supervised everything that went down as the driver attached my car to the tow truck's flatbed.

I met him outside of the salon.

"You know you didn't have do all of this. I could've driven to the shop. It was just the mirror that got messed up," I teased.

"You're straight. If you got stopped by the cops on your way to the shop, they would hit you with a ticket for a missing mirror."

"Good lookin' out, then."

"No doubt. Now, tell me again what the hell happened to this mirror?"

"Some dude was comin' to pick up his cousin. He claimed his cell phone was ringing and distracted him. All I know is I heard glass breaking. One of the barbers came out and told me that my car got hit."

"Did you get his insurance information?"

"He offered me money on the spot. Told me to estimate a price, and he would pay it." I lowered my voice and imitated Solomon, "along with a little extra for all my trouble."

"Why didn't you estimate real high?"

"You know I'm not like that. Besides, he's my client's cousin. I wouldn't do them like that. So, how much is it gonna cost?"

"You know I wouldn't charge *you*. But I'm not about to let old boy get off without coming outta his pocket."

"How much will it run him, Jinx?"

"Well," he started getting all-technical talking about casings and other stuff that went over my head. I stood there pretending to understand.

"For your car, that model BMW, everything is more expensive. I'll say $260.00 for parts and labor."

"Is that fair?" I questioned.

"Hell yeah it's fair. Besides, if he got it, you shouldn't worry about it."

"I'm not worried about it, but the dude who hit my car is Summer's cousin. You know Summer Weddington? She used to live next door to my father."

He nodded. "Yeah, I remember her."

"She told me to tell you to make sure you play fair. She said dude is crazy and he'll be hot if you overcharge him."

"I don't overcharge customers. I'm givin' him a discount, but if he gotta problem with that, you tell him to holla at me."

I pulled out my cell phone. "Okay, I'ma call him and tell him the estimate."

"You want me to call him?" Jinx asked. "Your car will be at the shop in a minute. I can take over from here."

"Nah, I'm a big girl. I got it." When I told Solomon the price, he was cool with it and easily agreed to pay it.

"What did he say?"

"He said he'll bring the money to the salon tomorrow."

"So, who is this cat that I'm supposed to be scared of?"

"His name is Solomon, but I think they call him Solly."

"Man, I know Solly. He told you that he had you

regardless of the price? That cat must hustle now. Uhm, he's big time now, huh?"

"You know him?"

"I rep the streets. I know everybody." No matter how long he'd been out the game; Jinx still thought he was the man.

I laughed, and playfully pushed him on the arm. "Whatever, Jinx. So, when is my car gonna be ready?"

"Gimme a few days, I might have to order the part. Tomorrow is Friday. It should be ready by Wednesday, Thursday at the latest."

My mouth fell open. "What am I supposed to do for a car until then?"

"Rent one."

I pouted silently.

"Ay, don't even sweat it. You wanna drive one of my cars, Baby Girl? We can go to my crib tonight and get you one. You can hold my CTS. It's real sporty. You'd like it."

I was sure I would like it. It was a Cadillac. What female didn't like riding around in luxury?

I really did want to drive the CTS. I could imagine myself in it, looking hella fine. Still, I was hesitant. My father raised me to have my own stuff and not to borrow from others.

"That's sweet, but I can't borrow your car, Jinx." I knew that my father would flip at the thought of me leaning on Jinx for help, rather than coming to him. I couldn't do it.

"I could just pick you up and drop you off until your car is finished."

"Nah, that's too much. You got your own life, and your own moves to make. I can't ask you to do that."

"How would you get to work tomorrow?"

"I'll walk." I only lived about nine blocks from the salon. It wasn't that much of an inconvenience.

"No, you won't," he stated. "I'll be in front of your building tomorrow morning. What time is your first appointment?"

"Jinx, I can't let you do that. I'm straight, really."

He looked over at me. "On the strength of Lay – Law, Passion, I'll always look out."

That was one of the few times I could remember him ever calling me by my given name.

"My first appointment is at 9:15."

"I'll be outside by 8:50. Be ready."

"Okay." I said giving in.

"Get in my truck. Let me take you home."

I climbed into the passenger side of his Escalade EXT. He sold the Ford Expedition a few days after Lorenzo's funeral. I think it had too many memories for him to hold on to.

"You hungry? You wanna get something to eat?" He put the truck in gear and sped off.

I sighed softly. Sometimes having Jinx around was like having another daddy. He was always worried about me. "No, I have food at home."

He pulled to a stop in front of my building. "You straight?"

"Yes Jinx, I'm fine."

"Good. I'll holla at you in the morning."

Even though I didn't turn around as I walked into the courtway of my building, I knew Jinx was still sitting there; watching; making sure I got inside okay.

Chapter Four

On Friday, I waited all day for Solomon to show up with the money that he promised me. I finished with my last client at 10:45pm, and Solomon still hadn't shown. That had me a little upset.

I walked over to Keena's station, where she was putting the finishing touches on her last client. "Hey Keena, you think you can give me a ride home?"

"Solly never showed up with the money he owes you? Uhm, typical." She picked up a can of holding spray, and generously covered her client's head with the light mist. "You know he got loot. I wonder why he's playin' with you like this."

I didn't want to talk about Solomon. I was pissed at him for being a liar. What I needed to talk about was how I was getting home. "I don't know why he's playin'. Can I get a ride home or not?"

"I guess so. I'm supposed to be hookin' up with Junebug tonight."

"You know what? If it's gonna take you out of your way, don't worry about it. I'll see if I can get somebody else to take me home." I turned to walk back over to my own station.

Sometimes, Keena just got on my nerves. We were cool, but whenever I asked her for a favor, she

41

was always shady when it came to looking out.

"Stop trippin', Passion. I'll drop you off at home. You just gotta be ready… like now," she stressed, looking down at her watch.

"I am ready now." I watched as she collected the payment from her client, and sent her off.

"Uhm, Passion…" Keena began.

I waited for the inevitable. She was the type of person that you couldn't ask for a favor, without expecting her to ask you for one back.

"To make things go faster, could you sweep out my station while I wash my combs and brushes?"

I started to say no, and just walk home. But I had been on my feet all day, and I really didn't feel like walking the nine blocks to my house.

"Yeah, whatever," I sighed, getting the broom.

I helped her clean up her work station and when she was finally ready to leave; it was after 11:30. I spent 45 minutes helping her and the heifer didn't even thank me. As we stepped out of the salon, a Hummer H2 was slowly approaching.

"Uhm, who is that?" Keena adjusted the gold chain that she always wore around her neck, and finger-combed her hair.

"I don't know. Let's go. Where did you park?"

"Yo, Passion!" A voice called.

"Whoever it is, they know you, girl. Who do you know that drives a Hummer?"

"Nobody."

The H2 came to a stop. Keena and I stood there as Solomon stepped out. He was wearing denim Enyce shorts, an Enyce striped polo, and K-Swiss that looked fresh out of the box. He had on a baseball cap, and Dolce & Gabbana sunglasses. It was almost midnight, and dude had on sunglasses.

"Damn, he's fine," she whispered, as he approached us.

I rolled my eyes up towards the sky and I ignored her comment.

"You must not want this money." Solomon parted out of his mouth, without so much as saying "Hello".

"Well, I was expectin' you to drop it off earlier."

"My bad, time got away from me," he responded.

My stomach started to hurt. He was bringing back bad memories of Lorenzo, reminding me of all the things that I hated about having to deal with ballers. First of all, you were always on *their* time. And in their world, it was appropriate to handle business at 12:00 midnight. Second of all, they were too used to women fawning all over them. Here was this idiot, grinning in my face at 11:50pm. And, he had the nerve to be talking about, time got away from him. He thought his grin was enough to get him over. Apparently, he didn't know Passion Hill. I wasn't having it. I didn't have to accommodate him.

"You know what? I don't need your dough. Keep it." I turned to Keena, who was glued to Solomon. "You ready?"

"What you mean, you don't need my dough?" He stood there puzzled, with the money in his hand.

"It's 12:00. I've been waitin' on you all day, and you show up at 12:00 with a grin on your face. Well, I ain't ya girl. I shouldn't have to wait on you. This is business, and business should be handled like business. I don't need your dough. *My brother owns a body shop!* He'll fix my whip for free. You can take your money and bounce. Peace." I started walking away. I didn't know where I was going, or if I was even going in the right direction. I didn't know where Keena parked.

He approached me with an attitude. For the first time, I felt a little bit shook. I didn't know him. I didn't know what he might do. All I knew was that I couldn't count on Keena for help if he started choking me or something.

"Who do you think you're talkin' to?" He stared at me.

I wasn't about to let him see that he had me spooked. I looked up at him defiantly. "You."

He started to laugh. "Oh, so you tough, huh? You a bad bitch."

"I'm not a bitch. I'm about my business."

"No disrespect. I meant that as a compliment."

Only a thug would think that calling a woman a bitch, under any circumstances, could be considered a compliment. I didn't reply.

He addressed his next comment to Keena. "Yo, you about to give her a ride to the crib?"

She gave him a bright smile. "Yeah, I'm about to drop her off."

"Ay, why don't you let me take care of that?" Solomon insisted. He pulled some bills out of his pocket and handed them to her. "Me and ya girl, we got some unfinished business."

Keena took the money and as she put it in her purse, I couldn't help thinking that my alleged friend had just sold me to the highest bidder.

"Girl, give him the money back. I'll walk home."

"No, you won't, Passion. It's 12:00 at night. It's too late for you to be out here by yourself, and I gotta go. I told you that Junebug is waitin' on me." With that being said, she made her way to her own car, without looking back.

"You wasted your money. I'm not gettin' in your truck. I don't even know you."

I headed back towards the salon. Solomon followed me. I pulled out my cell phone and called Jinx.

"Holla, Baby Girl," he answered.

"Hey Jinx. Uhm, Keena left me stranded at the salon. I don't have any way to get home."

"Damn, word? There's nobody there that you can catch a ride with?"

I didn't expect him to say that. Jinx always came through for me. I just knew I could count on him.

"There's only two stylists still here, and I don't know them like that."

"Look P, I would come and scoop you, but I'm over here with Ebonie." He lowered his voice. "We're about to get into somethin'."

Ebonie was his newest woman. I couldn't get mad at him for putting her before me. After all, it was late and he was enjoying himself.

I sighed softly, "Okay."

"Don't say it like that, P. Take a cab to the crib. I'll be there to scoop you up tomorrow night when you get off. I promise."

"Yeah, I'll do that." As I responded to Jinx, I cut my eyes at Solomon. He was leaning against the vacant reception desk taking in every word of my conversation.

"Ay, did dude ever show up with my money?"

"He's here now. He showed up about ten minutes ago. He keeps tryin' to get me to ride home with him."

"It's only a few blocks, P. Let the man take you home. Damn, you keep lettin' him off the hook. Dude owes you!"

"What?" I was outdone. "Jinx, I don't want this cat knowin' where I stay. His own cousin said he's crazy."

"Put Solly on the phone."

"No."

"Stop trippin', Passion and give Solly the phone." That was the second time in two days that Jinx called me Passion.

"My brother wants to holla at you," I said handing Solomon my cell phone. The two of them talked for a few seconds. When he handed the phone back to me, he was smiling.

"What's up?" I asked Jinx.

"I talked to him. He's gonna drive you home, Baby Girl. He knows you're family to me. Just hit me up when he drops you off."

"You're wrong for that, Jinx."

"Call me when you get home. And quit poutin'."

"Bye Jinx." I placed my cell phone back inside my purse.

Meanwhile, Solomon decided it was time for him to get in my business.

"Jinx is your brother? Small world. I ain't know that cat had a younger sister."

I ignored him.

"Let's roll."

I followed him out to his pewter colored H2. I climbed inside, and was engulfed by the luxuriousness of the interior. The leather seat seemed to conform to my body. The truck smelled good, too. It smelled like some kind of sexy cologne. I didn't say anything, though. I didn't want dude to know how much I was enjoying being in his truck. Especially after way I showed my ass about riding with him in the first place.

Solomon hit the stereo and the sounds of 106.3 fm, the soul station filled the truck. Not typical for a hustler. I thought he was about to blast Pac, Biggie, Jay-Z or Scarface.

"So, where do you stay, Passion?"

"72nd and Coles," I directed.

"Jinx ain't your real brother, is he?"

"What difference does it make?"

"None really. I was just wonderin'."

"No, he's not my biological brother. We're just close like that."

"What a dude gotta do to get close to you…on that level?"

I sighed. *I hope that whack garbage ain't his best pick-up line.* I thought to myself.

"I don't need any more big brothers. Between Jinx and my father, I'm straight. Thanks."

"How do you know Jinx?"

I was getting aggravated with his line of questioning. "Maybe I should ask you the same thing. How do you know Jinx?" I wasn't like most females, who loved to run off at the mouth. Who told their life story to a complete stranger? My father raised me to be a private person. There was no way in hell I was answering a gang of questions.

Solomon was blunt in his answer. "From puttin' in work. And I don't think you know nothin' about puttin' in work. So, I'm just wonderin' how you know him."

I didn't feel the need to lay down my street credentials to him. "Sweetie, you don't know what I know."

"True. You gotta point. Did you and Jinx used to deal?"

"Are you givin' me a ride home, or are you trying to pump me for information?"

"Both," he admitted.

I hesitated. I didn't expect him to be so honest with me. "Why would you want information about me?"

He stuck a piece of gum in his mouth. "Because I'm fascinated by you. You're different from other females that I come across."

I sucked my teeth. "You don't even know how different I am from other females, Solomon."

"So, you never messed with him?"

"I messed with his best friend, Lorenzo. They called him..."

"Lay-Law--," he interrupted. "You used to deal with Lay-Law?"

I nodded my head.

"You were his wife when he got killed, huh?"

"I was his girlfriend," I said, pointedly. Street recognition as Lorenzo's wife hadn't done a damn thing for me, but caused me pain.

"So, that's why Jinx considers you family. Man, I was devastated when Lay-Law got killed."

"Join the club," I murmured. "Anyway, ever since then, I don't mess with hustlers... on any level. I don't date them. I don't screw them. I don't befriend them."

"Oh, you wanna make sure I know that right off the bat, huh?" he teased.

"No doubt. So, you can keep all that flirtin' and stuff to yourself."

"We'll see."

"No, you'll see. Anyway, don't you have a woman? I heard Summer say something about somebody named Isis."

He blew out a big breath of air. "Isis ain't my woman. She's my son's mother."

"Uhm," I said, with disinterest.

"We broke up over a year ago. That bitch is just psycho. She wants me back, so she started stalking me and whatnot."

"You call your son's mother a bitch, huh? Interesting. If you don't respect your child's mother, how do you respect other females?"

"That bothers you?"

"No, but it should bother you."

I looked out through the tinted windows. We didn't seem to be getting any closer to my block.

"Are you takin' me home or what?" What should've been a five minute ride was lasting much longer.

"Yeah, I'm takin' you home. What you think, I'm tryin' to kidnap you?"

"I don't know. It's takin' you a minute to get to my house."

He pulled up to a stop sign and looked over at me. "I guess I'm drivin' slow, trying to keep you with me a little bit longer," he winked.

"Why would you wanna do that?"

"I told you, you fascinate me."

He was reminding me too much of Lorenzo. I "intrigued" Lorenzo. That wasn't what I was looking for in a mate. I was looking for a guy who expected a female to present herself the way I presented myself. He finally pulled to a stop in front of my building.

"You sure you don't wanna take this money?"

"Nope, learn to handle your business better. It'll help you in the long run."

"I'll take the money up to Jinx's shop tomorrow. Give it to him."

"That's fine," I agreed.

"Yo, since it's my fault your car is jacked up, I could come by and scoop you up for work in the morning," he offered.

I looked over at him in annoyance. I didn't wanna be bothered with him. What didn't he get?

"No thanks, Solomon. I'm straight."

"Well, later then," he said, as I climbed out of his truck.

CHAPTER FIVE

Jinx parked his truck as close to Lorenzo's grave as he could at 10:15 Monday morning. I took a deep breath. The only thing I hated as much as cemeteries were funeral homes. I stepped out of the truck slowly. I wasn't looking forward to walking across the grass to Lorenzo's grave. I hated the way the grass at the cemetery always sunk down under my feet. Like it wasn't stable. I hated how it always seemed damp, and murky and humid there.

Jinx took my hand. As we approached Lorenzo's burial plot, I spotted a woman and a little boy standing there. As we got closer, I could hear the woman weeping uncontrollably. I was confused. She didn't look like anybody I knew, nor did she look like any of Lorenzo's family members.

"Who is that?" I asked Jinx.

He looked as confused as I did. "I don't know."

As we advanced, I heard the woman say to the little boy, "Tell papi that you love him, Renny." The little boy spoke in jibber-jabber. He was too young to make real sentences.

I let go of Jinx's hand and quickened my pace. "Hello." I walked right up to her. She was a Latina, either Mexican or Guatemalan. Cute, with long brown hair, light brown eyes, a round face, and full lips. She was shorter than me, and thicker than I was. She wasn't small by any stretch of the imagination. I knew that Lorenzo liked thick women, but this girl was large. She was thick-thick.

I startled her.

"Hey," she jumped, looked me up and down.

"Who are you?" I had to know.

She regained her composure, and wiped her tear stained face. "Who are you?"

"I'm Passion. How did you know Lorenzo?"

"He was my fiancé."

Her fiancé? Lorenzo was engaged to her? I couldn't believe anything like that.

"He was my son's father. We were to be married. You're his sister, right? He told me that he had a sister named Passion."

I turned around and looked at Jinx. He wouldn't make eye contact with me. I was getting really pissed and really suspicious.

"What's your name, Sweetie?"

"Gabriela."

"Gabriela, Lorenzo only mentioned to you that I was his sister? Do you know Jinx?" I needed to know if Jinx was in on it. After all, Lorenzo was his best friend.

She looked over at Jinx noticing him from a distance for the first time. A huge grin spread across her face. I had my answer.

She ran over to him, and threw her large arms around his neck. He wouldn't hug her back. She didn't seem to notice. "What's up, Jinx? I haven't seen you in so long." She placed her hands on her wide hips. "How come you ain't been by to see your godson?" She picked up the little boy.

I got a good look at his face, and he was the spitting image of Lorenzo. I didn't need any DNA test to prove it to me. That little boy was Lorenzo's son.

"Renny," she cooed, "this is Jinx. Your godfather. Give him a hug." Gabriela thrust the little boy into Jinx's arms.

Jinx took him reluctantly.

"So, you do know Jinx?" I asked, giving him the evil eye. My heart was pounding in my chest.

"Yeah, Jinx was my home boy, until he stopped comin' around. After Lorenzo died, everybody stopped comin' around."

"Were you at the funeral?" I was trying to remember if I had ever seen her before.

"Nobody even told me when it was. I didn't find out about the funeral until a week later. Lorenzo never mentioned me?" She asked me when I shook my head. "Never?"

I looked into her unhappy face. "No, but don't look all sad. The reason that he never mentioned you is because I'm not his sister. I was his girlfriend. We were living together when he was killed."

Her face dropped, and she looked exactly how I felt. Like somebody had kicked her dead in the stomach. "What?"

"He was my boyfriend."

She looked really hurt, then really pissed. "Impossible!" she yelled, "That's impossible."

"Ask Jinx," I said easily. "Maybe he'll tell *you* the truth."

She turned towards him. He looked like he wanted the ground to open and swallow him up.

"Papi, is that true? Was Lorenzo messin' around on me?"

He didn't respond to her.

"Did Lorenzo give you an engagement ring?" I had to know. He had never given me an engagement ring.

She pulled a necklace out from under the collar of her shirt. On the end of the necklace dangled a gold ring with a few tiny diamond chips. It was cheap. I could tell just by looking at it. Cheap wasn't Lorenzo's style. I wondered why he had given her that joke of a ring. He had given me a nicer ring for my 21st birthday. It was platinum with a 2 carat emerald, flanked by diamond baguettes. That was his style.

"Lorenzo loved me, Chica. Do you see this ring?" She held it closer to my face. "We were to be married."

I wasn't going to argue that fact. The man was dead. It wasn't like I could get in his ass about what he had done.

"Yo, Lay-Law loved Passion. He considered Passion his wife." Jinx said, finally finding his tongue.

"Whatever that was good for," I mumbled.

"Do you have children by him?" she asked, as if that verified whether he loved me or not.

"No, I don't."

"But you were living with him?"

"Yes."

"I don't understand this." Her eyes filled with tears. "Why would he do this to me?" Her son wrapped his arms around her leg, and started crying, too.

"He did it to me, too. How long was you engaged to him?" It was killing me to know.

"He proposed two weeks before he was killed." She blew her nose on some crumpled up tissue. "How

54

long were you two livin' together?"

"Three years."

She sucked in a deep breath, and started crying. "Papi, why? Papi, why?" She wailed stomping on his grave.

In all my pain and confusion, I actually felt bad for her. I could tell that she was really hurting. I looked at the bouquet of flowers that I was holding in my hand. Then I looked at Lorenzo's headstone. I flung the flowers down.

"Enough is enough. I need to go, before I do something really disrespectful." I stated to Jinx.

"Not like this. Come on, P."

I gave him a cold, hard stare. "I'm ready to go, fuck Lay-Law. I'll be by the truck when you get through paying your *respects*." I walked across the grass, back over to where we were parked.

Gabriela followed me. "I don't know what to think." She chased me to catch up.

I didn't care what she thought. I had my own damn problems.

"This explains so much." She continued with her sobbing.

I looked back at her and couldn't help but agree. Seeing her, and her son did explain a lot about Lorenzo's behavior. "You're right." I told her.

She threw up her hands. "Now, I know why he could never spend the night at my house. I can't do this." She said getting upset. She picked up her son, and practically ran away.

I looked up at the beautiful blue sky. "How could you do this to me, Lorenzo? I was down for you. I rode for you!" My eyes started welling up with water. I was totally confused. While I was living with him, he was living a double life. A fiancée and a son?

I wanted to fling myself in the bed, and kick and scream like I did when I was five years old. I wanted to put the blanket over my head, and block everything out. I wanted my life to stop spinning.

Jinx met me at the truck. I could barely stand to look at him. I would have called my daddy and had him pick me up, but I had some questions. And I knew Jinx was the only one who could answer them.

"Baby girl," he began.

"Can you please call me, Passion? Only family calls me that."

He looked over at me with pain in his eyes. I couldn't concern myself with his pain. I had my own pain to deal with.

"So, I'm not family now? Passion, I know I should have told you…"

"Who is this chick?" I interrupted. "Who is she? Where did she come from?"

"Lay-Law met her at this club that we kicked it at."

"He had a baby with a damn stripper?"

"She wasn't a stripper. It wasn't a strip club. It was just a club. We handled a lot of business there. Gabriela was a waitress."

"How long were they together?"

"They weren't together, Baby Girl."

"She sure seems to think they were together. She thinks they were engaged, and that ring he gave her kind of says that they were."

"Women believe what they want to believe."

"You got that right," I sighed.

"I didn't mean you."

"Well, who did you mean, Jinx? Because I sure

as hell believed all of Lorenzo's lies."

"I'm just sayin', why would Gabriela think that she was engaged to somebody who would never spend the night at her house? Why would she think that she was engaged to somebody that wasn't there when she had her son?"

"I have a question for you. Why would he propose to her?"

He shook his head.

"To be honest, I can't answer that question. I asked him that a million times, and each time he came up with a different answer."

"You think he asked her to marry him, because he actually loved her?" My feelings were beyond simply being hurt.

"He loved you, Baby Girl."

"Well, what did he need her for? Why was she even around?" Tears started falling down my face. "He had a baby with her, Jinx."

"He didn't think you wanted kids."

"I'm too young for kids. I wanna go to college. I don't wanna spend my life doing hair." I said, still crying.

"And Lay-Law wanted to marry you. He told me that he wanted to marry you. But he knew you wouldn't marry him until he got out of the game."

"How long were they together?" I asked him again.

He shrugged. "I don't know. Maybe a year and a half."

"How old is that kid?"

"Probably a little over one."

"You said that Lorenzo wasn't there when she had the baby. Where was he?"

He paused before he answered. "I don't know. Maybe he was with you. He asked me to go to the hospital, instead."

I sat straight up and leaned forward. What kind of mess was that? "Did you go?"

"Hell naw. What I look like going to the hospital while his kid is bein' born? I think he proposed to Gabriela as a way to apologize for not showin' up at the hospital."

We rode in silence for about twenty minutes.

I took a deep breath. "Did he have other chicks on the side? Chicks besides this one?" It was all out now, I figured that he might as well tell me the deal.

"With the way Lay-Law was ballin' outta control? You know women were forever throwin' the ass at him."

"That's not what I asked you." I stated firmly. "Did Lorenzo have other women?"

"Yeah, there were other chicks. What you wanna know this stuff for, P? Lay-Law is dead. He can't right them wrongs. Let him be dead."

"Did he have other kids?" I questioned persistently.

"Not that I know of."

"Why didn't you tell me about this hoe and her kid? I thought you were my guy. My big brother." That was hurting me just as bad as what Lorenzo had done. "I mean, I know he was your boy. But he's been dead a year. You couldn't have told me by now? I gotta find out by walkin' up on them at the cemetery?"

"I know. I know."

"This makes me question our whole friendship, Jinx. Now, I wonder if you're so nice to me, because you genuinely care about me, or because you feel guilty about the way your guy dogged me."

"I love you, Baby Girl. You know that. We're fam."

"Are we? Cuz the fam I have would've told me something like this. They wouldn't have sat around and let me cry my eyes out over some asshole that got some other broad pregnant, and proposed to her." I turned to him as he pulled to a stop in front of my building. "You know I'm through messin' with you, right?"

"C'mon P, don't be like that. I know you're pissed right now, but through with me?"

"I'm through messin' with you, Jinx. As far as I'm concerned, you're as dead as Lorenzo." I got out of the truck, slammed the door and walked into my building.

*****

I went into my condo, and fell out on my sofa. I had about a billion thoughts running through my mind. I started dissecting my relationship with Lorenzo. I started playing back conversations, things he said to me. I tried to see if I could pinpoint when he started cheating with old girl. I tried to put my finger on when he started spending time with *Gabriela*, but I couldn't do it.

When my head started pounding to the extent that I couldn't take it anymore, I got up, packed an overnight bag, and took a cab to my father's house.

CHAPTER SIX

My father's wife, Lynne, answered the door for me. I had keys to my father's house, but I didn't want to disrespect him by entering his house unannounced.

"Hey, Passion," she smiled, but still looked surprised to see me.

"Hey, Lynne."

She noticed my overnight bag. "So, this isn't a casual visit, huh?" She embraced me.

I shook my head, and tears started to well up in my eyes.

She grabbed my arm. "Get in here. Come on. Your room is always ready for you."

I went up to my old bedroom and started to unpack. I had just put my suitcase in the corner, when Lynne appeared in my doorway.

"I had Anna Rae make us something to eat." Anna Rae was their cook.

"I'm not hungry," I replied sullenly.

"Well, come downstairs and keep me company while I eat."

* * * * *

Anna Rae hooked things up. There was fried chicken, mashed potatoes, string beans, a garden salad, and corn bread muffins. In spite of the fact that I said I wasn't hungry, the food smelled so good that I fixed myself a plate, and followed Lynne into the breakfast nook. I sat down across from her at the table.

My father met Lynne while we were living in Dallas. She was a teller at his bank. He dated her on the down low for months before he brought her home and introduced her to me. I hated her instantly. I didn't want some woman dating my father. I had already lost my mother; I didn't want to lose my father, too. I did everything to drive Lynne away. I acted as spoiled as I possibly could, but she wouldn't budge. She kept hanging around and hanging around until one day, my father proposed to her. I was thirteen and devastated. He was about to make the woman that I despised more than anybody, a permanent part of my family. I didn't speak to either one of them for almost a month. Then one day, my father suffered a mild heart attack. Lynne sprung into action and took up his responsibility.

She picked me up from school two days after my dad's heart attack and took me down to the bank where she worked. She introduced me to the financial advisor. I didn't even know what a financial advisor was. She walked me through all of my dad's businesses. She put me up on how much money he had, how much he was worth, how his money was invested, how his businesses ran... everything. She broke out his will, and showed me that I was to inherit everything, and she was to act as my trustee.

Not only did she look out for me on the financial end, she moved into our house while my dad was in the hospital. Since she wasn't the domestic type, she hired a housekeeper and a cook to make sure that I was well fed and looked after. She drove me to school and picked me up everyday. She took me to the hospital to see my father, and sat in the waiting room for hours, while I spent time with him alone. When I cried, she gave me hugs and kisses. Hugs and kisses were something I hadn't received from a woman in years. Even though she was only twelve years older than me, I started to look at Lynne as a mother figure. I started to love her.

"What's the problem, Sweetie pie?" She asked gently.

"I just found out some really devastating news."

"What do you mean, devastating?" She was genuinely concerned. I could tell.

"The whole time I was with Lorenzo, he was leading a double life."

"Leading a double life?" she repeated, "Oh Passion, don't tell me he was gay!"

I cracked a small smile. "You watch too much Oprah, Lynne. He wasn't gay. He was messin' around on me with some Mexican or Guatemalan chick. I'm not sure what her nationality is."

"Say what?" she asked, loudly.

Anna Rae poked her head into the breakfast nook. She was nosy; she couldn't help it.

"Yeah," I nodded. "He had a baby with this girl and everything."

"If he wasn't already dead, I would whip his ass."

"He proposed to her and everything. She showed me the ring." I sat my fork down. I couldn't enjoy the food, even though it was delicious.

"How did you find out?"

"Jinx took me to the cemetery and there was old girl, crying at the grave."

"You talked to her?"

I looked at Lynne like she was crazy. "Yeah, I talked to her. If you saw some broad crying at my daddy's grave, wouldn't you talk to her?"

She nodded. "You have a point."

"I asked her who she was, and how she knew Lorenzo. She told me that she was his fiancé... the mother of his son." Tears started falling again. I grabbed a linen napkin and dabbed at my eyes. "And she was thick, Lynne! He was cheating on me with a big girl. She wasn't even any kind of competition for me. But he got her pregnant!"

Lynne looked sorrowful. I knew that she felt for me. Not only did Lorenzo hurt my feelings but he hurt my pride by cheating on me with somebody who I thought wasn't even as pretty as I was.

"Are you sure everything the girl said was true?"

"Jinx was standing right there, he didn't deny any of it. He knew that broad. She gave him a big hug. That kid is his godson!"

"So, for sure the kid is Lorenzo's?"

"Lorenzo spit him out, Lynne. The little boy looks exactly like him. I wanted to dig him up and kill him again!"

"I know you did, Sweetie. I know you did." She shook her head in disbelief.

"I don't know who to be more pissed with, Lorenzo for not telling me, or Jinx for not telling me."

"Did you talk to Jinx?" she asked gently.

"I talked to him on the ride from the cemetery. I asked him why he didn't tell me," I paused. "I told him I can't mess with him no more."

She raised an eyebrow. "What do you mean; you can't mess with him no more?"

I knew what she was thinking. "Not like that, Lynne. I meant I can't be his friend. We can't be close anymore."

63

"You don't think that's drastic, Passion?"

I shook my head.

"You don't think you're gonna miss having Jinx in your life?"

Lynne knew how close we were. She and my father loved Jinx for the way he looked out for me after Lorenzo was killed.

"I'm gonna miss him, but I'm used to missing people. I miss my mother. I missed Lorenzo, until earlier today. I'll miss Jinx, but I'll survive. I always do." I took a breath. "The only thing is he has my car."

"What is he doing with your car?"

"Some guy was trying to double-park in front of the salon and he knocked off my side view mirror."

"Why is this, the first I'm hearing about this? Does your father know?"

"No, he doesn't know. Jinx took care of it. He had my car towed to his body shop. He's been working on it for me."

"How have you been getting around?"

"Jinx."

"Why didn't you come here and get a car? It's not like we don't have one you could borrow."

I looked over at her. "You know how my father feels about borrowing things from other people."

"Not from him, Passion, you know that."

I was silent.

"Well, why didn't you at least get a rental car?"

"I didn't want to waste money on a rental car."

"Your dad and I could've paid for it."

"I didn't need a rental car, then," I said. "But I do now. I am not trying to ride with Jinx, and my car won't be ready until Wednesday."

My father arrived home and walked into the

breakfast nook.

He was a handsome man, 45 years old, and didn't look a day over 35. He was butterscotch colored, with sandy brown hair, dancing hazel eyes, deep dimples, high cheek bones, and thin lips. I was the spitting image of him.

He was dressed casually, in olive Tommy Bahama deck shorts, a white Tommy Bahama polo and golf shoes. He had just returned from playing a few rounds. He bent down and gave Lynne a kiss on the cheek. He looked over at me and smiled brightly.

"To what do I owe the pleasure of seeing my beautiful baby?"

I accepted the kiss he placed on my jaw. "Hey Daddy."

"What's going on, Baby Girl?"

"I got some devastating news today."

The smile quickly disappeared as the corners of his mouth turned down into a frown. "And days after the anniversary of Lorenzo's death. I'm sorry, baby. I wish I could protect you from all of this pain..."

"I know."

"What happened?"

"Chad, let me tell you about Lorenzo," Lynne said. She told my father the story, the same way I told it to her. When she was finished, my father's handsome face was a mask. Emotionless.

"I guess he's lucky he's already dead," he stated, softly. "What about Jinx?"

I didn't even want to think about what he meant by that.

Lynne stood up, and placed her hands on my father's shoulders. "Now, we can't hold Jinx responsible for what Lorenzo did."

"We're not. We're holding him responsible for knowing, and not telling."

I finally spoke. "Lorenzo was his best friend. He was caught in the middle of a bad situation."

"And it seems like he made the wrong decision about where his loyalties should lay." He gave me direct eye contact as he spoke.

I was mad at Jinx, but I didn't want to see anything happen to him. He had looked out for me on too many occasions. I couldn't just let him blow in the wind. My father didn't play when it came to his family. He was especially protective of me. I knew that he had gotten out of the game, but he still had major connections. I knew he could make violent things happen with one phone call.

"Daddy, I need to make some moves," I said, to change the subject.

"I'm listening."

"Well, I bought my car with money from Lorenzo, that's not gonna work for me anymore. I don't want anything around me that reminds me of what he did."

I knew my father would understand. He knew all about the disrespect that surrounded betrayal.

"What are your plans?"

"I need a new car."

"You bought your condo with money from Lorenzo, too. What are you gonna do about that?"

"I'm gonna wanna move eventually, but not yet."

"So, you need a new car?"

"Yes."

He looked over at Lynne. "Are you free tomorrow? Can you help Baby Girl take care of her business?"

"I can't do it tomorrow, daddy. I have to work."

He stared at me blankly. He didn't like the fact that I was a hair stylist. He thought that I was wasting my potential. He wanted me to go to college, get a degree, and take over the financial aspects of his businesses. I planned on doing that... later on. First, I wanted to do what I wanted to do. I enjoyed doing hair.

"When are you going to college, Passion?"

"Classes start at the end of next month," I said, smiling and showing him my dimples. They were identical to his.

I was enrolled at the University of Illinois at Chicago and ready to begin this new journey.

"Good," he said, kissing me on the forehead. "You get your car. We'll consider it an early birthday present." He winked at me.

I winked back showing the same love. "Uhm daddy, somebody needs to get my car from Jinx's body shop. I can't face him right now."

"When will it be ready?"

"Wednesday."

"I'll pick it up myself. I wanna talk to Jinx, anyway."

Lynne and I looked at each other, but neither of us spoke. I would have loved to be a fly on the wall for that conversation.

CHAPTER SEVEN

Jinx was waiting outside of the salon for me on Wednesday night when I finished with my last client. I wasn't surprised. I was more surprised that he wasn't out there on Tuesday night.

"P!" He called, as I tried to ignore him.

Honestly, I didn't know how to act with him. A part of me wanted to give him my booty to kiss. Another part of me couldn't do him dirty, no matter how bogus he had played me.

"P, I know you hear me. You done sent your old man down to my body shop, the least you can do is talk to a brotha."

I stopped walking towards my rental car, and looked in his direction.

"Can I holla at you?" I could tell that he was frustrated by the way I was treating him.

I looked down at my Bulova watch with the diamond bezel. It was still early: It was 8:15. "How long is it gonna take, Jinx?"

He looked hurt. I knew it was because I never talked to him like that. "Not long. I'm on your time."

I walked over to his truck. The only reason I wanted to talk to him was to find out what my father said. He unlocked the door for me, and I climbed inside.

"What's up?" I asked, with my arms folded tightly across my chest.

"You hungry? You wanna grab something to

eat?"

"I guess."

"So, you've been stayin' at your father's, huh?"

"Yeah."

"I wondered where you were. I waited outside your building this morning...yesterday morning, too. You never really gave me a chance to apologize to you."

"What's to apologize for? I'm not new to the game. You know this. I completely understand why you kept Lorenzo's secret while he was alive. He was your boy, and I was his girl. You didn't owe me anything. It just hurts me that you kept his secrets after he was gone and we got so tight."

"Come on, man. You know I wouldn't purposely hurt you. I made the decision that I thought was best at that time. You were goin' through a lot of bullshit. I didn't really see the point of me pouring more dirt on top."

I was quiet.

"Your father picked up your car this morning."

"I know. I asked him to. I wasn't tryin' to face you."

"You still haven't faced me, P."

"I guess I'm still not ready to." I shrugged my shoulders.

"Your old man was pissed about the whole shit."

"Do you blame him?"

We were both quiet for a minute. Then curiosity got the best of me. "What did he say?"

"He asked about Gabriela, about her son. He asked if Lay-Law had other females on the side."

"Can you take me back to the salon?" It was too

much information. My pain was still too raw, and I couldn't handle it.

"I thought you wanted to eat."

"I thought so, too, but I can't do it. I can't sit across the table from you, Jinx. I can't even look at you right now. I feel like I'm about to be sick."

No man wanted vomit in his truck, so he drove me back to my rental car without saying another word.

* * * * *

I cancelled all of my appointments the next day, and went with Lynne to the car dealership. I picked out an ash blue Lexus GX470 truck. My truck was off the meter. It had all the bells and whistles a girl could hope for.

"You seem happy," Lynne stated, while we were waiting to take delivery on my new truck.

I grinned at her. "I am happy."

She hugged me. "Look at you. Girl, you got a lot of your daddy in you. All the madness you've been through, and you're still standin'."

"Barely, I really thought this stuff with Lorenzo was... whew!" I sighed. "I spent three years thinking he loved me. I spent three years living in a fantasy. And the thing that bothers me the most is that I wasn't even happy with him most of the time. I just stayed with him, because he stayed with me." I shook my head. "Isn't that the saddest thing you ever heard?"

She looked at me strangely.

"What?"

"You know Passion, you think really deeply for a girl your age. I wish I would've been as smart at your age as you are."

70

"I've been through a lot in my 23 years. Something good ought to come out of all this pain."

She hugged me again. "Are you coming back to the house with me?"

"Nah, I need to go home. I can't run away from my life forever."

"Well, your father and I are here for you whenever you need us."

"Thanks Lynne. Tell my daddy that I love him and I'll call him."

* * * * *

Summer showed up fifteen minutes late for her appointment.

"Hey, Summer," I greeted, grabbing a cape for her.

"Hey Passion, girl I'm sorry I'm late. It's been mad drama all mornin'. I called a cab to bring me over here, but it never showed. As you can see, I ain't even really put myself together. I just threw on some sweats, and came. I didn't want you to make me re-book."

I assessed her outfit. It was a casual look, different from the way she typically dressed.

"What's wrong with your car?" I asked taking down her ponytail. "The last few times you've been here, you haven't been in your car."

"Girl, while I was in Miami, doing the damn thing, my little sister, Autumn, tore my whip up." She threw up her hands. "See, that's why you can't be nice to young girls. I was pissed. She did $3,700.00 worth of damage. I was hopin' my insurance company would just total the car out, but you know that wasn't happenin'. They wanna fix it."

"How'd she tear it up?"

"Drivin' high, girl. Not drunk, high. Can you believe that? She wrapped my whip around a light pole. I wanted to beat her ass"

I gasped. "Was she all right?"

"She was fine...with her high ass." She sucked her teeth. "Then the body shop that my insurance made me take the car to, is takin' forever to fix it. It might not be ready for another few weeks. You know how they do. They tell you that they have to order this part, and that part. And of course all the parts gotta come from Antarctica or some damn where."

That type of stuff made me glad that Jinx owned a body shop and took care of my car.

* * * * *

Later, while I was styling Summer's hair, Solomon walked into the salon. He was still as fine as I remembered. He looked mad sexy in his baggy Rocawear denim shorts, and matching shirt.

He ignored Summer and addressed his comment to me. "What's up, Passion?"

I smiled in spite of myself. I didn't want to like him, but he was so damn fine that it was hard not to. "Hey Solomon."

"Your car wasn't out there. Don't tell me Jinx still ain't fixed it."

"Nah, I got it back earlier this week. I felt like walkin' this morning."

"Walking? Why would you wanna do that, when you could've requested a ride?"

"It's only a few blocks. Anyway, it's good exercise." I pretended not to notice as his eyes traveled over my body.

"Shorty, you don't look like you need exercise. Your body is straight just the way it is."

I made the mistake of looking up at him, and he winked at me.

"Uh Solly, I have to pay Passion. Can you meet me outside?" Summer watched as he flirted with me.

"Make sure you give her a tip for me." He turned and walked away.

"Oh I will," she said back to him and pulled me to the side. "Boo, I thought you said that you weren't interested in my cousin?" Summer looked at me sternly as she spoke.

"I'm not."

"Sure don't look that way to me." She reached into her purse, and pulled out $30.00. It was a white monogrammed multicolored Louis Vuitton bag. I hated those purses. I thought they were the ugliest things I had ever seen.

"Whatever," I said, taking the money.

"You know, we've known each other for a long time."

She was right. We had known each other for five and a half years.

"And I know how you are. You're a daddy's girl. A princess. I know you probably don't wanna hear me say this, but I gotta be honest, you don't know nothin' about the streets, Passion."

I looked at her like she was crazy. How the hell was she going to tell me what I knew about the damn streets? Did her mother get killed, because her father was a shot caller? Did she lose her man to an act of violence?

She held up her hand like she could read my

73

thoughts. "I know your daddy ran the city. And I know Lay-Law ran his business, but both of them sheltered you, Passion. They kept you at a respectable distance from the game. They kept you innocent." She threw up her hands, like I was exhausting her. "There's so much you don't know. You ever rode that bus down to Statesville to see your man in prison? Solly's been locked up four times. You didn't know that, did you? You don't know nothin' about his world. He don't mess with females like you, Passion. He messes with thugged-out females. Females that's willing to hide vials of crack up in their coochies. He messes with chicks who know how to measure weight, and who carry guns. That ain't you. He ain't your average, ordinary boyfriend, girl. Messin' with him ain't all shopping sprees and trips to concerts. Here's your tip… you need to think long and hard before you keep flirtin' with him the way you did today."

She was right. I didn't know anything about Solomon or how he got down. And he was a baller. I promised myself that I wasn't messing with any more ballers. I told myself that I didn't want any part of that world. I needed to put my hormones in check, and stay away from dude.

"I'm not interested in your cousin, Summer. I have enough problems."

"That's the perfect way to describe Solly – a problem. All he could bring into your life is problems. If he wasn't my flesh and blood, I would stay the hell away from him, myself."

I didn't respond to her tirade.

"Anyway, same time next week, girl. A wash and curl, you know how I do."

I waved at her. "See you next week."

* * * * *

At 7:25, I finished up with my last client, and cleaned up my booth.

"So, can a sister catch a ride to the crib or what?" Jainelle asked, plopping down in my chair.

"My car is at the crib. You have to walk home with me."

"All the way to your house?"

I laughed. Lazy people tripped me out. I only lived a mile from the salon, but some people acted like I lived on the other side of town. "Yep, all the way to my house."

She seemed to think about it as she sat there silently.

"Or you could just take the bus home," I suggested.

She rolled her dark eyes. "See, this is why I need a new man. I'm tired of being dependent on other people."

"You don't need a new man Jai, you just need your own car."

"No, my own car would come with my own car note. If it's my man's car, then the car note is his problem."

"That sounds like some true gold digger stuff." I told her.

She shrugged. "Whatever, Passion. I ain't tryin' to mess with you. You don't know about paying car notes and whatnot. Dudes hit you off with new whips, paid in full."

Usually I let her comments like that slide, but I didn't feel like it right then.

"Jai, you don't know what the hell you're talkin' about." I fumed.

"Whatever."

I sighed deeply. "I guess you gotta believe what you gotta believe. Do you want a ride home or what?"

"Yeah. You know I have to take three busses to get to my house from here."

I picked up my Gucci bag. "I'm ready." I announced.

I saw him as soon as the two of us walked out of the salon. I was surprised, but then again, not really.

"Uhm," I said aloud, but I was talking to myself.

"What's the matter?" Jainelle asked.

She didn't see the silver Chevy Avalanche parked to the east of the salon. I didn't know how she had missed him, Lloyd Banks was blaring from the stereo. I watched as he got out of the truck and started to approach us.

"Uhm," I said, again.

"Who's that?"

"Solomon."

"The cutie who tore up your mirror?"

"Yeah, that's him."

"What the deal, Shorty?" He asked looking me up and down.

"Nothing? What are you doing out here?" I asked, even though I knew damn well what he was doing out there. He was waiting for me.

"I came by to see if you needed a ride home. I remembered you said that you walked to work today." His lips were glistening, like he had just licked them.

I knew I was staring, but I couldn't seem to stop myself. He was too damn handsome. I felt Jainelle pinching me.

"You remembered that, huh?"

"Yeah." He nodded slowly.

"I'm all right." I told him, and Jainelle pinched me harder. I gave her the evil eye.

"Passion, you sure you don't want a ride?" She asked sweetly.

I knew she was dying to get inside dude's Avalanche. "This is my girl, Jainelle. Jainelle, this is Solomon."

"Solly," he corrected. "What's up, Jainelle?"

"What's up wit' chu?" she asked, blatantly checking him out.

"I promised Jainelle a ride home. We're about to walk to my house and get my whip."

"I'll drive you to your house, get in." Solomon volunteered.

Before I could protest, Jainelle practically ran over to the truck. I followed her and slid into the front seat.

"Why do I get the feelin' that you're tryin' to avoid me?" he asked, putting the truck into gear.

I didn't know how to answer that question. I was damned if I did, and damned if I didn't. The more I seemed disinterested in ballers, the more pressed they seemed to get with me.

"I'm not tryin' to avoid you. I just don't see any reason for us to spend time together. You're not my type, and I don't think I'm your type," I said, honestly.

Jainelle hit the back of the seat. I turned around and looked at her. I was about five seconds from whipping her ass for acting all wide open, "Chill out, Jainelle." I demanded with attitude.

Solomon was oblivious to the drama between Jainelle and me. He continued on with his

77

conversation. "How do you know what my type is? You don't even know me. From my cousin, Summer? She don't even really know me."

"Well, she knows you better than I do."

"You shouldn't judge me based on what Summer says. You should get to know me for yourself."

"I don't mess with hustlers, on any level." I shared my philosophy again. "I thought I told you that. I don't date them. I don't sleep with them. I don't befriend them. What's left?"

"You befriended Jinx."

I looked over at him. "Circumstances in my life made me and Jinx become friends. And even we didn't become friends until *after* he got out of the game."

"Well, I wanna be your friend, Passion," he said, point blank. "What I gotta do to be your friend?"

Why couldn't I get away from men that meant me no good? Why did I have to be relentlessly pursued by thugs? Why wasn't I ever pursued by a college graduate or a corporate dude who was doing something positive with his life?

"I'll be your friend, Solly," Jainelle offered, from the backseat.

I wished that she would shut the hell up.

"Thanks Jainelle," he responded, swelling up.

He pulled to a stop in front of my building and Jainelle got out of the truck.

Solomon picked up a few strands of my shoulder length hair, and twirled them around his fingers. The sensation sent a tingle down my backbone.

"I usually get what I want, Passion." He told me bluntly.

I moved my head, so that my hair fell away

78

from his fingers. I needed to stop the damn tingling.

"I'm sure you do."

"I wanna get to know you."

I shrugged my shoulders. "I'm sorry to hear that, Solomon. I can't help you."

"Yeah, you can."

"Don't you need to go?" I asked him. "I mean, I know there's a drug deal goin' down somewhere that you need to be part of."

He put his hand to his chest like I had hurt his feelings. "So, you gotta little mean streak, huh? I like that."

I wasn't surprised. There was no getting around it. He planned to pursue me. I could see it coming. I briefly considered inviting him upstairs to my place and just giving him the panties. That would've gotten rid of him. One of the quickest ways to get rid of a baller was to give up the sex too quickly. But I dismissed the idea just as fast as it came to me.

I opened the truck's door. "Bye Solomon."

Jainelle and I stood there and watched him drive off.

"Where's your whip?" she asked, looking around.

I grinned at her. "I got a new one."

She grinned back at me. "For real? Where is it?"

I hit the remote control ignition starter on my Lexus.

"Oh Passion, you lying heifer!" she blurted, looking from the truck to me. "This ain't your truck!"

I smiled, and nodded. "This is my truck. I got it yesterday."

"Oh hell no, this truck is hot to death! I can't believe my girl is flossin' a Lexus truck."

I climbed into the driver's side. "Come on, get in."

She climbed in next to me. "How did you get this?"

"I traded in my BMW."

"I know that didn't cover the whole price of this."

"Nah, my father made up the difference. He told me to consider it an early birthday present."

She looked over at me. "Your father wanna adopt any more children?"

I started laughing. "You're crazy."

"What made you get rid of the Beamer?"

I loved Jainelle, but I had a thing about telling my business to people. I didn't like doing it. People would use your weaknesses against you. My daddy taught me that lesson. It was better not to let people know where you were vulnerable. I wasn't about to tell her that Lorenzo cheated on me, or that the BMW reminded me of his betrayal.

"You know, it's been a year since Lorenzo died and it's time for me to move on. That car reminded me too much of him. I needed to make a clean break," I admitted.

"I understand."

She settled back into the supple leather interior of my truck. We rode in silence for a few blocks.

"Solly is makin' it real obvious that he wants to get with you." She said finally.

"Yeah, I know."

"He is too damn fine," she said, dreamily.

"Yeah, he is." I agreed. "And his swagger. Whoo-whee! Dude is definitely a rider."

"You're actin' like you're feelin' him."

I sighed, before I admitted the truth. "I like his style. The way he presents himself, but he's not my type."

"I don't know how you do it. As fine as he is, I'd be all over him. He's paid, too. Girl, he'd been got the panties from me."

"Loot doesn't turn me on. My daddy has loot. I'm more attracted to a dude's self-confidence. His swagger."

"You're feelin' Solly's swagger. Why don't you wanna give him a chance?"

"He's a hustler, Jainelle. I don't mess with hustlers. All they do is bring unnecessary drama into your life."

"You had one bad experience with Lorenzo. Now, you writin' off every brotha that balls. Everybody ain't gotta rich daddy. Some brothas do what they gotta do to get that paper."

"I can appreciate that a cat gotta do what he has to do. I just don't wanna link up with none of those brothas, feel me?"

You can't trust them. I thought to myself.

She cut her eyes at me. "So, how many brothas are checkin' for you that work legitimate jobs? How many 9 to 5 brothas are on your tip, Passion?"

She had a point.

Even after I dropped her off at home, that question kept replaying in my mind. *How many 9 to 5 brothas are on your tip, Passion?*

I sighed to myself. At the moment? None. But I was willing to hold out for one. I was willing to hold out for somebody I could trust.

CHAPTER EIGHT

Flowers showed up at *Platinum Plus* for me every day for a week. At first, I thought they were from Solomon. Butterflies danced in my stomach while I fumbled around for the first card. I was mad disappointed when I discovered that the flowers were from Jinx. I gave them to a different stylist everyday. Finally, after eight days of flower deliveries, I called him.

"Enough with the freakin' flowers!" I yelled when he answered his cell. "I keep giving your flowers away. You're wastin' your money."

"Not really. They did what I wanted them to do." He told me.

"What's that, Jinx?"

"Get you talkin' to me again. How are you not gonna talk to me, P?"

"I'm through dealin' with you. I told you that. It's a wrap."

"Nah, it can't go down like this, Baby Girl. You know I got mad love for you. It's killin' me, you not talkin' to me like this."

"I'm sorry to hear that." I wanted to hang up on him. I wanted to slam the phone down in his ear, but I couldn't. We had been too close for me to do him dirty like that.

"You gotta kill this madness, Baby Girl. Things ain't about to go down like this. Tell me what I gotta do for you to forgive me."

"That's just it. I don't know what you gotta do. What could you do to make up for the fact that you kept all that stuff from me? Nothin' can make up for that." I flatly stated.

"Well, something's gonna have to be enough, cuz I'm not about to go out like this."

I didn't respond.

"What time are you gonna be through with your last client?"

"I don't know. Why?"

"I'm comin' up there. We need to talk."

"No, we don't, Jinx. I don't have anything to say to you."

"Maybe I have somethin' to say to you," he responded, calmly.

"Maybe I don't want to hear it."

"What time are you gonna be finished tonight? Give me a time, Passion."

My heart was pounding. I didn't want to see him. "No."

"Well, check this out, I'll be outside of the salon at 9:45. If you don't wanna see me, then you better be gone by then."

I looked at my watch. It was after 5:00, and I still had four heads to do. There was no way that I would be finished before 9:45.

"Don't come up to my job, Jinx," I pleaded. "Please don't come up here."

"I'll see you at 9:45."

* * * * *

At 10:40, I grabbed my purse, and prepared to face Jinx.

Jainelle approached my station. "Is that Jinx out there?"

"Yeah. He says he needs to talk to me." I waved my hands dismissively.

Keena walked over to us. "Passion, Jinx is out there waitin' on you."

"I know."

"Are y'all a couple?" she inquired.

I looked at her like she was crazy. "Hell naw, we ain't no couple. He's like a brother to me."

"You should think about gettin' with him. He's a cutie. Besides, your man's been dead over a year. It's time for you to fill that position. And if you ain't gone get with fine ass Solly, you might as well get with Jinx." Keena had it all figured out for me.

I gave her the evil eye. She was an insensitive heifer at times. "I'm not gettin' with neither one of them."

She eyed me. "Well, if you don't get with somebody soon, I'ma start thinkin' you're gay."

I couldn't tell if she was joking or not.

Jainelle obviously thought she was, because she started laughing.

"I don't give a damn what you think, Keena." I replied. "But I know nothin' like that better get around this salon. If something comes back to me about you sayin' that I'm gay, I'ma beat ya ass."

Both of them looked surprised. They weren't used to seeing that side of me.

"I was just playin' with you, Miss Thing," she responded coolly.

"You shouldn't play like that."

"Go talk to Jinx," Jainelle advised, trying to lighten the situation. "He's been waitin' to talk to you for almost an hour."

I took a deep breath.

"See you on Tuesday." Jainelle waved her goodbye.

"See you."

I left the cool confines of the salon, and walked into the sweltering heat of a summer evening in Chicago. I immediately started sweating around my hairline.

"Hey," Jinx greeted, when he saw me.

"Hey," I said back.

He looked too handsome. His hair was freshly cut and he smelled good, like Ralph Lauren's Romance for Men.

"Can I get a hug?"

I thought that was pushing it, considering that I hadn't even spoken to him in almost two weeks. But my body seemed to have a mind of its own. It went into his open arms. Pressed up against him, I could feel the muscles in his chest. My hand touched the gun that he kept in his back holster. I pulled away from him quickly. I hated guns. And he knew that.

"Where's your whip?" he asked, to ease the awkward moment. He knew that I felt his gun.

"At home."

"How did you get up here?"

"I walked."

"Why'd you walk up here? You're gonna pass out in all this damn heat. Is something wrong with your ride?"

"No, walking is good for you. I like the exercise.

Plus it gives me time to think."

He looked like he didn't really believe me. I didn't care. I just stood there, swatting at the gnats and mosquitoes that were buzzing around us.

"It's hot as hell out here," he complained. "Come on, get in the car. Mosquitoes are eating me up."

I followed him to his Deville, and climbed into the passenger seat.

"Ay Passion, I'm sorry," he apologized as soon as he started the car.

I smiled to myself, because I understood that it was a big thing for him to apologize to me. A lot of dudes would never apologize to a female, no matter how badly they messed up.

"You're sorry about what?" I asked just to mess with him.

"For not tellin' you about Lay-Law. He was my dog. I know since he's been gone, we've gotten close, but I still had a commitment to him. I know you understand that."

I sucked my teeth. "You know what, Jinx? That's over. I wanna move pass that."

"I wanna move pass that, too. But when you move pass it; I don't wanna get left behind." He paused. "I don't want you to feel like you gotta cut yourself off from me, in order to cut yourself off from Lay-Law."

I hated that he knew me so well. "That's exactly how I feel," I said, honestly.

"I don't want you to feel that way. We need to fix this thing."

"I don't see how."

"I don't see how not!"

I switched gears. "Can I ask you a question?"

"Yeah, you can ask me anything."

"How did you feel when Lorenzo told you about that chick, Gabriela?"

"What do you mean, how did I feel?"

"I mean, how did you feel? What did you think?"

"Honestly?"

I looked over at him. "Yeah, a little honesty would be nice."

"I thought he was crazy. I was like, 'Lay-Law, you fuckin' up'. I told him none of those tricks compared to what he had at home."

"And what did he say? Be honest, he's dead. He can't get mad at you for tellin' me now," I prompted.

"He said that you were his baby girl, his wife. The other chicks were just ass."

"What did he say when he found out that Gabriela was pregnant?"

"He begged her to get an abortion. He begged her. He got on his knees and all that. He was petrified you were gonna find out. She wouldn't do it, though. She told him some garbage about it being against her religious beliefs." He took a breath. "So, he got her a condo out in Cicero. Close by where her parents stay, where nobody knew who he was."

We were almost to my block, and I had some more questions that needed answers.

"Jinx, I'm hungry. Can we go somewhere and eat?"

He looked over at me and grinned. He knew that meant that I was willing to spend more time with him. "Yeah, we can go somewhere and eat."

CHAPTER NINE

Summer pranced into the salon for her standing Friday appointment wearing a Lilly Pulitzer patch print dress, and pink Ralph Lauren sandals.

"Girl, I'm lovin' those shoes," I complimented her, as I draped the cape around her neck.

"Thanks. What's really hood?"

"Nothin'. What's up with you? What ever happened with that trip you were plannin'? Weren't you trying to get back down to Miami?"

She waved her hand. "I had to let that dream go. None of my friends could do it. Broke chicks. I guess I'm the only one on the come up."

"I guess so." I marveled at her confidence.

We were both quiet for a few seconds.

"You still with Rico?" I asked. She changed men as frequently as she changed purses.

"For now," she said. "I did meet a real interesting dude last night, though. My girl and I went out to this place called the *White Star Lounge*. You ever heard of it?"

I shook my head. I hadn't heard of too many clubs. I wasn't a nightclub person.

"It's downtown."

"What made you go there?"

"We were tryin' to go someplace different. I got

tired of going up to *Secrets*. Everybody up there knows my name."

I figured she didn't like that. "So, who's this guy you met?"

"His name is Roman. He's half Trinidadian, half Venezuelan."

"Uhm." I was a fan of Latin men.

"Yes girl, that cat is *damn* fine. Ballin' out of control, paid like crazy! Girl, he had the drinks flowin' like water all night long." She paused. "I'ma chill, though. I'm not gonna get too excited. I'ma ride this thing out. See if he's real or not."

We were both quiet, while I applied the blonde highlights to her hair.

"Whatever happened with your car? Did you ever get it back?" I asked finally.

"Nope."

"Your insurance won't let you hold a loaner?"

"Nope. They're bootleg. That's what I get for buyin' insurance from somebody I used to let hit it."

I chuckled. "Did you buy the insurance while he was hittin' it? Or after you stopped messin' with him?"

"Afterwards," she admitted.

"Well, you know you were a damn fool," I teased.

"The mechanic guy hollered at me yesterday, though. He said my car should be ready by Monday."

"Do you believe him?"

"I don't know what to think, Passion. I've been without a car for a month now. It's drivin' me straight crazy to depend on other people. But if it's not ready by Monday, I'ma break down and rent me a car."

"I don't blame you." I paused for a second. "So, is Solomon picking you up today?"

"Why?" she asked suspiciously.

"Because I'm tryin' to avoid him. I know you think I want your cousin, Summer. Honestly I don't."

"Uhm huh," she said with disbelief. "He sure seems to want you. All he talks about is you."

I wasn't trying to hear that. "What?"

"You heard me. You're all he talks about. Every time I see him, he's askin' me about you. He wants to know if I seen you, if you're hollering at anybody. I told him over and over again that I ain't helpin' him hook up with you. I don't even want y'all together," she sighed.

"I keep telling you I don't want him. Is he picking you up today or what?"

"Yep."

"Damn!" I mumbled to myself.

"Passion!" Jainelle called from the front of the salon. "You got some flowers up here."

I looked up just in time to see the flower deliveryman leaving the salon. There was a bouquet of pink Oriental lilies sitting on the reception desk.

"Okay," I replied.

"If you wanna give those away, I'll take 'em." Keena volunteered with a smile.

I smiled back at her. "No, I think I'll keep those."

I handed Summer off to the shampoo girl, and went to claim my flowers. Almost every female in the salon was oohing and ahhing over the beautiful arrangement.

"So, who are they from?" Jainelle asked, with a grin.

I shrugged my shoulders. "I don't know."

My first guess would've been that they were

from Jinx. But since we had made up, I didn't see any reason for him to be sending me flowers. I picked up the beautiful vase of flowers, and carried them over to my station. I took out the card, and read it silently.

Baby Girl,
A brotha appreciates you giving him a second chance.
~ Jinx.

"Damn!" Summer yelled when she returned to my workstation. "Who sent the flowers, Passion? They're gorgeous!"

Before I could answer, she put her hands on her hips and gave me the eye.

"I *know* those didn't come from Solly," she declared.

"It ain't none of your business, but the flowers didn't come from me." Solomon denied appearing at my station. "Who they from, Shorty?"

I looked up at him. "Why Solomon? Like you said, they didn't come from you."

He made eye contact with me. I broke it quickly. There was something about his eyes that was just sexy. L.L. Cool J sexy.

"What you doin' after work?" He asked me.

That made me and Summer look up.

"Huh?"

"Solly, no. I told you that I didn't want you tryin' to get with my girl," she whined.

He looked at her and spoke through gritted teeth. "Since when do you tell me what the hell to do?"

She changed her tone. "Come on, please, leave Passion alone."

"What's up, Passion?" he asked, ignoring Summer, "Can a don get a date or what?"

It seemed like all of the commotion and

conversation in the salon stopped. I looked around. It seemed like everybody was waiting on my answer.

I looked into his handsome face. "I'm busy. Sorry." I apologized, shrugging my shoulders.

"Busy, huh?" he repeated. "I guess you're busy with the cat that bought the flowers."

I didn't respond. I turned my attention back to Summer. "Fifteen minutes under the dryer. Let's go."

When I got back to my station, Solomon was chilling in my styling chair, like he was my next appointment. I ignored him, and instead started cleaning up my workspace.

"You're a trip," he said, bluntly. "You try to play so hard, Shorty. But the truth is I think you're scared of me."

I turned around, and faced him. "You're playin', right?"

He stared at me like, "Hell no!"

"I'm not scared of you, Solomon. I just ain't interested in you. That's probably a new thing for you, so it's kinda hard for you to comprehend."

"You wouldn't know how to act with me." He continued. "Cuz you know I wouldn't treat you like everybody else does. You seem like the type that's used to havin' people cater to you. Cats from off the block probably be killin' themselves to get at you," he paused. "And I wouldn't do that shit."

"I wouldn't ask you to." I assured him.

"Cats sendin' you flowers. You got Jinx ass settin' up rides home for you, and whatnot." He replied with disgust. "And I know your parents got you twisted. They probably spoil the hell outta you. You couldn't floss the way you be flossin' on what you make up at *Platinum Plus*. You're too accustomed to cats lettin' you walk all over them. You couldn't pull that with me, Shorty."

I shrugged my shoulders. "If you say so."

He looked me up and down. "You're the type that wants dudes to chase you. I'll tell you what, Solly don't chase females."

"And I don't date ballers, so I guess we never gotta worry about the two of us linkin' up." As far as I was concerned, that was the end of it.

* * * * *

The next day, Solly had the nerve to show up at the salon with some broad by his side. I did a straight double-take. I couldn't believe him. I peeped the whole thing from my station, as old girl took a seat in Jainelle's styling chair.

I tried not to be obvious. I tried to concentrate on my own clients and not notice him and his girl, but every once and a while, I would look down there. And every time I did, he peeped me.

That situation bothered me all day. I couldn't get over the nerve of his cocky ass!

* * * * *

I was still bugging when I drove Jainelle home later that night.

"So, who was that chick Solomon brought up to the salon?" I tried to be as nonchalant as possible.

"I forgot her name, but she ain't mean nothin' to him. I could tell by the way he was treatin' her. Plus, she was too amped up. I could tell she was new to a dude droppin' chips on her. She was an amateur."

"Uhm," I mumbled.

"Girl, you know that mess was just for show." She said, waving her hand superficially. "Why are you lettin' it get to you like this?"

"I just can't believe him. He was all in my grill yesterday, *beggin'* me for a date. And the next day, he brings some hoe up to the salon?"

She chuckled. "Why does she hafta be a hoe?"

"Whatever. That's just grimy," I continued.

She shrugged her shoulders. "Niggas, you know how they do."

"Asshole," I mumbled.

She laughed out loud. "Girl, Solly got you open already. All that talk about you don't mess with hustlers, that was some bullshit. You're diggin' Solly."

I cut my eyes at her. "No, I'm not."

"Yeah, you are."

I took a deep breath. "Okay, dude is fine. He's fine. If he was anything but a baller, I probably would holla at him. But I can't get with nobody I can't trust, and I don't trust ballers. Secret apartments, secret hoes, secret kids. I can't be bothered with that. Loyalty... that's like the most important thing to me, and I found out the hard way that most hustlers ain't loyal to nothin', but the hustle."

* * * * *

I dropped Jainelle off and then drove towards my own crib. When I pulled in front of my building, I noticed the blue Kawasaki Ninja right away. I had a thing about motorcycles. They were one of my weaknesses. And a cat that rode one, oh, that was just my stuff.

"What the deal?" He called, as I set the alarm on

my truck.

I recognized his voice immediately.

"What's up, Solomon?" I asked, but I kept walking.

"Ay, come here. Let me holla at you for a minute."

I stopped walking, but I didn't move any closer to him. "What do you wanna holla at me for?"

"Just come here."

I walked over towards him.

"Let me take you for a ride."

I shook my head.

"Quit trippin'."

I looked at him like he was crazy. "Quit trippin'? You're the one trippin'. How you gonna be tryin' to get at me one minute, then bringin' some random chick up to the salon?"

"That's my girl. She looks out for me and my workers from time to time. I owed her a favor. She wanted her hair done, so I got it done for her."

"At *Platinum Plus*?"

"What's the problem? You don't want me...right, Shorty?"

I looked him in his eye. "Right."

He smirked, "So, get on. Let's go for a ride."

I looked at the bike. The pearly blue was so pretty and shiny. And I loved motorcycle rides. I loved the feeling of the wind making my hair blow all wild, the speed, the excitement and the danger. I sighed asking myself, "What are you doing?" and climbed on behind him. I wrapped my arms around his waist, and put my head on his back. We rode up and down Lake Shore Drive, and all around the city. After about an hour, he pulled over.

"You hungry?"

"Yeah."

We ended up at T.G.I. Fridays. The restaurant was moderately crowded. We sat down in the waiting area with everybody else.

"Ay, who sent you those flowers yesterday?"

"Why?"

"I'm curious."

"A friend."

"You still got 'em?" he questioned.

"Yeah, I still have them. They're at the salon. That way, I can look at something that makes me smile while I'm workin'."

"So, dude makes you smile?"

"The flowers make me smile," I corrected.

"If dude sends you flowers that make you smile, why you out with me, Passion?"

Before I could answer, a tall, brown skinned female approached us.

"Hey Solly," she said, before making the gum in her mouth pop.

I thought I heard him mumble, "damn."

"What's up, Yolanda?"

"Nothing's up." She looked at me with hatred. "Who is this? It sure in the hell ain't Isis."

He looked at her coldly. "It ain't gotta be Isis."

"Uhm huhm." The girl said, and walked away.

I watched her go, and saw her pull out her cell phone and quickly start dialing.

"You wanna bet she's calling Isis?" I asked.

"Man, I don't care. I don't answer to Isis."

"Solly," the restaurant's hostess called over the intercom. "Table for two."

The two of us followed her to the non-smoking

section of the restaurant, and sat down at the table.

"Who sent you those flowers?" He asked again.

"Stop askin' me that."

"I wanna know."

"But you know that's none of your business, Solomon."

"Then, I have another question."

I didn't respond. I knew that he would ask it either way.

"Why did it bother you so much that I brought old girl up to *Platinum Plus*?"

I opened my mouth to speak.

He cut me off with a grin. "You don't even have to answer that."

"Yeah, I do."

"No, you don't," he said, continuing to grin.

I was getting upset.

The waitress appeared at our table, and asked to take our orders. I couldn't help noticing the way she was kicking flirtatious looks and stuff to Solomon. A couple of times, I started to speak on it, but I remembered that he wasn't my man.

"So, that waitress really wants you," I stated, once she walked away.

"I ain't interested in her. She's a regular hoe, just like the rest of them. I'm interested in you. I told you, you fascinate me." He smiled and shook his head. "I gotta tell you, it feels good to know that you dig me, too."

"I don't dig you."

"Yeah, you do," he winked at me. "You just proved it. But it's cool, cuz to be honest, I'm mad wildin' over you, girl."

I fought hard not to blush, but I lost the battle.

So instead, I concentrated on trying to stop butterflies from dancing around inside my stomach. I didn't want to like him, but something about him was damn near irresistible.

"I'm interested in you. So, when you get home tonight, you can call up dude who sent the flowers, and tell him it's over. He's being replaced."

"Solomon."

"What's up?"

"How do you make your money?"

"What?"

"How do you make your money?" I repeated.

"I'm a business man. I'm a professional hustler."

"Exactly, and I told you before, I don't mess with hustlers. Why do you refuse to believe me?"

He looked at me for a long couple of seconds. The flirtatious waitress brought our food to the table.

"If you need anything else, let me know. My name is Tori." She said, looking directly at him.

We both ignored her. Eventually she got the message and walked away.

"Everything you've shown me up 'til this point, tells me you ain't real."

I picked up a chicken quesadilla. "Huh?"

"I don't believe you won't mess with a hustler, cuz everything you've shown me up 'til now, tells me you're full of shit."

"Whatever."

"Girl, you know I'ma end up pullin' you."

I ignored his over confidant ass and kept eating, but on the inside I was tripping. I couldn't believe he had enough balls to say some stuff like that.

"Did you go to college, Passion?"

"I went to school for hair. I am going to college,

though. I start in August, at UIC."

"The University of Illinois, Chicago?"

I nodded, and took a sip of pop.

"I like your style, Shorty. You ain't like most of the bitch...uh...females that I meet," he said, catching himself. "You run your stuff. I dig that."

"Uhm," I grunted, not impressed or flattered. "You been to college?"

"I wanted to go." He eyed me. "I did pretty good in high school. Got decent grades. I even got accepted to a couple of colleges. I just chose not to go."

"Why?"

"I ain't the book, and homework type. I figured it would be a waste of time and money."

That didn't surprise me. Hustlers wanted fast cash not checks that came every 2 weeks that was too long for them.

We finished eating and he paid the bill. As soon as we stepped out of the restaurant, we were accosted. Some chick was coming towards us talking loudly and giving off attitude. I had never seen the girl in my life, but I knew right away that she was his baby's momma, Isis.

She was a pretty medium height girl, thick, with skin the color of ripe peaches. Her hair was pulled back in a ponytail. She was wearing blue jeans, a t-shirt, and gym shoes; fighting clothes.

"Why you always doin' this to me, Solly?" she asked loudly. "Why I always gotta be catchin' you out with other bitches?"

I saw the girl from earlier standing in the background. I knew old girl had called Isis, and told Isis to get her butt up to Friday's.

"Go home." Solomon sighed, like he was

exhausted.

"I was at home. But then I had to come up here. Cuz as usual, you runnin' around on me with some bitch."

"Don't call her a bitch," he fumed.

Her face fell. "You takin' up for this bitch?"

"I told you not to call her a bitch." He repeated.

"I can't believe this." She said looking at her friend. "I can't believe he's doin' me like this. Why you doin' me like this, Solly? I love you. We got a baby together. We got a baby, dammit!"

Drama queen. I thought to myself, as I watched the scene unfold.

"We ain't a couple. We have a kid together, that's all, Isis."

The entire exchange between the two of them brought back memories of Gabriela at the cemetery. Automatically, my stomach started hurting. "Solomon, can we go?" I asked calmly.

He looked glad that I asked. "Yeah, let's ride."

"Don't leave, Solly. I ain't through talkin' to you yet!" Isis yelled.

"Go home, Isis."

"Ooh, I hate you so much!" She yelled, as she started walking towards her car. "I hate you, you bastard! The next time you want some ass, don't call me! Call that hoe! I mean it! I hate you, you black bastard!"

The two of us walked to his bike. By that time, Isis was headed our way. She was holding the baseball bat she took out of her trunk. She ran towards the bike.

"She better not..." was all he got out of his mouth. Then, the bat made contact.

It wasn't nothing nice, either. Isis tried to outdo

Sammy Sosa. She pulled that stroke up from Mississippi somewhere. The sound the bat made when it struck the motorcycle was unforgettable. Solomon went nuts! He started going after her, before I could even react. And she might have been crazy, but she wasn't stupid. She tried to run.

"I'm sorry, Solly. I ain't mean to do that," she pleaded, realizing she made a big mistake.

"Too bad, cuz you did it." He replied, before he tackled her to the ground.

I didn't want to witness a beat-down, a choking, or a murder, so I went over to them.

"Solomon!" I yelled.

Over the years, I saw my father lose control of his temper too many times. He never hit my mother, but he broke and destroyed things all around our house, in the name of being mad. I couldn't tolerate that type of stuff.

"Solomon, can you please take me home? Please?" I begged. I didn't want to see him hurt his son's mother over a motorcycle.

He looked over at me, then down at Isis, who he had pinned to the ground. He slowly got off of her. He took a few deep breaths.

"You ready?"

"Yes, I am."

"Let's go then. Later for her ass."

The two of us got on his bike. Isis was still crumpled up on the ground, so we pulled off without incident.

When he pulled to a stop in front of my building, he turned and looked at me.

"Yo Shorty, you gotta understand, I don't usually act that way. She just made me so…"

"Mad." I said finishing the sentence for him. "Yeah, my father used to get mad like that. I can't be around that. Later."

He hung his head. I figured he was embarrassed about losing his temper and wilding out the first time I agreed to hang out with him. I left him sitting there on his bike and went inside my crib.

Hustlers, I thought to myself as I unlocked my front door, *they always bring drama.*

CHAPTER TEN

Early Tuesday morning, Jainelle came over to my station with a smile on her face.

"It's too early for you to be smiling like that. I haven't even plugged up my irons, yet."

"Girl, when is the last time you been out?"

"Why?" I asked suspiciously, as I went through my supplies.

"Mack is throwin' a party this weekend, and it's about to be off the chain."

Mack's parties were legendary to those in the know, but I had never been to one.

"Where's it gonna be?"

"The G Spot," she grinned deviously.

"Okay, I'll let you know," I said, still unfazed.

"You're gonna let me know?" she asked, like she couldn't believe me. "Uh uhn. You're the most boring heifer I know, Passion. You don't do nothin'. You don't go anywhere. You're not about to miss this party. You're goin'!"

* * * * *

I rode with Keena and Jainelle to Mack's party on Saturday night. I was feeling good. I hadn't seen or heard from Solomon since the episode at T.G.I. Fridays. I figured I managed to finally shake his ass.

I dressed to impress, that night. I wore a tan Ralph Lauren Polo V-neck top, with the matching Ralph Lauren Polo miniskirt and a pair of the cutest tan, Anne Klein slides. To complete the look, I carried my favorite brown, Dooney and Bourke tassel. My shoulder length hair was arranged in delicate curls that framed my round face. I smelled good, too.

The club was cracking when we approached. The line went on for more than a block, but Jainelle by-passed the line. We followed her through the crowd, and up to the door. I watched as she leaned over and whispered something to the bouncer. The next thing I knew, we were being escorted inside, like we were rolling with Beyonce or something.

"Mack's in V.I.P.," she yelled over the sound of the music. "Let's find him."

He had saved us a table in V.I.P. I figured that was for show, to impress Jainelle, since he wanted to get back with her. He had a complimentary bottle of champagne waiting on us. I quickly poured myself a glass. Since Jainelle had deserted us in favor of Mack, Keena and I sat at the table people watching together for a while.

I didn't even notice Jinx sit down at our table until he spoke.

"What's up, Baby Girl? You out trying to get your swag back?"

"Hey Jinx," I greeted, taking a sip of my champagne.

"Is Baby Girl the only one you see?" Keena asked, cutting her eyes at him.

He graced her with a dimpled smile. "Nah, what's up, Keena? I see you."

"You, and always have been," she said, forcefully.

Jinx seemed to put Keena on hold, and turned to me. "What you doing here?"

I grinned at him. "I could ask you the same thing?" He was like me; he didn't spend too much time on the club scene.

"I ain't been to one of Mack's parties in a minute. I didn't have nothin' to do tonight, so I decided to come out. What you doing here?" He asked again.

"The same thing. Gettin' out the house."

While I was talking to Jinx, the DJ mixed in one of my favorite songs.

"I'm about to go dance," I announced. I got up from the table and made my way to the dance floor. I was out there by myself, dancing like I hadn't danced in a while. A cutie pie started dancing with me. We danced the next three songs together. Finally, I was tired, so I went back to the table. Jinx was still there, but Keena wasn't.

"Where's Keena? You didn't just sit here ignoring her, did you?"

"Nah, I think she went to the bathroom."

I flagged down a waitress. "Can I get a tequila sunrise?"

Jinx looked surprised. He knew I wasn't much of a drinker. I would usually have one or two drinks a year, not a night. But I had been under stress, and I needed to unwind.

"What?" I asked smiling at him.

"You seem sort of... loose tonight."

"So, what's the problem with that?"

"I've never really seen you act like this."

"Well, take a good look, Sweetie."

"You wanna dance?" A short guy with a mustache asked me.

I stood up. "Jinx, can you watch my drink, when the waitress brings it?"

He didn't look too pleased, but he nodded. I went back out on the dance floor, and danced hard with the short dude, towering over his little ass. I was sweating and everything. Jainelle danced over to me.

"Can I holla at you by the restroom?" she yelled.

I nodded, and followed her off the floor.

"What's really going on?" She asked me, once we were by ourselves.

"What?"

"Girl, you out there dancin' with every Tom, Dick and Harry while Jinx is sitting at our table looking pissed."

"If Jinx wants to dance with me, he should ask, hell. The spot is jumpin' and I'm lookin' cute". Jinx will just have to be pissed. He is not my man. What do I care about his getting mad?" The champagne had me feeling too good. I wasn't about to let Jainelle kill my buzz with guilt-talk about Jinx.

"Uhm plus, your boy Solly done fell in the spot. I saw him layin' in the cut watchin' you. He ain't look too happy, either."

"Girl, I ain't thinkin' about Solomon. He don't run nothin'."

She looked at me disapprovingly. "Passion, are you drunk?"

"Hell no. I ain't never been drunk in my life. I

am a little tipsy, though. That champagne was too good. It got my head straight spinnin'."

She smiled at me. "How much did you drink?"

"Two glasses. I'm not drunk Jainelle. I'm just havin' a good time. It's been a minute since I chilled. "

"You're trippin'."

"What?"

"You're drunk."

I waved my hand at her. "I'm about to go dance." I left her standing there and went back out to the dance floor. I must have danced with five different guys before I knew it. Like I had told Jainelle, I was tipsy, but I wasn't drunk. I knew what was happening. Whenever a guy got a little too close on the dance floor, I simply danced away from him. I couldn't stand the way guys would gyrate all up on women, like they were getting off. I didn't play that. I made them keep their distance, and give me my personal space.

I went back to the table. Jinx was still sitting there. "So, you're not gonna dance at all?" I asked sitting down across from him.

He scowled at me. "I thought I was the hired drink watcher."

"Jinx, you didn't have to sit here and baby-sit this drink. Hell, I coulda just thrown it out and got a new one." I pushed the Tequila sunrise towards the middle of the table. I didn't want anymore to drink. The champagne was enough.

"I'm about to blow." He announced standing up.

I mentally debated whether or not to ask him for a ride home. I was tired. Plus, I knew my hair had to look a hot mess. I could feel that most of my curls had fallen out. But I decided to hang. It was rare that I even went out. I decided to make the most of the night.

I stood up, gave him a hug, and kissed his cheek. "See you."

"I'll holla at you tomorrow." He looked at me critically. "Don't drink nothing else, okay, P?"

"I'm not..." I began.

"I know you're not drunk." He interrupted. "But there's a lot of ballers up here tonight lookin' for a drunk honey to take home. I don't want nothing to happen to you. I don't trust these cats. Be careful."

"Okay," I agreed. I didn't want anything else to drink anyway. I watched him walk away from the table.

Jainelle sat down.

"Where you been?"

"Over there with Mack," she answered, nonchalantly.

"Is he winnin' any points?"

"Not really. He's still the same old Mack. I can't see us gettin' back together." She paused, and looked around. "Where's Keena?"

"I don't know. I haven't seen her in a minute."

"Well, I think we need to get ready to bounce. Mack told me that this dude Frisco and his people just came in. Mack's guys don't like these dudes. Somethin' might be about to pop off."

"Word?" I got alert real quick.

"He told me to get my girls, and get out of here."

"Word?" I asked again. That sounded serious. I didn't want to be around if guns were about to blow. With all of the gun-related tragedies in my life, I had a crippling fear of them.

"I don't know if he's feedin' me garbage or

what. Cuz you know he's a big liar," she admitted. "He could just be trying to get rid of me, cuz one of his bitches is comin' up here."

I didn't care if he was telling the truth or not. If guns were about to blow, I wanted to get the hell out of there. "You leavin' or not?" I asked her.

She eyed me. "We can't leave without Keena. She drove."

"Well, let's find her and get the hell up out of here."

The two of us made our way through the gang of people in the club. We checked the bathroom, the foyer, and all around the club. Keena's ass was no where to be found.

"Where could this heifer be?" Jainelle asked.

"You think she left us?" I asked over the music. I wouldn't have put it past Keena. I didn't really trust her.

Jainelle shook her head. "She wouldn't do us dirty like that."

"I don't know," I mumbled. "Call her cell."

She tried Keena's cell phone three times. Each time, she got the voice mail.

I hated to do it. I hated to bother him. But the only person I could think to call to come get us was Jinx. "I'ma call Jinx and ask him to come get us." I yelled.

"One of Mack's boys will take us home. Come on."

I followed her reluctantly. I didn't like the idea of riding home with a stranger. I really didn't want none of Mack's boys knowing where I stayed.

We were making our way back over towards the V.I.P. lounge, when I heard women start to scream.

"Damn," I cursed softly.

Screams weren't a good sign. That usually meant that either somebody was fighting, or somebody had pulled out a gun. A few seconds later, I heard the unmistakable sound of gunfire. Then, everybody started screaming. People started running and pushing. The club was in chaos. People were pushing past me everybody in there was wilding.

The blasts were coming so rapidly, I couldn't even tell what direction they were coming from. I was scared to run the wrong way. I didn't want to run right into the line of fire, but I knew I needed to get out of there. I tried to follow the crowd, but everybody was disoriented and panicking. I said a quick prayer, and started moving in the direction that I hoped the exit was in.

Then, somebody grabbed my hand and was yanking me through the crowd. I thought the person was going to pull my arm out of the socket. They were pulling me in the opposite direction that the crowd was running. I prayed that the person had a plan, as I followed them.

The next thing I knew, we were in the alley behind the club.

"You straight?"

I looked up. It was Solomon. I was happy to see him. I calmed down and tried to catch my breath. He didn't let me. "Come on," he demanded, then, yanked my arm again, and pulled me out to the street.

People were pouring out of the front door of the club. The cops were pulling up. We ran to his Hummer H2.

I sat in his truck shaking. The thought that I was so close to bullets really had me bugging. I hated guns.

I hated them! Neither one of us spoke while we rode to my house. I was still shaking when he pulled up in front of my building.

He looked over at me. "What's the matter with you?"

"Nothin'," I said, but a few tears fell down my face.

He wiped them away. "Let me park."

CHAPTER ELEVEN

Solomon sat on the couch in my family room, while I changed out of my club outfit, and put on jogging pants and a tee shirt. I walked back into the room, and sat down next to him. My legs were still shaking, but they were starting to slow down.

He placed his hand on my right leg. "Why you shakin' like that?"

"It's a long story."

"Why was you cryin'?"

I was silent.

"Yo, do you usually act like this when you're drunk?"

I got upset. "I'm not drunk, Solomon. Hell, I only had two glasses of champagne."

"I can't tell, the way you were shakin' your ass all around the dance floor, with every dude in there."

It was typical that he would say that. "I wasn't shakin' my ass. I was dancin'."

"Where was those dudes when you was about to get shot?"

I threw my hand up at him. "Whatever!"

"Where was those dudes when you was about to get shot, Passion, huh?"

I eyed him defiantly. On one hand I was pissed.

Who the hell was he to tell me how to run my business? On the other hand I was grateful. He basically saved my life.

"Thank you for gettin' me out of there." I relented after a minute.

My cell phone started ringing.

"Don't answer that." He instructed me. "We're talkin'."

I figured he was used to females doing what he said, but I wasn't the one. I answered my cell.

"Hello."

It was Jinx. "Where you at, Baby Girl? I heard some buster shot up the club."

"I'm at home."

"Who is that?" Solomon asked, just loud enough for Jinx to hear him.

"Who is that?" Jinx asked.

"That's Solomon."

"Who is that?" Solomon stood up from the couch.

I took the phone away from my mouth. "It's Jinx."

That seemed to calm him down.

"What's Solomon doin' in your place?" Jinx asked.

"He brought me home. Keena left me and Jainelle stranded at the club."

"Why is he still there?"

"I was shakin', Jinx. Somebody started shootin' up the club, and I had a panic attack. Solomon got me out of there."

Jinx knew how I felt about guns. He knew that gunfire petrified me. "Are you straight, P? You need me to come over there?"

"Nah, I'm cool."

"I knew I shouldn't have left you up there." He said more to himself than to me.

"Yeah, I shoulda left when you left." I agreed.

"How long is Solly gonna be there?"

I didn't think that was any of his business, but I answered anyway. "Not long."

"You sure you're straight?"

"I'm cool, Jinx." I assured him.

"Holla back if you need me."

"I will."

"I'll check on you tomorrow."

"Talk to you then. Bye."

"Jinx must think he's your daddy or somethin'." Solomon said after I hung up.

I rolled my eyes at him. "He's been there for me through a lot of foul stuff," I replied.

He eyed me suspiciously. "And you're sure y'all ain't never messed around?"

"What difference would it make if we did?" I was getting tired of him trying to act all possessive over me, when I wasn't his girl.

He watched me for a while. "I don't think you messed around with him. I think he wants you, but I don't think you ever messed around with him."

"He doesn't want me." I schooled him.

"Ay, he's a better man than I am, then. I couldn't spend as much time around you as he does and not want you."

I was uncomfortable, but flattered by his compliment.

"If you can't tell, I'm kinda jealous of Jinx,"

"Why, you wanna be a big brother to me, too?" I teased.

He shook his head, and licked his lips. "Nah, but I wanna get to know you like that cat knows you. He knows a lot of things about you, and you won't tell me nothin'."

I cocked my head to the side. "Just tell me what you wanna know? Maybe I'll tell you."

"I wanna know why you were shakin' like that in my whip," he asked, gently.

"Uhm."

"See, you ain't gone tell me, but I bet Jinx knows. And since he knows, I wanna know why you won't tell me."

"I will."

"Tell me, then."

"I'm scared of guns. Ever since Lorenzo got killed, I can't stand being around them," I admitted, leaving out the fact that my mother was killed by a bullet too. "I have anxiety attacks. That's what causes the shaking and stuff."

"That's messed up, Shorty," he said, then pulled me to him. I put my head on his shoulder. He smelled really good. It was the same scent that always seemed to follow him. It was the same scent that permeated his truck.

"What is that cologne you're wearing?"

"Happy For Men," he responded, easily.

I sat straight up. My dream man wore Happy For Men, but Solomon wasn't my dream man. My dream man worked a 9 to 5. He worked in an office building. He wore suits to work. My dream man wasn't a thug.

"What's the matter?"

"Nothing," I lied.

"You don't like it?"

"No, it smells good."

"Then, why did you get up? I like the feelin' of you layin' your head on me."

I put my head back on his shoulder. I was walking on dangerous ground with him, but I couldn't seem to stop myself. Even though he was the last cat I would've chosen to get with, I had to admit that I was attracted to him. I wasn't sure how much longer I could fight it.

"Shorty," he whispered sweetly.

"Huhm?"

"I wanna kiss you."

My heart started pounding. I couldn't let him kiss me. That would just lead to all types of trouble. Before I could respond his soft lips came down on top of mine. I opened my mouth and accepted his tongue. He kissed me hard and deeply. After about the third kiss, I put my hand to his chest and pushed him away gently. He was turning me on, and I wasn't trying to let things go further than I was ready for them to go.

"No Solomon." I stopped him.

"Why?"

"You said it yourself. I'm not like the girls you're used to hollerin' at."

He stared at me, looked into my eyes to see if I was feeding him bull. When he realized that I was serious, he pulled back.

"I wanna see you tomorrow."

The next day was Sunday. I had plans to spend time with my daddy and Lynne.

"I'm busy tomorrow."

"With what?"

My whole demeanor changed. Lorenzo was a control freak, too. He always had to know where I was, who I was with, what I was doing. I wasn't getting into anything like that with Solomon.

"I'm busy tomorrow, Solomon. I don't know what else to tell you."

"So, it's like that, huh?"

"It's like that."

We were both quiet for a few seconds.

"I wanna ask you a question." I said innocently.

"What's up?"

"Are you gonna tell me truth?" I knew he was gonna lie. Ballers hardly ever told the truth. It wasn't in their nature. But I had to ask anyway.

"It depends on what you ask me."

I was shocked. He was more honest than I thought he would be. "Are you still hittin' your son's mother?"

He brought his gaze down to mine. "What made you ask me that?"

"I wanna know. I'm curious."

That wasn't the whole truth. I wanted to know because he kept hinting that he wanted to holla at me. I wasn't about to get with him if he was still having sex with Isis. I remembered what she said, as she went to her car to retrieve the baseball bat that night up at T.G.I. Fridays. She told him that the next time he wanted some booty, not to call her. To call me.

"I was still hittin' her for a minute after we broke up. But then she started acting all psycho and whatnot. She couldn't separate the sex from a relationship. So, I had to leave it alone."

"How long has it been since you stopped havin' sex with her?"

He eyed me. "You ask a lot of questions."

"If I don't ask, how am I gonna know? You want

me to break all my rules. Get involved with you. I need to know what I'm gettin' myself into. If you can't handle that, then you need to get in the wind."

He sighed heavily. "I stopped hittin' her about six months ago. I'm not real comfortable hollerin' at you about stuff like this, Passion. The past should be the past."

"You're full of mess." I told him.

He looked surprised. "What? I ain't lyin'. I ain't hit Isis in at least six months."

I rolled my eyes. "That's not what I'm talkin' about. You're full of mess with your comment. *The past should be the past.* You weren't sayin' that when you were askin' me all about Jinx."

He smirked and his eyes lit up. "You're a trip."

"No, I'm just real."

"Whatever, man," he said, standing up.

I winked at him. "I know this is all new for you. I'm a different kind of female. That's what *'fascinates'* you about me, right?" I teased.

"Oh, you wanna be jokin' me."

"You keep screamin' you wanna get with me."

"Is that what I'm screamin'?"

"You know that's what you're screamin'. Well, this is me." I walked him to my front door.

"When are we gonna get up? When are you gonna make some time for me?" he asked.

"You can holla at me Tuesday after work. I'ma need a ride home."

"Tuesday?" he questioned. "What are you doin' Monday? Ain't you off on Mondays? Why can't we get up then?"

"See," I began, "this is exactly why things between us probably won't work. I'm my own woman,

Solomon. I only answer to Passion. I'm tellin' you, either you can pick me up on Tuesday night or you don't have to. The choice is yours."

"I'll scoop you on Tuesday. Hit me up and let me know what's up."

"See you Tuesday."

He bent down, and kissed me. I wrapped my arms around his neck, and enjoyed the sensation. It had been a long time since a brotha kissed me like that.

*****

I didn't speak to Keena on Tuesday. I couldn't get over the fact that she left us at the club. Jainelle talked me into going to lunch with them. I didn't want to go, because I was feeling like I might snap out, but the three of us went up to Burger King anyway. Being around Keena made me lose my appetite. I didn't even order anything. I just sat down at the table with them.

"So, why did you leave us up at The G Spot?" Jainelle wanted a response after asking Keena.

"I looked all around that club for y'all," she claimed.

"Why are you lyin', Keena? You know you didn't look for us. The club ain't that damn big."

"I did look for y'all," she insisted, getting angry with her.

I knew that broad was lying. I could just tell.

"So, when you didn't see us, you just decided to bounce?" Jainelle frowned.

I watched her think up another lie.

"I didn't know if y'all left me, and I was ready to go."

"Bitch please!" It slipped out before I could

catch myself. She ignored me.

"How could we leave you, when you were the one who drove?" Jainelle asked.

"Exactly," I seconded.

"Did you even care that we didn't have a way to get home?" Jainelle was getting angrier.

Keena sucked her teeth. "Hell, Jinx was up there. I know he wouldn't have a problem droppin' his girl, Passion off." She said it real nasty, too. Envy mixed with jealousy.

"Jinx left." Jainelle informed her.

Keena looked surprised. "Jinx left without giving y'all a ride?"

"Yeah, Jinx left. We told him we were straight. Did you know somebody shot up the club?"

"Yeah, I heard that."

"Did you even care that Passion and I got caught up in that mess?"

She looked agitated. "Hell, y'all are grown. I can't protect y'all from bullets? What did y'all expect me to do?"

"We expected you not to leave us up there. We expected you to holla at us, and tell us you were about to bone out." Jainelle schooled her. "Plus, I called your cell three times. You didn't even answer that."

She sighed. "I went over Junebug's that night. My phone was probably off. We were into somethin'."

"So, you were screwin', while we was gettin' shot at?" Jainelle was about to beat her ass.

I couldn't say anything. I was too pissed. I was a second from grabbing Keena by the throat, and choking the hell out of her.

"Whateva," she said unmoved.

I got up and walked out of Burger King. I had to

leave. I was too close to doing or saying something I would regret. I was too damn pretty to go to jail. Too pretty for a chick named Big Bertha to be staring at.

* * * * *

When I got off work that night, Solomon was outside waiting for me, just like he said he would be. I smiled when I saw him. He was so damn fine. And he always dressed so nice.

I grinned at him. "Hey you."

"Hey yourself. You ready?"

I nodded and walked with him over to his truck. He took me to the movies.

"Yo, Shorty," he started, as we were driving out to the movie theater.

"Yeah?"

"You still got those flowers dude sent you?

I was lost for a second. I didn't know what flowers he was talking about. "Oh, you mean the pink lilies? Yeah, I still have them."

"If I send you some flowers tomorrow, what are you gonna do with dude's flowers?"

He probably never sent a girl flowers in his thug life. I thought to myself.

"You're gonna send me some flowers?"

He looked over at me. "Maybe. Answer my question first."

"I can't just throw the flowers away, Solomon."

He got a little upset. "Why? Why are they so important to you? Who are they from?"

I started to lie, and tell him that they were from my daddy. I always felt like I had to lie to Lorenzo, just to keep the peace. I wasn't about to start that stuff with

Solomon. He was going to have to roll with me or leave me alone.

"They're from Jinx. I was pissed at him for something, and he sent me the flowers to apologize."

"I knew they were from that punk," he fumed, like he was pissed.

I sat there silently.

"Why were you pissed at him?"

"I don't wanna talk about that, Solomon."

"He must have tried to get with you or something."

I rolled my eyes. I had been looking forward to spending time with him all day, and he was pissing me off. He needed to shut up talking about Jinx.

"Why are you messin' up our time together worryin' about Jinx? I'm not with Jinx, am I? If I wanted him, I wouldn't be here with you." I didn't say another word to him until we left the theater.

* * * * *

When he pulled up to my building later that night, he turned to me. He was looking all-pitiful and stuff. He grabbed my hand. "My bad, Shorty. I ain't mean to trip over Jinx. I know y'all gotta friendship thing happenin'. I'ma respect that. I've been in a lot of relationships, filled with a lot of stupid, petty arguments. I don't want it to be like that with me and you."

"It won't be." I assured him. "Because I don't like arguing like that."

He pulled me to him, and kissed me deeply.

"I've been waitin' all day for you to do that."

"Say word."

I chuckled, "Word, Solomon."

"I'll hit you up tomorrow."

"Later," I said, waving at him.

* * * * *

"What in the hell did you do to my cousin?" Summer asked when she came in for her weekly appointment.

I smiled at her. "What do you mean?"

"If I knew you were gonna have this kind of affect on him, I woulda tried to get y'all together sooner." She continued. "Girl, that ain't the same Solly. I don't know who that is."

"Word?"

"Word." She lowered her voice. "Passion, I know you ain't hit him off with no booty already."

"Naw," I admitted. Summer and I weren't close like that. She usually didn't get in my business on that level.

"I didn't think so. I guess it's just you that's got him actin' this way."

"Actin' what way?"

"I don't know. He's just different. He's more calm... more relaxed. Something matters to him besides the hustle."

That made me smile. Since Solomon came in my life, I felt more relaxed, too. Kissing those soft lips helped take away some of my stress.

The telephone rang at my workstation.

"Hello?" I asked, wondering who was calling me.

"Passion, it's me, Kimberly. I have some flowers up here for you. Can you come get them?"

"Okay," I said and hung up the phone. "They have some flowers up there for me." I told Summer.

"Damn, you get more flowers than any other stylist up in here. I know they must be jealous."

I left her at my station, and headed towards the front of the salon where the receptionist desk was located.

"I can't believe Jinx is still sendin' you flowers." Keena commented as I walked past her station.

I ignored her. I hadn't spoken to her since she left us at the club.

Sitting on the receptionists' desk was a bouquet of purple roses, and a purple teddy bear.

"Aaww," I cooed, picking up the vase of flowers, and teddy bear.

I carried them back to my station. I sat the flowers down next to the ones that Jinx had sent me. I put the bear in Summer's lap.

"Hold this."

"Who sent the flowers?" she asked.

"Probably Jinx." I guessed. I dug around for the card. When I found it, I read it to myself.

Yo Shorty,

I never sent any female flowers, so I really didn't know what to put on this card. I just like your style, and when I saw these flowers, they made me think of you. The color purple is real feminine, just like you. As far as the teddy bear, I know females like stuff like that. You can name him Solly. He can chill on your bed until the real Solly gets a chance to chill there.

~ Solly

I must have been smiling, because Summer grinned at me.

"I know those flowers aren't from Solly," she

stated.

I didn't reply. I just took the teddy bear from her lap, and placed it on top of my workstation.

"Are those flowers from Solly?"

"Yeah, the thug sent me flowers." I stated in disbelief.

"Girl, you got him wide open. I can't believe he sent you flowers. You gotta have him buggin'."

I just kept smiling.

"Apparently, he has you buggin', too, huh?" she observed.

"I'm feelin' him," I confessed.

"Passion, I wouldn't usually get in your business like this, but I have to say somethin'."

"What's up?"

"Don't sex him yet. Females always cater to him. Make him work for the booty. That way, he'll treat you different than he treats these regular hoes out here."

"Okay," I agreed, since that was my plan anyway.

"Okay." She replied, then, smiled. "Solly sent my girl a bouquet of flowers. Wait 'til I tell Autumn this! She's gonna flip the hell out."

CHAPTER TWELVE

Lynne had four tickets to see Bernie Mac in concert that she and my daddy couldn't use, so she gave them to me. I invited Solomon and Jainelle to go with me. I told Solomon to invite one of his boys, so Jainelle would have a date.

I was real specific with him about who he should bring. I told him not to bring anyone that would make the metal detector at the venue go off. I told him not to bring nobody with an insane baby's momma. I told him not to bring anyone with a *main* girlfriend that still saw other women on the side. And finally, I told him not to bring no damn druggies.

By the time I finished giving him my list, he looked at me like I was crazy. "Do you really want me to invite one of my boys?" He second-guessed me. "I don't fuck with squares, and that's who you're askin' me to bring."

I laughed but I was dead serious.

Finally, he decided that his cousin Tippy would be the best bet. Tippy was a baller from the north side of the city. I didn't care that Tippy was a thug...as long as he was a refined thug, and knew how to act in public.

Jainelle came home with me from work that evening. I set her up in my guest bedroom, so she could spend the night, after the show.

"Girl, I hope Solly's cousin is as fine as he is."

"I hope he knows how to act. I would hate it if

Tippy turns out to be some ignorant type cat."

She eyed me. "Ooh, I would hate that, too."

The two of us sat down and ate Popeye's fried chicken, while we watched television. We chilled for about an hour, then, it was time for us to get ready.

Jainelle and I were both into fashion. I spent more loot on clothes than she did, though. But I admired the way she was able to make her paper stretch. She knew how to work what she had to get the most out of it. As soon as I slipped into my black Kate Spade pumps, Solomon called my cell phone to let me know that he and Tippy were downstairs in front of my building.

"You ready?" I asked her.

She picked up her Coach bag, while I grabbed mine.

"Yeah," she said. "Man, I hope you and Solly ain't set me up with no sucker."

* * * * *

Solomon and his cousin were double parked in front of my building. They were standing in front of a red Hummer H2 talking.

"Is that dude's Hummer?" Jainelle asked me, like I would know.

"He looks comfortable leanin' on it. It must be." I hyped her.

"He gotta Hummer? That's a good sign. He must be paid."

I shook my head at her. She was destined to be a damn gold digger.

"I can't really see his face. Is he ugly?"

"From what I can see, no," I said.

128

We walked up to the guys.

"Hey," I greeted Solomon.

He bent down and hugged me tightly. Then he slowly took in my outfit, "You look nice."

"So do you."

And he did. He was wearing Sean John and it was loose in all the right places.

"Yo Tip, this is my shorty, Passion." Solomon introduced. "Passion, this is my cousin, Tippy."

"Hey," I said smiling. "It's nice to meet you."

Tippy was attractive. A lot like Solomon, except he was shorter, and broader. His face was round and friendly. They both had the same smiling brown eyes, thick eyebrows, small nose, and lush mouth as Solomon.

"What's up?" Tippy acknowledged.

Solomon pulled Jainelle up front and center. "Yo, this is Jainelle. Jainelle, this is Tippy."

"Hi," she smiled shyly.

I tried not to laugh. She wasn't shy by a long shot.

"What's up, Ma?" Tippy asked. "You ready to have a good time?"

"Sure am," she said, happily, looking all pleased.

"Well, let's do this." He took her hand.

I got into Solomon's truck.

"So, you think your girl is feelin' my cousin?"

"I'm sure she is. Y'all look alike."

"Everybody says that."

"He seems cool."

"He is cool."

"You think he's feelin' Jainelle?"

"He's diggin' her. They'll hit it off."

* * * * *

After the show, and a late dinner at Shaw's Crab House, Solomon and Tippy drove us back to my condo. Solomon walked me to the front door, while Tippy and Jainelle stood at his truck and talked.

"Since you had the tickets, I guess I should thank you for showin' me a good time." He teased. "Do I gotta give you some ass for comin' outta your pocket?"

"Not this time." As I laughed, I touched my hand to his chest. He was so silly.

He caught my wrist, and pulled me to him. Our bodies were touching, and the fabric of my dress was much too thin. I could feel every inch of him.

"So, where are my flowers?"

"They're at work."

"Where's the bear, Little Solly?"

I laughed. "You're crazy. I guess he's upstairs asleep in my bed."

"Lucky him."

I stared into his eyes.

"When do you think it's gonna be my turn?"

I put my finger over his lips. "Slow down, Boo." I whispered, then, I leaned forward and kissed him. He put his hand on the back of my head, and held my mouth to his. Then, he let his fingers play in my hair. That stuff was turning me on, for real. I could feel my nipples hardened under the material of my halter top. He put his hands on my butt, and pulled our pelvises together. I could feel that he was getting hard.

Then I heard the tap of Jainelle's footsteps on the concrete. She was approaching us. He kissed me again then released me. "I'll holla back tomorrow," he said.

His mouth was right on my ear and I could feel the heat of his breath.

"Okay." I practically melted.

"Bye Solly," Jainelle said, grinning at him.

"Later, Jainelle."

* * * * *

Me and Jainelle changed into our pajamas, and met in my family room.

"So, what did you think of Tippy?" I asked.

She threw her hands up in the air. "Oh my goodness. Dude is fine, fine, fine! I think I'm in love, Passion," she gushed.

"Love?" I asked, doubtful. "You just met him."

She was a real dramatic person. Everything with her was over the top. "You don't understand." She tried to explain it to me. "Dude is what I been lookin' for. He's fine, paid and he's real sweet. Passion, he has conversation. He actually talked to me."

Most thugs didn't have long drawn out conversation. Usually, they were basically out to hit it. I figured Tippy was really feeling her.

"What did y'all talk about?" I asked, thinking that maybe I had hooked up with the wrong cousin.

She fell out on the sofa. "Everything."

I sat there and waited for her to get to the point.

"We talked about growing up, our parents, relationships, and the election. We talked about everything. And he had stuff to say on every topic."

"Did he kiss you good night?"

She shook her head sadly. "Nah. He ain't even try," she paused. "I did give him my number. He said he would hit me up tomorrow. You think he likes me?"

131

I smiled. "I think he's interested."

She sat up abruptly. "What makes you say that?"

"Solomon told me."

She gave me a Kool-Aid smile. "Good. Cuz I really like this cat already, Passion."

"I can tell," I said chuckling, "but you need to slow down, Jai. You need to get to know him. He could have a lot of kids. Or he could be one of those brothas who likes to beat the hell outta his women."

"I don't think so, but you're right. I do need to slow down."

We were both quiet. She looked over at me.

"What?" I asked smiling.

"You're thinkin' about Solomon, aren't you?" She teased with a grin.

"Maybe."

"Passion, that boy is gone over you. You should see how he looks at you."

"I ain't messin' with you, Jai." She wasn't about to blow my head up.

"I'm serious. Solomon looks at you, like a well trained dog looks at a sirloin steak."

I raised my eyebrows. "What?" I giggled.

The look on her face was serious. "I'm straight up, Passion. Solomon looks at you, like a well-trained dog looks at a steak. A well-trained dog wants that steak so bad he can taste it, but he knows better than to jump, before the master gives the command. So, he'll wait, pretend to be patient, but when the master lets him loose...you best believe that dog is gonna do damage to that steak."

"What kind of damage is he plannin' on doin' to me?"

She winked at me. "Sexual damage, girl. That boy wants you. And when you let him off that leash, you better be prepared."

Don't worry. I thought to myself. I was already fantasizing about what sex with him would be like.

"Since the first day that boy laid eyes on you, he's been sweatin' you. Showin' up at the salon, givin' you rides to the crib. He even sent you flowers. Girl, please. As fine and as paid as that bastard is, do you really believe he's ever been checkin' for a broad the way he's checkin' for you?" She lay back on the sofa, and stared up at the ceiling.

"Nah, I know he's givin' me special treatment."

"Your ex-guy was a hustler, too, right?"

"Who Lorenzo? Yeah, he was."

"How long did you make him wait before you gave him some?"

I thought about it. "Four, maybe five months," I admitted.

"How in the hell did you do that? I see you one of those ancient chicks." Before I could answer, she spoke again. "I hope you don't think Solly's gone wait that long for some ass."

I didn't respond. I didn't expect him to wait as long as Lorenzo did. Lorenzo caught me when I was a virgin. I was scared to death to have sex with him the first time. Solomon was a different story. He had me feeling too good every time he touched me. I was hoping I would be able to hold out on him for another week, but I wasn't sure. A few more kisses like the ones he gave me today, and I knew my panties would fly off.

"Solomon and Lorenzo are two different people." I explained. "I was a virgin when I linked up with Lorenzo. Ain't none of that happenin' now."

"You were a virgin?"

I nodded proudly.

"So, how many guys have you linked up with, Passion?"

"One, Lorenzo."

Her mouth dropped. "So, Lorenzo is the only dude you ever dropped the panties for?"

"Yeah." She acted like I was lying or something.

"Does Solly know?"

"No. That ain't none of his business. I never asked him how many females he's been with."

"If he ever starts movin' too fast for you, just tell him that Lorenzo is the only person who ever hit it. That should slow him right down."

"Please. Things between me and Solomon could never move too fast."

She bugged her eyes. "Oh, you're talkin' big now, huh? Solly got you feelin' all tough."

I laughed. "I think I'm just horny."

We both exploded into a fit of laughter.

CHAPTER THIRTEEN

The first Saturday in August started out like any other day. I made it to the salon at 7:30 in the morning for my 8:00 appointment. I parked as close to the shop as I could get, which wasn't all that close. I went inside, set up my station preparing for my first client of the day.

Around 11:00 that morning, the spot was cracking. Everybody was trying to get their hair done and get out of the salon. I was working on two clients and had another one waiting for me to start on her head. I heard a commotion at the front of the building. I sat one client under the hair dryer, and moved towards the front of the shop to see what was going on.

"There that hoe is." I heard an irate female say.

The crowd parted like the Red Sea, and the next thing I knew, I was face to face with Isis. She had two chicks standing behind her. I assumed that they were her back-up.

"I've been lookin' for you, bitch." She hissed at me.

She caught me off guard, and it took me a minute to recover. I was indecisive at first. One part of me was tripping, because I couldn't believe the heifer had brought some garbage up to my job. The other part of me wanted to mop the floor with the hoe.

"Me and Solly have a son together. That there is my property, and if you touch what's mine one more time, I'ma fuck you up."

135

"What?" I couldn't believe she was up at *Platinum Plus* wilding out. How did she know where I worked? I was gonna kill Solomon.

"You heard me, bitch."

I made eye contact with her. "You got one more time to call me a bitch," I warned. I was trying to remain calm. A soldier needed to remain calm, especially in the face of a war. My father had taught me that. A hot head never prevailed.

"Stop fuckin' my man, hoe! Stop messin' with my damn husband!" She yelled loudly.

Everybody in the salon had their eyes on the two of us. I was humiliated, and pissed. I hadn't even had sex with dude, and his psycho ex-girl was up at my job calling me out.

My pride overruled my desire to remain calm. I rushed the broad, and popped her dead in her lying mouth. While she was stunned and confused, I grabbed her by the hair, and flung her to the ground.

"I ain't no punk, bitch! Don't be comin' up to my job talkin' trash about me." I had her on the floor, choking her. "You been lookin' for me? You been lookin' for me? You're gonna mess me up? Huh? Huh?"

A crowd gathered around us and after a minute or so, strong hands were pulling me off of her.

"What?" I yelled. "What?"

Daniel and a couple of the other barbers were holding me by the arms. I was still kicking with my feet. They made good contact with her ribs a couple of times. Isis' girls had congregated around her.

"Passion, calm down." That was Jainelle. She was trying to wrap her arm around my shoulder.

I was huffing and puffing, trying to catch my

breath. The barbers released me. I straightened up my clothes, and ran my hands over my hair. I was still pissed, but I was calming down.

"Everybody get back to work!" Shonnie Davis demanded loudly. "I called the police, and they're on the way up here." She walked over to Isis and her girls. "I suggest y'all leave, before the police get here. Cuz I do believe in pressin' charges."

Shonnie was the closest thing to an assistant manager at *Platinum Plus*. When Taffi was away at one of the other locations, we looked to her for help and guidance. She had worked at the salon the longest, and had tons of experience in doing hair.

"Uh, Passion, can I talk to you?" She turned and made her way towards the back of the salon.

I followed her into Taffi's office. I knew that she couldn't fire me, but she could tell Taffi. And Taffi could fire me. My heart was pounding. Shonnie was a down to earth person. She had grown up in the hood, so she understood hood situations. I knew that I could talk to her about the whole Isis - Solomon situation.

"Shonnie, I apologize." I began as soon as we sat down. "I can't believe I lost my temper like that. That's never happened to me before."

"That's understandable, but this is a place of business. You handle hoodrats in the hood. Who is that broad anyway?"

"That's Solomon's baby's momma."

"So, she's mad that you got him, now?"

"Basically."

"Crazy heifer. Look, I wouldn't tell Taffi about this, but there are too many big mouths in this salon for it not to get back to her. I'm gonna call her and tell her what happened, but I'ma tell her that you were defending yourself. I'll probably say that broad had a weapon. I don't know, hell, she could have had one. And when the police come, I'm gonna give them a statement."

"Okay."

"Are you straight? Can you finish workin' on your clients?"

"Yeah, I can. That is, if they let me. I hate that my clients saw me wilding out like that. I like to present myself as a professional. I hope I don't lose business over this bullshit." I walked back to my station with all eyes on me. I picked up my utensils, and went back to work. Regardless of the thoughts that were running through my mind, I made sure that the rest of the day was business as usual even when the police arrived.

* * * * *

Solomon was outside of the salon when I got off work that evening.

I was surprised, because in all the confusion, I didn't have a chance to call him and tell him what happened. I was happy to see him, though. I smiled at him.

He frowned in return. "What the hell happened between you and Isis?"

No, hello, no hug just a question about Isis.

"Hey, Solomon. How're you doin'?"

"Quit playin' with me. What the hell happened?"

"She came up here on my job startin' that bullshit. How did she know where I worked?"

He looked annoyed. "I don't know. She says you

attacked her."

I almost laughed. "Well, if that's code for, I beat her ass, yeah, I guess it's true."

He looked at me with disgust. "You 'beat her ass'?"

I couldn't tell if he was pissed with me, or pissed with her. "What's the deal? Are you mad at me?"

"I don't know. I'm still tryin' to figure out what the hell went on. Isis been blowin' up my cell all day, talkin' about you attacked her, and called the cops on her. Then you come out here, actin' like some regular bitch, talkin' about you beat her ass. Ain't you better than that, Shorty?"

I couldn't respond. I was stuck on the fact that he called me a "regular bitch". That was total disrespect. That was the same as calling me gutter trash, ghetto hoe or something like that.

"Bye Solomon." I said, and walked to my truck.

"Shorty! Hold up!" He called.

I ignored him. Just like a *regular bitch* would do. I got in my whip and headed over to my daddy's house. I knew that if I went home, he would just show up there. So, I flipped the script on him. He did blow up my cell phone, though. He blew it up so much that I ended up turning it off. I popped Nas,' *I Am* CD into my stereo, and hit track number eight.

I sang along with Aaliyah. *"You won't see me tonight, you won't see me tomorrow. I'll be gone by daylight, and you'll be so full of sorrow."*

* * * * *

Jinx invited me to lunch with him on Monday afternoon. After lunch, he followed me back to my place in his car. I saw Solomon's Avalanche parked in front of my building as soon as I bent the corner. I didn't acknowledge him. I waved to Jinx as he pulled off, then, walked into my building. No sooner than I locked the door to my apartment, did Solomon ring my bell. I buzzed him up.

While he was making his way to the second floor, I kicked off my Via Spiga sandals.

He banged on the door three times.

"Who is it?" I asked, even though I knew it was him.

"Solly."

I unlocked the door and let him in.

"Where have you been?"

"Around," I replied going into my kitchen. "I'm gettin' a pop. You want something to drink?"

"Nah, thanks." He followed me into the family room and sat down on my sofa. "Saturday was crazy." He said. "I ain't like the way things played out."

I was silent.

"I told you before that I've been in a lot of relationships with a whole lot of unnecessary arguing and whatnot. I thought we agreed that we weren't gonna have that in our relationship."

"We did, but a relationship involves two people, Solomon. Not three. I didn't appreciate the fact that you came to me with some garbage that your son's mother told you."

"You gotta understand, Shorty. She was hysterical when she called me."

"Of course she was hysterical. She came up to my job talkin' major garbage, then, she got her ass whipped. You woulda been hysterical, too."

He cracked a smile. "What happened?"

"Does it even matter?" I asked, but I knew it did. He had a baby with Isis.

"I just wanna know. You tell me what happened."

"Your girl Isis came into the salon wildin', all bugged eyed, talking about she was lookin' for me. When she saw me, she started callin' me out. Talkin' about, you're her property, if she catches me with you again, she's gonna mess me up. Everybody in the salon was watchin' us. Then, she told me to stop sexin' her husband. So, everybody in the salon starts lookin' at me like I'm some type of home wrecker. I was so embarrassed that I lost it. My temper got the best of me. I hit her in the mouth. Then, I started choking her." I took a breath. "I'm not some *regular bitch*, Solomon. I don't usually get down like that. She pissed me off."

"I didn't mean to say that, baby. I know you ain't a regular bitch. That came out the wrong way. I was mad."

"That's not an excuse to me." I didn't want him to get in the habit of verbally abusing me every time he got mad.

"True," he agreed.

"I've never called you outta your name and I never will. I don't roll like that, and if you ever call me outta my name again, it's a wrap."

We were both quiet.

"Did you ever figure out how Isis knew where I worked?" I asked him.

He shook his head. "I'm still workin' on it." He shook his head. "That broad is crazy. She probably followed me up there one day. She follows me every now and then."

"What?" She followed him every now and then?

What type of stuff was that? That sounded like some psycho-stalker stuff to me.

"Yeah, she likes to follow me. Every now and then, I'll look in my rear view mirror and see her car."

"And you don't check her about that?"

"At one point, I felt like she was gonna push me to kill her. I really did. I had to reevaluate the situation. So, now I ignore her. She's like a real high-strung person. She loves attention and drama. When I ignore her, it tears her up on the inside. It works better than me gettin' pissed off."

I decided not to comment on his taste in his past women. He was with me, so he had obviously figured out some things.

"Did she tell you that she came up to *Platinum Plus* wildin' out?"

"She made it seem like she was walkin' past the salon and you came out and jumped on her. The details were real shady, except for the fact that you jumped on her. I shoulda known she was lyin'."

I couldn't help but agree. He should have known she was lying.

"Where were you and Jinx comin' from?"

"Applebee's. He treated me to lunch."

"Why?"

"We're just cool like that. We go to lunch, dinner, and the movies. We hang out all the time."

"Even since you've been messin' with me?"

I nodded, "Yes."

"So, where have you been since Saturday? When you left the salon, where did you go?"

I knew that was bugging him. Especially since he saw Jinx's truck pull up behind mine. I decided to let him off the hook. "I went out to my father's house. I stayed over there until this afternoon. After lunch, I came home."

"Where's your father stay?"

I was starting to notice a pattern with Solomon. Every time Jinx's name came up, the third degree came into play. "In Frankfort."

"Frankfort?" He repeated.

"It's in the southern suburbs."

Solomon's cell rang before he could question me any more. He answered it and said a few words. When he hung up, he turned to me. "I gotta blow. That was Isis. I told her that I would pick up my son today." He paused. "You wanna come?"

I briefly entertained the thought, and decided against it. "Nah, that's okay. I don't wanna impose on your son's time."

He hugged me and kissed me deeply. "I'll holla." He told me, and left my apartment.

* * * * *

The next day when I got to work, Taffi was waiting to talk to me.

I walked into her office, and sat down on the chair. She sat across from me at her desk.

"Passion, I heard what happened on Saturday with that client attacking you." She said sadly.

I didn't know what Shonnie had told her, so I just nodded my head.

"I don't know what's wrong with women nowadays. Everybody's so ghetto. All these young girls think that fighting is the way to solve problems. Are you okay? Is everything all right?"

"Yes."

143

"Good," she said. "I want you to know that Shonnie did file a report with the police. If that little girl ever comes in here again, she will be removed for trespassing."

I smiled. "Okay."

"That's all, Passion. Have a good day."

"Thank you, Taffi," I exhaled.

I'll have to look out for Shonnie, I thought to myself. Maybe pick her up a nice little present for making things all good with Taffi for me.

* * * * *

I only had four clients, so I was at home, and eating dinner by 7:30 Tuesday night. I was washing up the dishes when my telephone rang. I checked the caller ID; it was Solomon's cell phone.

"Hey."

"What the deal?"

"Nothing. What's the deal with you?"

"I'm sittin' up here lonely."

"Word?"

"Word."

"Where are you?" I pried.

"I'm at the crib."

"And you're lonely?"

"Yeah. I rented some movies. I don't wanna watch them by myself. I need somebody to come over here and keep me company."

"Is that an invitation?"

"Yeah," he said. "You wanna get up with me tonight?"

I couldn't help noticing that he sounded really hopeful. "Yeah, I'll get up with you."

"How long is it gonna take you?"

"About an hour."

"Cool, see you in an hour."

I showered, and dabbed Noa perfume on all of my pulse points. Next, I put on my favorite La Perla thong and bra set. Over that, I wore denim shorts, and a tee-shirt. I threw on a pair of white K-Swiss gym shoes, grabbed my purse, and hit the door.

CHAPTER FOURTEEN

Solomon didn't live far from me. He lived in Hyde Park. He stayed in a high-rise building, with beautiful views of Lake Michigan. I made it to his place in about fifteen minutes. He answered the door wearing blue jean shorts, a blue wife beater, and whiter than white socks.

He wrapped me up in a hug. "Hey Shorty, get in here."

I walked into his apartment for the first time. It seemed like he had been getting ready for me to come over all day. His house was immaculate and I could smell the unmistakable scent of incense burning.

My apartment was real feminine, with lace curtains and colorful throw pillows. Solomon's apartment was just like him, all man. The furniture was big and dark. His couch and loveseat were black leather. His cocktail table, end tables, and entertainment center were a deep mahogany.

"You gotta nice place." I told him, taking in his art work, and his plasma television.

He smirked. "I know it's not as nice as yours, but thanks."

146

I playfully pushed him on the arm. "It's as nice as my house…it's just different."

"Yeah, my furniture ain't got no ribbons on it and whatnot."

I rolled my eyes at him. "You tryin' to talk about my taste in furniture?"

"Nah, Shorty. I like your place. It's real feminine, just like you. It's easy to relax there, but I can't seem to get no invitation to your crib."

I ignored him.

"You can sit down."

I sat down on the sofa next to him.

"Since this garbage with Isis, it seems like our relationship's been…I don't know, strained," he stated.

I nodded in agreement.

"I don't want that. I don't want no third party thinkin' they gone come in and disrupt our flow. I know what you're thinkin', and you're right. I was the one who let it happen. I realize that, and I've handled that situation. As long as we together, Shorty, that'll never happen again."

"Okay, Solomon."

He changed the subject. "Yo, I got these movies." He handed me the DVDs.

While I went through the movies, I could feel his eyes on me. I looked over at him, and caught him staring. I grinned. "What?"

"Nothin', you look good."

That was when I noticed what Jainelle was talking about, the look in Solomon's eyes when he looked at me. I didn't know about the "well trained dog" thing, but I could definitely see desire in his gaze. I started feeling turned on.

"Thanks." Warm feelings enveloped me.

"You're a good girl, Shorty. I like your style."

"Thanks."

"Sometimes, I can't believe you actually messin' with a cat like me."

I smiled, but didn't respond. I wasn't sure if he was being sincere or talking slick.

"You're like mad different from other females. It's like, everything about you is official."

"Are you tryin' to gas me?" I asked suspiciously.

"Nah. I'm straight up. You're like, mad classy. You gotta job. You got your own dough. You got your own whip. You got your own place. It's like, what do you need a man for? What can I do for you that you can't do for yourself?"

I looked over at him slowly. "You're right. I don't need a dude to hit me off with a whip or loot. But shoot, I do get lonely. I do wanna talk to somebody sometimes. I do want some companionship." I took a deep breath. "It's nothin' nice being out here by your damn self all the time. Please believe me."

"But you could get any cat. Why are you messin' with me?" He asked like he couldn't accept his good fortune.

"You could get any chick. Why are you messin' with me?"

"None of these other females out here can touch you, Shorty."

"Remember that."

He put the movie in the DVD player. I rested my head on his shoulder. He was good for about the first fifteen minutes of the movie. He sat there and watched, like a good boy. But then, he started playing in my hair.

"Stop Solomon," I teased. "You're supposed to

be watchin' this movie."

"I am," he lied, then leaned over, and kissed me on the lips.

Before I knew it, I moaned. "Uhmmm."

He kissed me again, and again. His hands went from holding my head, to traveling down my body. First, they were on my breasts then on the sides of my hips. I lied back on the couch, and let him climb on top of me. We were kissing and grinding like nobody's business. He was running his hands through my hair, and I was running my hands over his back.

"Uhm," I moaned over and over.

"You gotta stop moanin' like that, Shorty. You're makin' my dick hard."

I tried to be quiet, but I couldn't. It was too long since I last felt the sensations he had me feeling. He lifted up my tee shirt, and bra, and started sucking on my right breast. I put my hand on the back of his head and held him there. I enjoyed the feelings his mouth was giving to my body.

"Take your shirt off. I wanna feel your skin."

He pulled off his wife beater. Things were moving quickly, but we weren't being wild like animals. We were moving at a comfortable pace.

"Let's go in the back."

I figured the bedroom was in the back.

"Okay," I agreed. At that point, I was down for whatever. I followed him to his bedroom. It was pitch black in there. He let up his mini blinds, so the moonlight would stream in. It was a nice effect.

I climbed in the middle of his king sized bed. He climbed in next to me.

He took off my shirt, then, winked at me. "I wanna feel your skin." He ran his hands over my breast. "Damn Shorty, this bra is sexy as hell."

"Thank you."

"Even your underwear is classy."

I giggled.

"Lose it."

"Huh?"

"The bra, everything, Shorty. Lose it."

I unfastened the clasp, and let the bra fall over the side of the bed with my shirt. Then, I took off my shorts and thong, while Solomon took off his clothes. He came to me real easy. He grabbed me in his arms and held me close. Made me feel like I was the only chick he wanted. He laid kisses all over my neck, with sucks and nibbles in between. I moaned and groaned like he was already sexing me.

"Stop moanin', Shorty," he whispered between kisses. Then, he moved down to my breasts. He took my left, perfectly rounded size 36D breast into his mouth. I wrapped my arms around his neck. I dropped kisses on his forehead, while he reminded me of the pleasure being in a man's arms could bring. Then, I lied naked in the middle of his bed. I was dripping wet, and ready for him to do practically whatever he wanted to me.

He rolled over and reached into his nightstand for a condom. Once he had it on, he trailed little kisses down my stomach. My breath caught as he spread my legs and dropped kisses in my sweet spot. He licked soft at first. My legs started to shake. He applied more pressure, and went to work. My back arched, and I pushed his face all up in my candy.

"Ooh, ooohhh," I moaned.

Solomon knew exactly what the hell he was doing. He was a master at eating the candy. Just when I thought I was about to explode, he moved up my body. I was tingling everywhere and ready for the real thing. I needed to have sex. I needed to feel the sensation of penetration. I climbed on top of him. He positioned his head at the opening of my center. I pressed my pelvis down. He put his hands on my waist, and helped me down slow. He let me feel him inch by wonderful inch. Let me control the pace. I rode the hell out of him.

I bucked and moaned, threw my head back and everything. After a year without sex, I was like a nympho. I tried to take every inch of his sexiness, and he tried to give it to me. He pinched my nipples hard as hell, while I bounced up and down, wilder and faster than I ever did before. The feeling of pleasure was multiplied by the way he was pinching my nipples.

He flipped me over, and got on top. He hit it deep like it was good to him. Like it was a minute since he had some booty as good as mines. I moaned and screamed like I was being tortured. The two of us pounded out a rhythm. The more I moaned, the harder he gave it to me. Solomon pumped the hell out of me. And I loved every stroke. I came like two times. The second time, I squeezed my muscles and caught him up. That and my screams made him bust like five seconds after me.

He groaned and shook. Then, he collapsed all on top of me.

I held on to him. For some reason, I didn't wanna let him go. I wrapped my legs around his middle. He didn't protest. He held me tight, too. We stayed that way a few minutes.

My eyes were closed while I rode the last of the waves. He kissed my eyelids.

151

"You cool?" he asked in typical thug fashion.

I nodded. I wasn't ready to talk. I was still enjoying the sensations.

"I dig you." He kissed me on the forehead.

I smiled to myself. I wondered if that was the most sincere form of emotional expression he could show. I wondered if the "L" word ever exited his luscious lips.

"I dig you too, Solomon."

The two of us laid in his bed, with our bodies curled up to each other.

* * * * *

"Shorty! Shorty!"

I woke up slowly. I was disoriented for a minute. I wasn't sure whose big, old bed I was laying naked in. I looked towards the direction of the voice.

Solomon was standing over me, holding my cell phone. He had on his shorts, but his chest was still bare.

I remembered the lovemaking he put on me, and smiled at him.

He smiled back. "Somebody's blowin' your cell up." He handed me the phone.

I looked at the clock on the nightstand. It was 1:37 a.m. "Hello?"

"Baby Girl, where the hell are you?" It was Jinx, and he was talking mean to me. Something wasn't right.

I sat up straight. "What's wrong?"

"I've been callin' you for almost an hour, and you ain't been answering your cell."

"I was asleep," I admitted.

"I called your crib, too. You didn't hear that phone either?"

I responded without thinking. "I'm not at home."

"You're not at home? It's 1:00 in the morning. Where the hell are you?"

"What's wrong, Jinx? Can you just tell me what's wrong?" I thought maybe something happened to my father.

"It's Lynne."

"What about Lynne?" I was hesitant to ask, because I was petrified to hear his answer.

"Who's Lynne?" Solomon asked.

I looked in his face and saw concern. I held up my finger, and asked him to give me a minute.

"Your father found her unconscious in her office at the house." Jinx repeated what my father had told him.

I gasped, "Where is she now? Is she okay? When did he find her?"

"She's at the Olympia Fields Medical Center. I'll come and scoop you. Take you out there."

"No," I said quickly. "I got it. I can drive myself. Just give me the address."

Solomon handed me a pen and a piece of paper. I wrote down the information. "I'll be there in a minute." I hung up my cell phone and started looking around for my underwear.

"What the deal, baby? What's wrong?" Solomon asked.

"My father rushed my step-mother to the hospital. He found her unconscious." I searched the entire bed, frantically looking for my clothes. "Where're my clothes? I can't find my clothes."

He watched me silently for a minute. "Calm down, Shorty." He said finally, and handed me my clothes. "Where you gotta go?"

"To Olympia Fields Medical Center."

He went to his closet and pulled out a shirt. "I'ma drive you."

I looked over at him. "Nah, Sweetie, that's okay. I can drive myself."

"You kinda hysterical Shorty and I don't want nothin' to happen to you."

"I'm cool really. I need to be by myself right now."

He looked skeptical.

Once I was completely dressed, Solomon rode the elevator down to the street with me.

"Yo Shorty, I don't think it's too cool for you to drive all the way to Olympia Fields by yourself. You're upset. I got a bad feelin' about this."

I didn't respond. I couldn't deal with arguing with him. All I could think about was that I was about to lose another mother. He walked me to my truck, and when we got there, my sadness turned to anger. My truck was sitting on four flats. The tires weren't just flat they had been slit. And I could see where my truck was keyed. Somebody had taken the time to go back and forth along both sides, just ruining my entire paint job.

I stomped my foot. "I'ma kill that bitch when I catch her!" I yelled. "I know ain't nobody did this, but your girl, Isis."

"Damn!" He fumed, looking as mad as I felt.

I leaned against my truck, and started crying. I was pissed off, and scared.

He pulled me to him, and hugged me tightly. "Don't do that, baby. I got you. I'll drive you anywhere you need to go." He seemed to know that I needed him to hold me.

I followed him to his truck.

CHAPTER FIFTEEN

I despised hospitals; absolutely despised them. The only things I hated worse were cemeteries and funeral homes. I especially hated the emergency room. It was a haven for infected people. That smell, those germs, and the sick people. I just hated it.

I bent the corner of the waiting room cautiously. I peeped Jinx leaning against one of the ashy gray walls. I ran right up to him.

"Where's Lynne? Is she all right?" I blasted him with questions.

"I'm not sure. I just got here myself," he responded.

Just then, Solomon came in from parking his truck.

Jinx looked from Solomon to me. "What's up, Solly?" Jinx asked extending his hand.

Solomon gave him dap. "What's up, Jinx, man?"

"So, you were at Solly's crib when I called?" Jinx asked me, as Solomon stood right by my side.

"Solomon, I'm really thirsty. Could you get me something from the pop machine?"

"Yeah," he agreed.

Once Solomon was out of earshot, Jinx started in with the questions. "Is your boy insecure or what? Why'd he have to come up here with you?"

"My truck was on a flat. Actually, it was on four flats. He drove me up here."

"Your truck was on four flats?"

I nodded, feeling anger rise in me.

"Your brand new truck?"

"Yeah, my brand new truck."

"Did it have something to do with the little altercation I heard went down at the salon?" he asked. "I heard your boy's ex-woman came up to *Platinum Plus* wildin' out."

It seemed like he had an "in" on everything that happened in my life.

"Can we talk about that later?" I asked getting agitated. I wanted to know what was going on with my step-mom.

Solomon came back with a Sprite for me. I smiled at him as I took the cold drink from his hand.

"Passion..." Jinx began.

"Ay Jinx, fall back." Solomon felt the need to protect me. "She's been through a lot tonight."

Jinx looked like he wanted to say more. My father approached us before he had the chance.

"Baby Girl," my father said, breathing a sigh of relief. I went into his open arms, and let him hold me close.

"Daddy, what's wrong with Lynne? Is she all right?"

"She's all right. She'll be fine."

I exhaled. I didn't even realize that I was holding my breath.

"She fainted from exhaustion and dehydration."

"Exhaustion and dehydration?" I repeated.

What did Lynne do that would exhaust and dehydrate her? I thought to myself. As far as I knew, she was a kept woman.

"Like I said, she'll be fine. They're going to keep her here tonight, run a few additional tests. She should be home by tomorrow."

"Oh, thank God!" I said, and hugged my father again.

"Jinx," my father said, extending his hand, "thanks for everything. I appreciate your concern."

Jinx shook his hand. "No problem, Mr. Hill, anytime."

My father noticed Solomon for the first time. "Hello," he said extending his hand.

Solomon shook it firmly. "It's nice to meet you, Mr. Hill. I'm sorry to hear about your wife."

"Thank you," he said, graciously. "And you are?"

"I'm sorry. I'm Solomon Kent. I'm a friend of Passion's."

So, Solomon had some home training? I thought to myself. That was a relief.

"It's nice to meet you, Solomon." He turned to me. "Passion, I need to speak with you in private."

I followed my father away from Solomon and Jinx.

"Baby Girl, who is this thug telling me that he's a friend of yours?"

"Daddy, he's my friend."

He eyed me, and I felt like a misbehaving seven year old again. "Is he the reason that Jinx and I couldn't find you?"

158

I didn't lie to him. My father wasn't a punk. He knew the deal. I couldn't pull a 'fast one' on my daddy. I had given up on that as a teenager.

"Yeah."

"Passion, I love you. You're my only daughter, and you mean the world to me. I've worked hard to give you all of the advantages that most people don't have. I've never asked for anything in return."

"I know, daddy."

"I never commented when you brought Lorenzo home, even though I knew his line of work. When he was killed, your pain was my pain. I thought you had learned this lesson. I thought you realized that a certain type of man is headed for a certain type of destiny."

How could I explain to my father that I had tried to stay away from Solomon? How could I explain that I didn't want to have feelings for Solomon, but I did?

"Daddy, I did learn that lesson. I learned it the hard way..."

"Obviously not well enough, Baby Girl." He interrupted. "The first guy you bring to me since Lorenzo, and he's a hustler? I don't understand this."

There were so many things that I wanted to say, but my father had enough on his mind.

"Daddy, I apologize for bringing Solomon to the hospital. I wouldn't have brought him, but he thought that I was too hysterical to drive. He was worried about me." I kissed his cheek.

I threw in the part about him being worried about me to win Solomon some points. My father seemed to like it when guys wanted to protect me. I figured it gave him a sense of comfort.

"Worried about you, huh?"

I knew that would soften his feelings towards

159

Solomon. "Yes."

"I know you're not stupid, Baby Girl. I didn't raise you to be stupid. I trust your judgment."

I gave him a gentle hug. "Do you want me to send Solomon and Jinx home?"

"I want you to go home, too. There's nothing for you to do up here. It might take hours for them to get Lynne admitted."

"I don't care," I whined. "I wanna see her. I wanna be here when she wakes up."

My father looked drained. "Passion, I need some time...alone."

I understood completely. I hugged him. "Okay daddy. I'll be back first thing in the morning. Tell Lynne that I'll see her no later than 10:00."

"I will."

"And tell her that I love her."

"Be safe, Baby Girl. Call me when you make it home."

"I love you, daddy. Bye."

When I got back to the waiting room, I spotted Solomon asleep in a chair. Jinx was leaning against a wall shooting bullets at Solomon with his eyes.

"What's up, Baby Girl?" Jinx asked, when he saw me.

Solomon opened his eyes.

"They're gonna admit Lynne. That could take hours, so my father told me to go home, and come back later on today."

Solomon stood up and stretched. "So, you ready to rotate?"

"Yeah, I guess."

"Where's your whip?" Jinx reached out to me. "I'ma have one of my tow trucks pick it up. We'll start workin' on having the tires replaced tomorrow."

I was just about to respond, when Solomon cut me off.

"You're straight, Jinx. I got this. I mean, I'm partly responsible for it happenin'."

"Partly?" Jinx asked, sarcastically. "The way I see it, you're totally responsible for the shit happenin'."

His comment totally caught me off guard, but it didn't seem to startle Solomon one bit.

"Why the fuck is you in my business, Playboy? I'ma take care of Passion."

"Oh yeah?" Jinx was sarcastic.

"Ay!" I said interrupting. "Cool out, it's not this serious." I turned to Jinx, and gave him a brief hug. "Thanks for calling me...over and over." I teased, to ease some of the tension.

He hugged me back, which I knew pissed Solomon off. "You sure you're straight?" His eyes never left Solomon.

"I'm fine. Be safe going home. I'll get up with you tomorrow."

"I'll holla," he said, then, walked away.

I turned to Solomon. "You want me to drive? You seem sleepy?"

"I'm straight. Let's blow," he stated, his eyes filled with suspicion.

* * * * *

I called in sick to work the next day and had Kimberly reschedule all of my appointments. Jinx picked me up at 10:00 in the morning, and we were at the hospital by 11:45. I was loaded down with gifts for Lynne. I had flowers, candy, and even a diamond tennis bracelet from Rogers & Holland's. It may have seemed extreme to some, but in a family where my father gave a Lexus truck as a birthday present, it was the norm. Besides, Lynne loved diamonds.

We walked into her room. It was filled with balloon bouquets and vases of flowers. Lynne grinned at us, and put her fingers over her lips. My father was sitting in the chair next to her bed. He was asleep.

"Hey," I whispered, giving her a hug. "You okay? Don't ever scare me like that again."

"I'm fine. I'm just embarrassed. I can't believe all the fuss your father made over me."

"Well, he loves you."

"I know he does. Hey Jinx, you're still just as handsome as ever."

"Hey, Mrs. Hill, it's good to see you're doin' better. You had us all worried."

"I'll be almost perfect, once they get me off all these machines. Give me a hug."

He hugged her gently.

"I brought you a gift." I said, and handed her the bag from Rogers & Hollands.

"Ooh," she was so thrilled. "What can this be?" She pulled out the long, slim velvet box. Then she opened it and removed the tennis bracelet.

"Ooh, Passion," she cooed. "You didn't have to do this."

"You love it." I teased with a smirk. "I want you to have something pretty to look at while you're stuck in this hospital."

"Well, put it on me," she said, holding out her wrist.

I clasped the bracelet on her wrist. She held it up and admired it. She twisted her wrist to the left and to the right acting like my father didn't give her gifts like that all of the time.

All the fuss Lynne made over the bracelet woke my father up. He opened his eyes slowly.

"So, you finally made it, Baby Girl? I thought you said that you would be here no later than 10:00," he teased.

I put my hands on my hips. "I had to wait for the mall to open."

"The mall?"

Lynne held up her wrist. "Look at what Baby Girl picked up for me." She practically gleamed.

He examined the bracelet. Then he looked up at me and grinned. I knew that I did a good job. He kissed Lynne on the cheek, then, turned to me. "Passion, I want to talk to you."

He walked out of the room and I followed him.

"Why is Jinx here?"

"He drove me."

"Why?"

"My truck had a flat tire." I was evasive.

He stared at me for a long while. He knew something was up. "This Solomon cat has something to do with that, right?"

I didn't answer right away.

His whole demeanor changed. He became his old self before my eyes. It didn't surprise me or scare me. I knew exactly who my daddy was. He could wear expensive clothes, buy a huge house, make all of his businesses legit, but he was street. I knew, and he knew it.

"What the fuck? I just bought that damn truck."

"His son's mother put my truck on four flats last night," I confessed. "And she keyed it. She messed up

163

the paint job completely."

He was pissed. His eyes were two little slits. "What kind of man lets his old bitch, mess with somethin' that belongs to his new bitch?"

I understood that he wasn't calling me a bitch. He was making a point. And he wanted me to understand the disrespect that Solomon was showing to me by not protecting my personal belongings.

"If somebody came out of the woodwork and laid a hand on *anything* that belongs to Lynne, I would dead 'em."

I knew he was serious. He wouldn't care if it was man, woman or child. He didn't play when it came to his family. Since my mother's death, protecting the people he loved had become his top priority in life.

I didn't say anything.

He sighed heavily, "Tell Jinx to have your truck towed to-fucking-day! I mean it, Passion."

"Solomon's taking care of it," I said, finally.

He eyed me. "As well he should. As well he should," he paused. "What is he doing about this crazy bitch?"

I was embarrassed. I didn't know what he was doing about that.

My father let me off the hook. "You let him know who I am, Passion."

He kept calling me by my given name. So, I knew he wasn't messing around with me. I hung on his every word.

"You mention my name. If he's as large in the game as he's supposed to be, he'll know who I am. You tell him that I said if something like this happens again, I'm holding him personally responsible. And if he likes his life, he'll make sure that nothing like this ever happens again."

"Okay daddy."

"If this dude won't protect your material possessions, how can you expect him to protect your life, Baby Girl? Ballin' ain't no game for the weak at heart. I refuse to lose you the way I lost your mother. I'll put this whole city in the ground, before I lose you. This cat needs to step up. He can't date my daughter if he's bullshittin'." He eyed me. "You think I'm playin'?"

"I know you're serious, Daddy."

"I've never dictated who you should and shouldn't date, but I will make an executive decision."

"Understood Daddy."

"As a matter of fact, I want you and Solomon to come by the lounge tonight," he instructed. He owned a lounge off of 87th and Stony Island. "Sometimes, young boys pick things up better, if they hear it from the horse's mouth."

I didn't say a word.

"Be there by 9:30."

"Okay."

"And don't be late."

"Okay," I repeated.

As he started to calm down the glazed over-look left his eyes, and I became Baby Girl, again, instead of Passion. "Wear something pretty tonight. I wanna show you off."

"All right, daddy."

He pulled me into his arms, and hugged me tightly. "You and Jinx get out of here. I'm gonna try to get these hospital bastards to let me take my wife home."

I kissed his cheek. "I love you, Daddy."

He looked at me with a seriousness that I had

never seen. "I love you, more."

Chapter Sixteen

When I called Solomon and asked him if he would take me to my father's place, he didn't ask me why. He just agreed. I figured that he felt bad, because his baby's momma messed up my whip. All I knew was that no matter how he felt, he was gonna feel worse once my father got through with him.

He picked me up at 8:45. When I walked out of my building and up to his Infiniti, he just stared at me. I asked him what was wrong, and he said that I looked really good. I didn't tell him I dressed up for my daddy. I just took the compliment and smiled.

I was wearing a wrap dress by City DKNY and Manolo Blahnik suede slides. My hair was pulled up into a bun, with delicate curls coming down along the side of my face.

* * * * *

My daddy's lounge, *Classified*, catered to an older and more upscale clientele than 'shake your booty' clubs did. *Classified* was decorated in muted tones of tan, camel and sand. The chairs, bar stools, and chaises were plush leather and suede. The long bar was the best oak that money could buy. The liquor served was top of the line. The music played at *Classified* was mellow. It was mostly all jazz. People didn't come to my father's lounge to jump and wiggle, they came for an experience.

When we walked into the door, I noticed that Solomon hesitated. "Whoa! This is your father's lounge?"

"Yep." I was proud.

He shook his head. "I didn't even know nothin' like this existed over in this neighborhood."

Most people didn't. I took his hand. "Come on."

We walked over to the bar. I smiled at the bartender. He had known me since I was in high school. "Hey Joe."

He smiled at me. Joe always greeted me with a smile. "Your father said you would be coming by, Baby Girl. How you doing?"

"I'm fine. How are you?"

"I can't complain." He looked over at Solomon. "Who is this?"

"My friend." I easily omitted Solomon's name from the introduction.

"Hello," Joe greeted.

"How you doin'?" Solomon responded.

"Fine. Baby Girl, your father said to tell you to come back to his office when you got here."

"Thanks Joe. I'll see you later." I led Solomon back to my father's private office.

"Yo Shorty, does everybody call you, 'Baby Girl', but me?"

I thought about it. "Pretty much," I paused. "Solomon, my father wants to talk to you. That's why we're here."

He looked confused. "What does he wanna talk to me for?"

"You'll see. I just wanna tell you, whatever happens, don't let my father see you act like no bitch. He can't stand weak men."

"Shorty, I don't ever act like a bitch. So, you don't have nothin' to worry about."

I wasn't convinced. I had seen my father break tougher men than him. I tapped lightly on the door.

"Come on in, Baby Girl."

He had surveillance equipment throughout the lounge. That was how he knew it was me knocking on his door. I turned the knob and walked into the room.

Lynne decorated the office to resemble a rich man's library. There were oak bookshelves, mahogany desks, leather armchairs with tons of books. It was also a very relaxing atmosphere for my father. It had a 60-inch plasma TV, a mini bar, an entertainment center, a pool table, its own restroom, and a leather chaise, big enough for two.

"Baby Girl, you look beautiful, gorgeous."

I was glad that he was pleased. "Thank you, Daddy. You remember Solomon."

My father looked over at Solomon. "Yeah, I do. What's up, Solomon?"

Solomon reached out and shook my father's hand. "How are you doin', Mr. Hill?"

"Thanks for coming, Young Blood." My father said, showing his age and taking a seat at his desk. "Have a seat."

The two of us sat down next to each other, facing the desk.

"Did my beautiful baby tell you why I asked you here tonight?"

Solomon shook his head. He looked cautious, but he didn't look spooked. I was impressed.

"Nah, not really, she just said that you wanted to talk to me, sir."

"*Yeah.*" He unloosened his tie. "How long have you been in the life, man?"

Solomon looked surprised. "Sorry?"

"Don't play with me, man." My father said, dropping all pretenses. "How long have you been in the fuckin' game?"

"Years," Solomon said, finally. "I can't say for sure. I've been around the game practically all my life since I was a shorty."

"Well, I used to run the damn game," Daddy retorted. "You were trying to get your first piece of ass, when I owned these streets, youngin. You've heard of a nigga name Pretty Hill, right?"

Solomon searched his memory bank. It didn't take long. "Yeah, I heard of him. He's a legend."

"Well, the legend lives, Young Blood. The legend lives."

It took him a second to catch on to what my father was saying. Then his eyes got all wide.

My father nodded his handsome head. "Yeah, you done lucked up and landed Pretty Hill's baby girl."

Solomon looked over at me. I knew he was probably hot that I didn't tell him who I was off the bat. I didn't make eye contact with him. I looked straight ahead, at my dad.

"And I gotta tell you; so far you ain't impressing me too much."

Solomon was silent.

He went on. "My daughter came by the hospital

170

this morning to see my wife. I got in her ass. And it's not fair for me to get in her ass, without getting in yours. It seems like you got a little situation."

"What do you mean?"

My father watched him. "Somebody messed up my daughter's brand new truck. I paid for that truck, and I don't stand for nobody messing with my paper," he eyed Solomon meanly, "Do you know what I mean?"

"Yes sir."

"It seems as though the perpetrator is somebody you did dirty. As far as I can tell, my daughter doesn't know this hoe."

"My son's mother fucked... messed up the truck."

"Why is my daughter paying for your situation? Why did this broad mess up my daughter's whip, instead of messing up yours?"

He didn't have an answer.

My father half smiled. "Don't play with me, you young muthafucka. You know why and I know why. You would have half killed that bitch, regardless of who she is, if she did to your whip, what she did to my daughter's," he paused. "Why aren't you doing that for Passion? Why aren't you takin' care of business?"

Again, Solomon didn't have an answer.

As I sat there, I was getting more and more pissed with him. My father was right. Why *wasn't* Solomon riding for me? Why *did* he let that heifer get away with coming up to my job, and clown me? Why did he let her get away with messing up my truck the way she did? He should've rode down on her that night after he dropped me off at home. He should've beat her ass, and made her call me with an apology.

171

My father looked in my face, and read me. "My daughter is getting pissed at you, Young Blood." He told Solomon. "She's starting to wonder why you're letting things go down the way you're letting them go down."

Solomon looked over at me. I closed myself up. It was a trick that my father had taught me as a child. I made my face blank, and kept all emotions to myself.

He placed his hands together, and made a steeple with his fingers. "What are you prepared to do about this situation, man?"

"I'ma get at her for what she did."

"Let me tell you what I told Passion earlier today. I have to wonder about the man who lets the old bitch get away with fucking with something' that belongs to the new bitch. If I can't trust you to protect my daughter's material possessions, then I can't trust my daughter's life in your hands. Now can I?"

I watched as Solomon shook his head.

"I don't bullshit when it comes to my family... especially Passion. She'll tell you. I have no qualms about doing whatever it takes to keep her safe. If you're not man enough to make sure she's safe when she's with you, then, she doesn't need to be with you."

"I'm man enough to take care of Passion. I wouldn't let nothing happen to her."

"What the hell happened with the truck? Where were you when the ex-bitch keyed my daughter's shit?"

He sat there silently while my father clowned him. I was looking at him in a whole new light, and I didn't like what I saw.

"I want this bitch dealt with." My father continued. "I don't care if she's your son's mother or not. Either you deal with her or, I'll deal with her. And if I have to deal with her, your son might be calling Passion mom because he didn't have a chance to grow up with his. You dig?"

Solomon didn't flinch.

"I'll deal with her," he promised.

"Good. Because one more incident...I don't care how big or how small. I'm holding you personally responsible."

"I'll handle it." Solomon assured him.

"Where is my daughter's SUV?"

"Uhm, my boy has a body shop..."

My father shook his head and interrupted him. "I don't play that, man. I can't have just anybody working on my daughter's Lexus. Who are these people?"

"Just somebody I know."

"You close with them? Do they work on your vehicles?"

"I ain't really close with them like that."

My father shook his head again.

I looked over at Solomon, and rolled my eyes skyward. He was losing major points with me. My father was making it real obvious that dude wasn't at the top of his game.

"Get my daughter's truck out of there. What's the address, man? I want it towed over to my guy Jinx's place."

"Jinx?" he repeated, before he knew it.

My father watched him. I knew he saw the way Solomon puffed up when Jinx's name was mentioned. I knew he was storing that in his mental rolodex. He spotted Solomon's vulnerability, and it had taken less than twenty minutes.

173

"Yeah, Jinx," he plainly stated. "You got a problem with that?"

"More like Jinx got a problem with me." Solomon backed up his last statement.

"He ain't got no problem with me, that's all I care about. I want my daughter's truck outta your *boy's* place tonight! If they're closed, then they need to open up and release my daughter's property. Is that gonna be a problem?"

"No sir."

"I don't want my name dropped. My daughter and I are very private people. I'm not looking for everybody to know she's my daughter. If you can't get the place to release her truck without name dropping, call me. I'll take care of it."

"I got it, Mr. Hill."

"And I expect that you will be paying for any and all damages. Is that correct?"

"Of course, I told Passion I'd take care of it."

"That was a brand new truck, man. When she gets it back, I want her to get back a brand new truck. I'm not playing. It better look as good as it looked when she drove it off the lot."

"If it doesn't, I'll buy her a new one."

My father eyed him and chuckled. "You sure about that? That truck wasn't cheap."

"I know."

"Now, she needs a way to get around until her truck gets taken care of. Can I assume that you'll be providing her with a rental car?"

"Whatever she wants, Mr. Hill."

My father stared into his face. "I know you, Young Blood," he recollected.

Solomon looked doubtful.

"You say your last name is Kent?"

"Yes sir." The level of respect Solomon showed my father was getting higher and higher.

"Is your father, Hooper?"

Solomon's mouth practically fell open. "That's my uncle."

My father stared at his face a minute longer. "Are you Yvonne's son?"

"Yeah, that's my mother," he confirmed.

I wanted to slide under the table. I hoped and prayed my father never had sex with Solomon's mother as a teenager or young adult.

"I know your mother very well, son."

I knew Solomon was probably wondering how my father knew his mother, too.

"She was good-friends with my first wife, Angel, Passion's mother."

Solomon's mother was good-friends with my mother? Small world. I looked over at my daddy. He had the same far away look on his face that he always got when he mentioned my mother.

"Oh Young Blood, you can't ever get away from me now. I know *all* your family. You better not fuck up with my daughter. They'd hand you over to me."

Solomon looked over at me. "I'm not gonna mess up."

"So, I expect you to get Passion's truck over to Jinx's body shop by tonight, and she'll need some form of transportation by tomorrow," he summarized the conversation.

"Yes sir."

Did dude recently join the army? I thought to myself. With all of his, "yes sirs" and "no sirs," I couldn't tell.

My father stood up, signaling that the conversation was over. He had said everything that he needed to say.

Solomon and I went out to the lounge area and mingled a little bit. My father introduced me to his regular customers.

"Y'all get on out of here," he motioned, releasing us.

He shook Solomon's hand, and hugged me.

"Bye daddy."

"I'll talk to you later, Baby Girl."

* * * * *

On the ride back to my house, Solomon seemed eager to talk.

"What the deal, Shorty?"

"Nothin'. My stomach kind of hurts," I lied. I couldn't tell him that my father had exposed his weaknesses and I wasn't really feeling him anymore.

"You hungry? You wanna grab some food?"

"Nah, I'm tired. And you still have to get my truck towed over to Jinx's. I just wanna go home and get ready for work tomorrow."

"I can't believe you didn't tell me your father is Pretty Hill." He was amazed.

"I never woulda, if Isis wouldn't have done that stuff to my whip."

A look of anger crossed his face. "Yeah, she's gonna pay for that."

"What are you gonna do to her?" I was interested to know if he had already formulated a plan, or if he was talking shit.

I remembered that I stopped him from hurting

her in the T.G.I. Friday's parking lot. I couldn't help thinking, that maybe if I had let him whip her ass then, I wouldn't be going through this now.

He looked over at me and grinned. "Come on, Shorty. You think if something goes down I want you to have prior knowledge? Let me handle my business."

The way you should've handled it before my daddy had to get in that ass. I thought to myself.

He pulled up to my building double parked his car, and walked me to my front door. I let him kiss me, but my heart wasn't in it. He ran his hands through my hair. Instead of turning me on, I didn't feel anything.

"I'll holla."

"See you, Solomon." I went inside wondering what had happened to thug in him. Where was the swagger that originally attracted me?

My father had shown me Solomon's hand and as far as I could see, he wasn't holding no aces.

CHAPTER SEVENTEEN

A couple of days later, I rode out to my father's house. I needed to talk to somebody, and the only female that I trusted 100% was Lynne. She was relaxing on the chaise lounge when I walked into the bedroom she shared with my daddy.

"Hey, Lynne."

She put down the book she was reading. "Hey, Passion. What are you doing here?"

"I need to talk." I expressed to her.

She looked up at me, to see if she could read my face. "Sit down." She made room for me on the chaise.

I sat down next to her, and covered myself with some of her blanket.

"What's going on?"

"My daddy did me dirty the other day," I announced.

"Does this have something to do with that talk he had with you and your new friend? What's his name?"

"Solomon," I provided.

"What happened?"

"You know, daddy is good at reading people."

Her mouth fell open. "Are you serious? Sometimes he's too good at reading people. He pulled Solomon's card, huh?"

"Yeah, he pulled Solomon's card real quick."

She rubbed my shoulders tenderly.

"The thing that pisses me off the most is that instead of just tellin' me what was up, daddy had to get me and Solomon together. Put it all in my face." I continued.

"You know how your dad is. He thinks people are better off when they see things for themselves. What did you see in Solomon that upset you?"

"His inactivity. I mean, he let his son's mother wild out on me. More than once. I didn't tell you this, but that hoochie showed up on my job one day."

Lynne was shocked. "Are you serious?"

"Yeah, I'm serious. She came in the salon talkin' slick to me in front of my clients. I ended up fighting her. Ooh, she pissed me off."

"See, you've got Chad's temper."

"All I know is I hit her in the mouth. The next thing I knew, people were pulling me off of her. I was choking that broad. When Solomon saw me later that day, all he did was ask me what happened. Him and I ended up gettin' into a big argument, while she chilled at home and nursed her wounds."

"He didn't correct her?"

"Not as far as I know. I asked him how the heifer even knew where I worked. All he could say was, 'I don't know'. Then she messed up my truck, and daddy had to bring it to his attention before he took action. What's that about?"

"I don't know, Passion. But I know it pissed your father off that homeboy was sitting on his ass."

She sighed, "I think your father would've found a reason to not like Solomon no matter what, though. He could have torn up the city behind your truck getting messed up, and Chad still wouldn't have been impressed. He doesn't think *anybody* is good enough for you. The only person that he'd be happy to see you with is Jinx."

"What!" That startled me. "Why would he wanna see me with Jinx?"

"He knows that Jinx will look out for you. Jinx has proven that to him, time and time again. He's always concerned about you, and he's always taking care of you. Chad knows that he cares about you."

"Yeah, he does," I agreed. I cared about Jinx, too. He was my guy - my big brother. I figured that my father saw that aspect of him, too. "But enough about Jinx. I ain't come over here to talk about him. I came to talk about Solomon."

"You don't even want Solomon. Why waste time talking about him?"

"I do want him," I protested.

She looked up at the ceiling. "Who are you lying to? I know you, girl. It's not the fact that he didn't take care of the situation with his son's mother that has you pissed with him. You're pissed, because your father manipulated you into seeing Solomon's failure to act, as a weakness. And if there's one thing he taught you to despise, it's a weak man."

"Why do you say that daddy manipulated me?" I asked, though her comment did have some truth behind it.

"I love your father. Goodness knows that I love that man, but he's a manipulator. He can't help it. It comes from his days in the streets. He doesn't want to see you with Solomon, because he sees him as being weak. All he had to do was get you to see him as weak, too. Then, Solomon would be out of the picture."

"An executive decision," I remembered him saying.

"What?"

"Nothing."

"Baby Girl, if you still want to be with Solomon, don't let your father's feelings about him, become your feelings about him. Just because your father *thinks* he's weak, doesn't mean he is."

"But what if he really *is* weak? What if when daddy pulled his cards, they showed me the real him? Daddy made him look real bad Lynne. If you woulda been there..."

"Well, if you think Solomon's weak, then you have to decide if you're gonna stay with him. You Passion, not Chad."

"He let that broad mess up my $60,000.00 truck."

"Was that really all his fault? I mean, you were there, too. You weren't watching out for your truck either. And I raised you myself, so I know that you know better than that. Ain't nobody gone take better care of your stuff than you. Is it fair to put all the blame on Solomon when you were there, too?"

I hated to admit that she had a point.

"See, that's part of Chad's manipulation. He put all of the blame for what happened on Solomon."

She was right to a certain extent, but I still thought Solomon was weak.

"Don't give up on your friend. He might surprise you."

I shrugged. I would have to wait and see on that

one. I stood up. "I've been talkin' about myself this whole time. I'm tacky. How are you feelin'?"

"I'm fine, sweetie. I'll be back to business tomorrow."

"You sure? You need to make sure you give yourself enough time to recuperate. You don't wanna fall out again."

"I'm well rested. I'm ready to get back to work in my garden. I can't stand being laid up like this. I like being busy."

"I have to go."

"Your father wants to throw a barbecue for you in a few weeks."

"Why? What did I do to deserve a barbecue?"

"You enrolled in school. He wants to celebrate that. He is so proud of you, Passion. He always wanted you to go to college, and now you're going. Start making your guest list, and tell me what you want to eat."

"Let me think about it, Lynne. I don't too much feel like partyin' right now."

"Passion, don't take this away from Chad. Let him do this," she exhaled noisily. "He really wants this for you."

"I don't know, let me think about it. I'll call you tomorrow."

"Give me a hug," she requested.

I bent down and hugged her. "I love you, Lynne."

"I love you, too, Baby Girl."

* * * * *

I called Jinx while I was on my way home from

my father's house.

"What's up, Baby Girl?" He asked as soon as he answered. "I got a good look at your truck this morning."

"Hey Jinx."

"That broad messed your truck up, P. She must really hate you."

That was not what I wanted to hear. "Can it be fixed?"

"Yo, I can definitely replace the tires. As far as the body, I think I'ma holla at this cat I know down at Windy City Customs. Basically, you're gonna need a new paint job."

I sighed heavily. "Yeah, I figured that."

"Don't sound so sad. You know I got you. I'ma do whatever it takes to get your truck fixed."

That was typical of Jinx. "Ay, you can charge Solomon whatever you wanna charge him. You don't have to give him no kinda discount on my behalf."

"Trouble in paradise?" he teased.

"You know dough is the only thing hustlers can really relate to. The more dough he has to shell out, the more serious the issue is."

"You seem upset."

"Are you being sarcastic, Jinx?"

"Nah," he said, and I could tell that he was being sincere. "I don't want you to stress over this."

"Jinx, I know you'll hook my truck up. I'm not worried about that. You always look out for me. I've got bigger things on my mind." I sighed. "So, how long are we lookin' at on my truck? A month, two months, what?"

"Damn, this sounds like a conversation we've had before. Seems like since Solly's been in your life your whips keep gettin' messed up."

How am I supposed to respond to that? I asked myself.

Jinx kept talking, though. "I'm orderin' special tires for your truck. I gotta wait for those to come in."

"You're not gonna have me sittin' on 22s, are you?"

He laughed at me. "Nah, I won't have you up that high, but I do want you sittin' on somethin' nice."

"Thanks."

"As far as the repaint...I don't know how long that's gonna take. Could go fast, could take a minute. What are you doin' for transportation, now?"

"Solomon rented me a truck. A Montero Sport."

"Uhm, I guess I didn't give him enough credit," he confessed.

I didn't mention that my father had to tell him to rent me a whip. "So, you'll hit me up with an update, right?"

"You know I'll holla back."

"Okay. I'll hit you later."

"Peace, P."

CHAPTER EIGHTEEN

Thursday and Friday, I didn't want to be bothered with Solomon. I still had beef with him over the way he handled the Isis situation. But by Saturday, I was bugging, because I hadn't heard from him. I called him a few times from the salon. I never got a call back.

When I finished with my last client of the day, I met Jainelle over at the washbowl.

"You talk to Tippy today?" I asked her. She was still seeing him. It was the longest relationship I had ever known her to have.

She shook her head. "Nope. Why?"

"I've been callin' Solly all day, and he ain't called me back."

"Girl, he's probably into somethin'. You know how they do. Mack used to disappear all the time. Didn't your ex-guy ever disappear?"

That was what had me upset. When Lorenzo disappeared, he was out romancing hoes, and getting folks pregnant. I didn't even want to think that Solomon might be out doing the same thing.

* * * * *

By Monday, I was through with Solomon. I

185

wondered which hoe that he was messing with, had booty good enough to make him blow me off for almost five days. Since the salon was closed on Mondays, I intended to drive to Hyde Park and sit outside his crib until he showed up. And when he finally showed up, I planned to let him have it. I planned to tell him exactly how to kiss my pretty, yellow ass.

I was tying up my K-Swiss gym shoes when my cell phone rang. I checked the caller I.D; it was Jainelle.

"What's up?"

"What's up, girl? I just called to tell you that Tippy found your boy."

"He found my boy?" For the obvious reason, her using the word "found" made me think of death. My heart locked up and my stomach dropped.

"Yeah, Solly called him this morning."

"Is Solomon alive?"

"Yeah, he's alive. He's been locked up. Tippy went to bail him out."

"What the hell was he locked up for?" I asked, then, I thought about it. "Movin' bricks? Hustlin'?"

I heard a noise that sounded like gum popping. "Nah, actually, he got picked up on battery. I think he beat up his baby's momma." She reported happily.

"Are you serious?"

"I'm pretty sure that's what Tippy told me."

"So, where is Solomon now?"

"Probably still at the county. You know how long it takes to get somebody outta there. I knew you were buggin' Saturday about why you hadn't heard from him. So, I just wanted to let you know."

I smiled to myself. Solomon wasn't somewhere cheating on me. He was holed up in jail. I knew it was messed up, but knowing that made me feel a lot better.

* * * * *

Tuesday, I took off work to spend time with my man. He was out of jail. He took care of the Isis situation. I was feeling him more than I felt him since my father pulled his card.

We had a good time together. He took me out to Oak Brook Center shopping mall. He ran me in and out of every store. Bought me anything and everything that I pointed at.

Later that night, we were at my condo chilling in the family room. I only had on my panties and a bra. My head was in his lap, and he was running his fingers through my hair.

"What happened with you and Isis?" I wanted to hear exactly what had gone down.

"She got her ass beat," he admitted with no hesitation.

"You jumped on her?"

"Let's just say, I made it happen."

"So, if you didn't do it, how'd you end up locked up?"

"The bitch filed charges against me. She told the police that I was the one who did it. So, they picked me up."

I adjusted myself to a more comfortable position. He kept talking.

"I would've been out Thursday, but my damn prints came back too quick. As soon as they saw that shit, I knew it was a wrap."

"How did you get out?"

"Nobody could place me at the scene. All the eyewitnesses told the police that females jumped on

Isis's ass, and wasn't no guy involved. They pretty much had to let me go."

"And you still had to make bail?"

"Nah, they threw the shit out."

"Oh, Jainelle said Tippy went down there to bail you out."

"Nah, he came down there to scoop me up."

"So, is the bitch in the hospital or what?" He hadn't personally taken care of it. I wanted to know specifically how much damage was done.

"She's at the crib. But she'll be outta commission for a minute. She'll think before she pulls some more dumb shit like that, again." He picked up a few strands and twirled them in his fingers. "What's up with your vehicle? You hear anything from Jinx?"

"Yeah, he ordered special tires for my truck but they ain't in yet. If that's what you wanna know."

I felt his body jerk, but I didn't react or comment.

"When are you gettin' your truck back, Shorty? That's what I'm tryin' to figure out."

"He said he doesn't know. After he puts on the new tires, it still has to go to some custom shop for a paint job. He said it could take a month, maybe less, maybe more."

"Damn," he fumed.

"What?" I asked, but I knew he was probably tripping on the amount of money that my truck and the rental truck were going to end up costing him.

"Nothin'."

I let it ride and didn't press him. I enjoyed his company all day, so I didn't wanna trip. Not only did he drop a nice amount of loot on me at the mall, he took me out to lunch, too. I didn't want to mess up our vibe. I wanted to see if I could actually make things work with him.

"I'ma be startin' school soon." I informed him.

"Say word."

"Word! In three weeks."

"Man that is soon. You got everything you need, Shorty? You got your book bag and your pencil case?"

I laughed. He acted like I was going to my first day of kindergarten.

"Yeah, I have everything. My father is throwin' a barbecue for me. I want you to come."

"Straight up? When?"

"The Sunday after next."

"Where?"

"Out at his house."

"Oh damn, in Franklin?" He was pressed about my father, and it showed in his eagerness.

I chuckled. "Frankfort, yeah."

"I'll be there."

"You better."

He leaned over and kissed my lips. "I better?"

"Yeah." I sat up, and took off my panties. "You got somethin' to say?" I asked, straddling him.

He placed his hands on my bare thighs. "Nah, I ain't got nothin' to say."

I pulled his shirt over his head, and pressed my chest up against his. I kissed him deeply, and enjoyed the way I could feel his penis start to grow. I could feel it even through the thick denim of the shorts he was wearing.

"I didn't think so," I said, seducing him with my light kisses on his neck.

He took off my bra, and bobbed his head down to my breasts. He sucked thirstily. I grinded myself against his middle. He increased the pressure that he was applying to my breasts.

I put my hand under his chin and lifted his head. I wanted to kiss him. So, I did. We kissed deeply. He ran his hands up and down my body.

"Get on the floor," he demanded lifting me up.

I waited as patiently as I could while he got undressed and took a condom out of his wallet. I watched anxiously as he put it on. He put my knees over his forearms, pushed back my legs and entered me. I was already wet, already anticipating the pleasure of his stroke. He set a moderate pace for us. I moaned his name, and he began to increase his speed. His strokes became faster and deeper. I wrapped my arms around his neck, and grinded my pelvis up.

"Solomon," I moaned.

As shaky as his street reputation was with me, dude didn't have any shortcomings when it came to his sexual skills. He had me going there in a matter of minutes. I shrieked and moaned, and dug my nails into his back.

"Get on top," he panted, after I caught my breath.

I climbed on top of him, and rode until he joined me in the land of sexual satisfaction.

CHAPTER NINETEEN

The day of my barbecue dawned sunny and clear. The temperature was supposed to go into the upper 80's. I was excited, because I was worried all night that it might rain.

I packed up everything that I needed for a couple of days and headed out to my father's house at 6:30 that morning. I would've gone the night before, but I needed to get up with Solomon. I needed him to get my body right with some loving. We had an all night sex session. We finally dragged ourselves out of his bed at three in the morning. He drove me home, and I fell asleep on my couch until six o'clock.

Over the last few weeks, things between us were intensifying. The shopping trips multiplied. Dude was buying me everything under the sun, spending chips on me like crazy. And the sex...it was crazy. We were going at it like bunny rabbits. I was dropping booty on him every chance I got. I was trying to sex him four to five times a week. I had to give props where they were due. Dude was rocking me right. He kept my mind on the loving. Sometimes I would be at the salon, just calculating when the next time I could get some would be.

* * * * *

I slept until 10:30 at my dad's house. Then, I

threw on jogging pants and a t-shirt, and went downstairs for breakfast.

Lynne and my father were in the breakfast nook talking. When I walked into the room, my father looked up and smiled.

"Good morning, Baby Girl."

"Good morning, Daddy. Hey Lynne."

"So, are you all ready for school?" He was too excited about the thought of his "Baby Girl" being college educated. "Do you have everything that you need?"

I nodded, and took a bite of turkey sausage.

"How many people are we expecting today?" Lynne asked.

"I don't know. Maybe twenty, thirty."

Lynne was back to her old self and ready to entertain.

"Is Solomon joining us today?" My father inquired.

"Yeah. So is your choice for most valuable player...Jinx."

Lynne looked over at me. "Passion!" she exclaimed.

I raised my eyebrows. "Yes?"

"Where did you get that ring?"

On the ring finger of my right hand, sat a platinum ring with a two and a half carat, pear shaped amethyst, my birthstone. The stone was flanked with channel set diamonds. It *was* an eye catcher. It caught my eye immediately when Solomon took me into the jewelry store.

"Solomon got it for me," I bragged.

He thought he concealed it, but I saw my father's eye twitch almost imperceptibly.

"Uhm, Solomon has an eye for nice things, doesn't he?" Lynne commented.

"Solomon is a low class, wannabe street hustler. You know Baby Girl picked out that ring." My father retorted.

"She may have picked it out, but he paid for it." Lynne said pointedly.

My father got up and left the room.

"He's mad."

"You're a grown woman, Passion. He can't decide who you date."

"Why does he dislike Solomon so much? Solomon didn't do anything to him."

She eyed me. "I told you before, he thinks Solomon is weak. He doesn't feel like he can trust him to look out for you."

"So, he's never gonna like him?"

"Don't worry about it. He doesn't have to date Solomon, you do. He'll get over it."

She went back to reading her newspaper and I went back to eating my breakfast.

* * * * *

The barbecue was cracking by 5:00 that night. The D.J. was bumping R. Kelly. The caterers were hooking up the food. The guests were laughing and enjoying themselves and I was looking cute in my pink denim Calvin Klein shorts, and matching pink and white striped shirt.

I was talking to Summer and her guy, Rico when Solomon pulled up in his Avalanche. Tippy and Jainelle pulled up right behind him in Tippy's other car – a Red Tahoe.

I excused myself from Summer and Rico, and went to greet my man and my friends.

"Hey," Jainelle said, giving me a hug.

"Hey, Jainelle. Hey, Tippy." I smiled at them. I hadn't seen him since the Bernie Mac concert.

"What's up, Passion?" He asked pleasantly.

Solomon walked over to me and grabbed me like he owned me. He kissed me on the lips. "What the deal, Shorty?" He looked me up and down while making a face. "Damn, you rockin' the hell outta them shorts. You think we can get away for a minute, and get into somethin'?"

My mouth dropped. "In my daddy's house? Oh, you must have some kind of death wish."

"Yo, I'ma take Tippy over there to meet your pops. Hooper, the one your old man knows, is his father." Solomon reminded me.

"Say word." I said, using his favorite phrase.

"Oh, you brought jokes. I'll holla."

I waved and watched them walk away. Then I turned to Jainelle. She was watching them walk away, too.

"So, what's up?"

We hadn't really talked in a while. Since she started messing with Tippy, she didn't need me to drive her home anymore. He was letting her drive one of his whips.

"Nothin," she responded, with a guilty smile.

"Why are you lookin' like that?"

"Like what?"

We were both giggling like we were in high school or something.

"Like that, Jai. You look like you have some good gossip or somethin'."

"Naw, I don't have no gossip."

"So, what's up with you and Tippy? You in love?"

She rolled her eyes to the sky. "Am I? I can't seem to stay away from him. Every time I'm with him, I don't wanna go home. When I'm not with him, I can't wait to see him again. Girl, he got me straight sprung. He wants me to move in with him." She confessed.

My eyes got as big as saucers. "What!"

She pulled something out of the front pocket of her shorts. "He gave me these."

I grabbed them from her hands. It was a set of keys. "Are these his house keys?"

She looked so ecstatic that I didn't want to rain on her parade, but all I could think was that she and Tippy only knew each other for a minute.

"Are you gonna do it?" I asked curiously.

"I'm thinkin' about it."

I started to tell her to think long and hard, when something caught my attention.

There was a black convertible pulling up to my father's property. It was the hottest car that I had seen in a minute.

"Who's that?" Jainelle asked.

I gave her the eye. "I thought you were sprung on Tippy?"

She smiled like I caught her hand in the cookie jar. "I'm just askin'."

The car pulled to a stop. The driver and his girl got out and started approaching.

He was wearing blue jean shorts that showed off his muscular legs, and a blue and gray striped Phat Farm polo. He had on a baseball cap and Gucci sunglasses. Dude knew how to dress and what to drive.

He's doin' that. I thought to myself.

I watched him advance. His walk was familiar. As he got closer, he took off his sunglasses and smiled at me.

I almost fainted. It was Jinx!

"What's up, Baby Girl?" He asked with a sly wink of the eye.

I wondered if he knew that I was checking him out like that. I was too embarrassed and could hardly look him in the face.

"Hey, Jinx. I see you."

He didn't seem to notice anything unusual. He hugged me in his typical way.

"Hey, Passion," Ebonie greeted me with a smile.

"What's up, Ebonie? I like that purse, girl." I lied. It was one of those multi-colored Louis Vuittons that I hated so much.

"Thanks," she said, grinning.

"Is that a Cadillac XLR?" Jainelle, the expert car booty asked.

"Yeah, it is," Jinx answered.

"Is it new?" Jainelle was nosy. She couldn't help it.

"Nah, not really. I got it about six months ago. I just don't really get a chance to drive it."

Before I could catch myself, I said, "I wanna get a chance to drive it." All eyes were on me.

"I'll take you for a ride, P." He offered easily. "Come on, Eb." He then called for her and started to walk away.

Ebonie hung back, and watched me for a few seconds too long, before she followed him. I knew instantly that she saw me as a threat to her relationship with Jinx. But she didn't have to worry. I didn't want Jinx.

Jainelle interrupted my thoughts. "Damn, Jinx is lookin' even better than usual."

"Ebonie must be good for him."

"She must be." Jainelle looked at me. "So, what's really good with you and Solly?"

"Same old, same," I said, waving my hand dismissively. Why did I do that?

Jainelle grabbed my hand, and studied my new ring. "Did Solomon put this big ass rock on your finger?" She gave me a knowing look. "He came outta the pocket like this? Oh, you must be hittin' him off with major ass."

"You know it," I sang.

"Got him open, huh?"

"Like 7~11," I joked.

Jinx walked up and joined us, just as our conversation ended.

"Yo, Baby Girl, I gotta run up to Walgreen's. Lynne needs her prescription picked up. You wanna drive me up there?" He dangled the keys to the convertible in front of me, like he was my brother and I was his pesky little sister.

I was about to grab the keys, and head for the car when I caught Ebonie through my peripheral vision. She was glaring at me. I knew that I could either mess with her by exploiting her insecurity by taking the keys from Jinx. Or, I could take the mature approach. I could take myself outta the picture. I decided to take the mature approach. I looked at Jinx regretfully. I really did wanna drive that convertible Cadillac.

"That's okay, Jinx. Why don't you take Ebonie,

instead?"

I watched as her facial muscles relaxed.

"I would, but I don't know where the hell Walgreen's is. You're the only one who knows where to find stuff out here in the country."

"It's cool, Passion," Ebonie said, a bit more comfortably. "You go ahead and show him."

I figured that by not acting pressed and whatnot, I won back her confidence.

Jinx handed me the keys.

"You wanna go, Jainelle?"

She looked indecisive for a second. "Nah. I'll stay here with my man."

"I'll be right back. Hold Solomon down for me."

As Jinx and I turned to walk away, I heard Solomon's voice. Jainelle was trying to explain to him where I was going, but he wasn't trying to hear her.

"Shorty!" he called.

"Damn," I cursed, and looked over at Jinx. "While I was makin' things all good with your girl, I shoulda been makin' things all good with my man. I'll be right back." I walked back over towards Solomon.

"Where you goin'?"

"My step-mom asked Jinx to pick up her prescription. He doesn't know how to get to Walgreen's. I'm about to show him."

"You're the only one who can show him where it is?"

He was as bad as Ebonie.

"Basically."

"Why don't you tell your step-mom that we'll go up to Walgreen's and get her prescription? Jinx can go to hell."

I looked at Solomon all bent out of shape and

198

threatened by Jinx. My father would have a field day if he saw that behavior. My father woulda been too happy to exploit his vulnerability. He was too worried about Jinx like he didn't have enough confidence in his own capabilities.

"Solomon--" I began as casually as possible. "Don't trip because I'm runnin' up to Walgreen's with Jinx. We said we weren't gonna let no third party come into our relationship and interrupt our flow."

He stared at me, like he wasn't buying.

"Come on, baby." I soothed, sweetening my voice. "Will it make everything cool if I go home with you tonight and let you rock me 'til my eyes roll back?"

"You think you're slick, Shorty," he said sternly, but his eyes were smiling.

I knew mentioning sex would bring him over to my side. Solomon was coochie-whipped.

"Are we straight?"

"We're cool." He gave in and kissed my lips. "I know you're just tryin' to drive that cat's whip, Passion. I ain't new to this. I saw the way you were lookin' when he rolled up. I know that's the reason you're pressed to go up to *Walgreen's*."

I couldn't help laughing. He pulled my card.

"Don't tear his shit up, Shorty. I'm already makin' major moves trying to get your truck out the shop. I don't wanna have to pay to get his out the shop, too," he joked.

"Whatever."

Jinx was in the passenger's seat waiting for me. I climbed into the driver's side.

"So, did you kiss and make up?"

I could have sworn that I sensed some jealousy.

"I don't know about all that, but I made sure

everything was cool."

"You got your license, right?" he teased.

"You got insurance, right?" I teased right back. I set up the mirrors, and adjusted the seat to suit me. "Jinx, this car is hot to death. I love this car."

He just smiled as I pulled on the main road.

"So, how far is Walgreen's?"

"It's a minute," I confessed.

"I see Solomon iced you."

"What? This ring?"

"Yeah, that ring. What, he still feeling guilty?"

"Nah, I don't think that's it."

Jinx got quiet.

"Are you and Ebonie gettin' serious?" It wasn't my business, but I asked anyway.

"I don't know. There are some things about her that are cool, but some things are missin'."

"Like what?" I didn't want to ask him. I didn't want to get all in his business, but my curiosity got the best of me.

"P, you're kinda nosy, aren't you?"

I laughed. I knew that meant he wasn't gonna tell me. I pulled the car into the parking lot of Walgreen's.

"You like the car?" he asked, changing the subject.

"I told you I love it. It rides so smooth, and handles so easy. I might need one of these."

"Tell your guy to rent you one."

Again, I heard the unmistakable tone of jealousy. Was I imagining it, or, did Jinx hate on Solomon and I?

I shook my head. "Nah, that's all right. If I want to rent one, I can do it for myself."

* * * * *

On the way back from Walgreen's I let Jinx drive, and I rode in the passenger's seat.

"You sure you don't wanna drive?" he offered.

I pulled my Miu Miu sunglasses out of my Coach purse, and slipped them over my eyes. "Nah, this is the kind of car that I should just ride in while lookin' good." I was acting all Hollywood.

"Well, you do look good."

He didn't think I caught the comment, but I did. I stared straight ahead.

He reached over, and hit the stereo system. A few seconds later, the car and the great outdoors were filled with the sounds of Jadakiss.

"What's up with my truck? Is it almost ready?" I asked over the volume of the music.

"You gettin' tired of drivin' that Montero Sport?"

"It's not that I'm gettin' tired of it. I mean; it's cool. But my truck is luxury."

"Yeah, I know. As far as I know, everything with your truck is straight. But I'll holla at them on Tuesday. Check things out."

"Are you for real?" I asked with relief.

"Yeah," he said, like I shouldn't have been surprised. "You know I always got you."

* * * * *

Later that night, after everybody left my father's house, Solomon and I sat on the steps of the cedar deck. He was holding my hands inside of his. My body

201

was leaned against his. He ran his fingers through my hair. "I thought you were comin' home with me tonight."

"I was, but I'm sleepy. I'ma stay out here."

"So, when am I gonna see you?"

"Tomorrow," I answered.

We were both quiet. I closed my eyes, and enjoyed the feeling of the warm breeze caressing my skin.

"What did you and Jinx talk about while y'all were gone to Walgreen's?"

I wondered how long he had been waiting to ask me that question. I hated that he was so pressed over my friendship with Jinx.

"Nothin' unusual. We talked about my truck. He said he would stop by the place where it's gettin' painted and see what's up for me."

He was silent.

"You ever thought about doin' that?" I asked him.

"Doin' what?"

"Hollerin' at the custom shop. Seein' what the hell is up with my truck." I chastised him. "I'm buggin' cuz Jinx offered to do it. But you're my guy, and you haven't said nothin'. Why didn't you think to do that?"

"Maybe cuz I'm too damn busy hustlin', tryin' to pay for your truck, to waste time goin' up to the shop," he replied. He was a little bit louder than was necessary. "Maybe Jinx got too much time on his fuckin' hands."

My father appeared at the French doors that lead from the kitchen out to the deck.

"How long are you gonna be out here, Baby Girl?"

202

"Not too much longer, Daddy."

I knew he didn't really care. He was probably in the kitchen listening, and heard Solomon getting loud. He wanted to let Solomon know that he better not get too loose with me.

"I'm about to blow," Solomon announced, feeling Pretty Hill's presence.

We both stood up.

"Walk me to my car."

We held hands while we walked.

"You want me to go by and check on your truck, Shorty? I'll take care of it."

"Not after I had to ask you to do it, Solomon. That's something you shoulda thought about on your own." I was frustrated. There was too much to teach him. "Your woman is out here without her vehicle, because of your baby's mama. Are you even concerned?"

"I got you the Montero."

I sighed heavily. He wasn't getting it. "That's not mine. I want *my* truck back. I want my *Lexus*, not some damn Mitsubishi."

"Look Shorty, it might not seem like it, but I'm concerned. Okay? But I got a lot on my mind that concerns me. I can't sit up and cry over your truck all day."

"I don't expect you to," I mumbled.

"I'm makin' moves, Passion. Tryin' to stay on top." He looked into my eyes. "I know it's not as nice as your Lexus, but I need you to drive the Montero for now. Can you do that for me? Please?"

I fought hard not to curse at him. I mean, at least he did make sure I had *something* to drive.

"Come on, Shorty. I know I ain't perfect, but a

nigga is tryin'. I'm tryin' to make you happy, Shorty. You can't do this one thing for me?"

"Yeah, Solomon, I'll drive the Montero for you. But I still want *my* truck back."

"I know you do. You're a straight brat."

"I'm startin' school Wednesday. I wanted to drive my truck. Now I gotta drive the Montero," I pouted.

"You could hold my Infiniti or my Avalanche. You're the one that has a problem with drivin' other people's cars."

"I don't have a problem drivin' other people's whips. I have a problem with borrowin' from people."

"So, you don't wanna hold my Hummer? Push it to school?"

I shook my head. "No thanks. I'll just have to drive the Montero."

He hugged me. "I dig you. You're mad different from any female I've ever messed with."

I continued to pout. "I dig you, too."

The longer I had to go without my truck, the more that feeling was diminishing.

CHAPTER TWENTY

School turned out to be way more demanding than I thought it would be. I hadn't been in anybody's classroom in years. It took every drop of concentration for me to stay on top of my class assignments and homework. I was taking fifteen credit hours, and it was kicking my butt.

I had to make changes in every other area in my life. The first thing to go was work. I cut my days at the salon down to Thursdays, Fridays and Saturdays only. The second thing to go was a lot of the time me and Solomon spent having sex. It wasn't easy for me to decide to give up the sex. Solomon's dick game was off the meter. He could've bottled his skills and sold them. Plus, I just missed being with him. I tended to get caught up daydreaming about the loving, or just wishing he was around to touch me when I wanted him to put his hands on me. I really didn't have a choice, though. I had to put school first. It was a sacrifice I felt like I had to make.

It pissed Solomon off when I cut back on the sex. All he did was complain about how he never got any booty. He made it real obvious that he wasn't happy with my commitment to school. That was his problem, though. I couldn't get caught up on that. Buckling down, and getting my education were my priorities.

* * * * *

205

During the second week of September, I got a big surprise. It was a Friday night, and I was waiting for Jainelle to finish cleaning up her station. We were going out for drinks after work.

I heard loud music blaring from a whip parked outside the salon.

"Somebody's jammin'." Jainelle said bobbing her head.

I grabbed my purse. "You ready?"

"I'm ready. Let's go."

As we exited the salon, we both looked in the direction of the truck with the blaring music. I almost fell out.

"My Lex!" I screamed. "My baby's back!"

Jinx climbed out of the driver's seat of my truck with a huge smile on his face.

Before I even thought about what I was doing, I ran over to him, and jumped in his arms. He held me to him.

"Oh my goodness. I can't believe it."

He was still smiling. His dimples were showing. "I figured since it was ready, you would want it back."

"Thank you. Is it straight? I mean, is it the same truck?"

"Yeah, baby. Nothin' was wrong with the interior. It just got a new paint job and new tires."

"So, are you still tryin' to do this, or what, Passion?" Jainelle asked me.

I looked over at her. I had practically forgotten that she was there. "Jai."

She held up her hand. "Don't even worry about it. We'll do it tomorrow after work. Okay?"

"Okay," I exhaled with relief.

I watched her walk over to Tippy's Chevy

Tahoe. She'd been driving it like she owned it for over a month.

Jinx watched her, too. "I see she found somebody to help her get back on top."

I smirked, "Yeah."

"He a baller?"

"Of course he is."

"Of course he is," he repeated.

There was a funny tone in the way he said it. I looked over at him. "You aren't disappointed are you?"

He looked surprised that I asked him that. "Hell naw. Jainelle ain't the one that I wanna get with."

"You got somethin' against ballers?" I joked.

He shook his head slowly. "Nah, I don't have a problem with ballers... as long as they stay outta my way."

We stood there with our eyes locked on each other for a few seconds. I got the feeling that he was trying to tell me something, without really telling me.

"Do you need a ride home?"

"I'm not going home. I'm about to stop through Ebonie's."

"You need a ride over there?"

"Nah, I got it."

I was confused. "How are you gettin' there?"

"You're about to let me hold the keys to the rental. I'll take it back tomorrow for you."

I went to reach into my purse, then, a thought dawned on me.

"I can't do it. Solomon would have a fit if he found out I let you drive the truck he rented."

Jinx looked at me like he couldn't understand why that would be a problem.

"You know he's not feelin' you, Jinx. He would be pissed. I can't disrespect him like that."

"Baby Girl, who do you think paid Windy City Custom?"

"You?" I asked dumbly.

I was so happy to get my truck back that I didn't even think about that. He paid them just to get my truck, and surprise me with it. I took the keys to the Montero out of my purse and handed them to him. I decided that there was no reason I should front on Jinx, when he went out of his way to handle Solomon's business.

"Tell your guy that I expect my money' first thing tomorrow morning." He paused. "And I ain't playin' with him."

"Okay," I agreed giving Jinx a hug. "Thanks again for gettin' my truck. I really appreciate it."

He held me a little longer than was necessary, but I didn't pull away.

"Do you?"

I was tripping he would ask me something like that. "Jinx, you know that I appreciate everything that you do for me. You do more for me than anybody I know, except my daddy. You don't think I see how much you look out for me?" I sucked my teeth. "I wish the people who are supposed to look out for me, would look out for me the way you do."

"You mean, Solly."

He knew I was talking about Solomon.

"That cat doesn't deserve you, Baby Girl. He got real lucky linkin' up with you. He's the luckiest dude I know."

Jinx looked angry. I stood there silently. I didn't want to say anything. I had a certain loyalty to

Solomon. He was my man. I couldn't dog him out to Jinx.

"If I knew you were gonna end up messin' with him, I never would've let him take you home that first night. I woulda scooped you up myself."

A thousand thoughts were running through my mind. Jinx was pissed with himself for accidentally hooking me up with Solomon? Goose bumps popped out all over my arms, even though it was over 70 degrees outside. He stared at me. The way he looked at me made butterflies go bananas inside my stomach. Before I could process what to say or what to do next, he spoke.

"I'll hit you up tomorrow, Passion," he said, and walked away.

Jinx just indirectly tried to push up on me, I thought to myself. I got in my truck and called my father to tell him that I had my vehicle back.

After we hung up, I called Solomon. I was too happy.

"I got my truck back tonight," I said to him, as soon as he answered his cell.

"Shorty, I'm on somethin'. I gotta hit you back." He hung up on me just like that.

I looked at the phone. He couldn't be serious. I saw things like that happen to other females before, but men didn't hang up on me. Who did he think he was?

I was pissed.

* * * * *

When I got home, I put Floetry's CD into my stereo system. Then, I chilled on my sofa and worked on my class assignment for an hour. I put on my pajamas at 11:55. Before I got in the bed, I picked up the telephone, and dialed Jinx's cell. I didn't know why I felt the need to talk to him, I just did. I thought my call would go to voicemail, but he answered. He sounded tired, but not like he was asleep.

"Jinx, it's me."

"What's up, Baby Girl? What's wrong?"

"Nothin'. I just wanna thank you again, for gettin' my truck for me. You're always so concerned about my happiness."

"No doubt. You're my girl. I always got you."

"I appreciate that."

"What time is it?"

"Midnight."

"What are you doin' up?"

"You act like its 3:00 in the morning. I was studyin'."

"How are you studyin' with music on?" He heard the smooth vocals of Natalie Stewart and Marsha Ambrosius in the background.

"I can study with the radio on."

"What's that you're listenin' to?"

"*Say Yes*. It's by Floetry."

"Turn it up, it's hot."

I picked up the remote, and turned up the volume of my stereo. We sat on the telephone listening to Floetry together. I never did anything like that with a dude before. It was romantic. I listened to him breathe, and pictured him lying on his sofa with his eyes closed, listening to the lyrics. I thought about how his dimples made deep gaps in the sides of his face when he smiled. After the song played for the fifth time, I spoke.

"I'm tired, Jinx," I said, regretfully. Secretly, I

wished we could've vibed like that all night. "I gotta go. I have a class in the morning."

"My bad," he apologized, "I'll let you go."

"I'll talk to you later."

"Holla back, P."

I barely slept. All night long, I dreamt about seducing Jinx while Floetry played in the background.
What was that about?

* * * * *

I called Solomon while I was on my way to the salon. It was 7:15, Saturday morning. I wanted to put him on blast for hanging up on me.

He answered his cell phone all incoherent. "What the deal?"

"Solomon, it's me."

"Yo, Shorty, what up?" he said, more clearly.

"I tried to call you last night. Why'd you hang up on me? I didn't appreciate that."

He laughed a little bit. "My bad. I was makin' moves. Last night was crazy. I was wildin'."

"I just wanted to tell you that I got my truck back."

"Say word."

"Word. Jinx brought it up to the salon."

"Jinx, huh?"

"Yeah, Jinx," I said, taking a deep breath. The beef between him and Jinx was getting on my nerves. "He paid the custom place. He said he wants you to holla at him about his money this mornin'."

"Who the hell told him to take it upon himself and pay 'em? I woulda picked up your truck, and paid them myself."

"He wanted to surprise me."

"Surprise my ass! Nah, that cat wanna get with you. He's about to make me fuck him up."

I didn't respond. He was bugging. The only way he could hurt Jinx, was with a gun.

"Ay, is dude tryin' to impress *you* or *your pops*? 'Cause he ain't impressin' me. He should feel fucked up wanting his man's girl."

I didn't wanna argue with him about Jinx. "Do you need his number or what?"

"I know where that cat be. I'll take care of it."

"Thank you."

"Shorty."

"Yeah?"

"I'm glad you got your truck back. I know you were buggin' about not havin' it." He finally realized that everything wasn't about Jinx.

"Thanks, baby."

"So, I'll ride through your place and pick up the rental. I wanna hurry up and take that back, so they can stop chargin' me."

I don't know what possessed me to lie. I promised myself that I wasn't going to lie to Solomon. But I felt like he backed me into a corner. I knew he would trip if I told him Jinx had the rental truck.

"My father has it," I lied. "He's gonna take it back today."

He didn't say anything for a second. I briefly wondered if he knew I was lying.

"Okay," he said coolly. "Yo, when am I seein' you? I ain't seen you in a minute."

"I know," I admitted. "You wanna see me tonight?"

"No doubt. Holla back when you get to the

crib."

"Okay. Bye," I said, smiling to myself. I needed some sexual healing, anyway.

"Later."

* * * * *

Solomon was outside of my building at 11:52 that night. As soon as I got in the truck, I knew that something was wrong.

"Hey." I greeted him.

"What up?"

We drove in silence from my place to his, which was unusual. He parked the truck, and we rode up the elevator to the sixteenth floor in silence.

I walked into his apartment, and sat down on his sofa.

"Yo, let's go in the bedroom," he instructed.

I followed him.

This time, Solomon's sex was different. He didn't give me any foreplay. He barely kissed me. Then, he was so damn rough with me that I just knew I was gonna have a yeast infection in a few days.

All I said during the whole situation was, "ouch", "wait", and "hold up."

My first thought was that he was trying to get rid of me. My second was that he was trying to pay me back for something.

We dressed the same way we undressed, in silence.

"What the hell is wrong with you?" I asked finally.

"What?"

And I could just tell by the look on his face that

213

he was fronting. He knew what I was talking about.

"I mean hell, you hardly talked to me since I been here. You ain't give me no foreplay, and you got my coochie throbbing! Why were you being all rough with me? What's wrong with you? You tryin' to tell me that you through messin' with me or somethin'?"

"Why the hell you lie to me?" He asked coldly.

Damn! I thought to myself. So, that was it. The one and only time I chose to lie to him, I got busted.

"About the Montero?" I asked, even though I knew exactly what he was talking about.

"Yeah, unless you lied to me about some other shit." He eyed me, and for a second I was scared of what he might do.

"I'm up at Jinx's shop, payin' this cat that I don't even like. Then, I spot the Montero that I rented, sittin' in his parking lot. I'm thinkin' that can't be the truck I rented. Shorty told me her old man got that truck. Then, Jinx whack ass starts tellin' me that he promised to take the rental truck back as a favor to you." He took a deep breath. "Why would you lie to me? I already don't trust females. Y'all are too fuckin' connivin'. I thought you were different, Shorty."

"I'm sorry. I only told you my father had the truck, because you were already trippin' so hard about Jinx. I knew if I told you he had the Montero, you woulda really bugged out."

"That ain't no excuse."

And he was right.

"Shorty, I don't know what the hell's goin' on between you and Jinx. First, I thought that he just wanted you." He eyed me. "Now, I'm startin' to think you might want dude, too. Just admit it. Be a woman. Tell me the deal."

"I don't want Jinx." I told him, but even as I was saying it, subconsciously, I wasn't so sure. I couldn't stop thinking about the dream I had of me seducing him. Did I really dig him like that, *like that?*

Solomon continued to eye me. "All I know is, I ain't about to compete with no other cat for your heart." He was serious. I could tell. I knew I messed up, and I felt real guilty about lying to him. Especially since, he caught me in the lie.

"You don't have to compete with Jinx for my heart. I don't want Jinx." I walked over to Solomon, and wrapped my arms around his waist. I tried to kiss him. He turned his head.

"I ain't feelin' you right now, Shorty."

"What?" I asked in disbelief.

"I don't trust yo ass. I got a bad feelin' about you. The more I look at you, the less I wanna be around you. Come on, I need to run you back to your crib."

"What?" I repeated. He was treating me like the side hoe.

"I need to take you home," he said, calmly.

It was almost like he was enjoying shocking the hell out of me. I knew it was payback. I knew he was trying to hurt me, because I hurt him by lying. I was still pissed, though. I didn't even speak to him. I grabbed my purse and marched out to the elevator. At that moment, I didn't care if he and I ever spoke again.

* * * * *

Jainelle and I went out to dinner on Monday evening. We met up at Chili's out by River Oaks Shopping Mall, in Calumet City.

"So, what's up?" she asked, once we sat down.

"Nothin'."

"Tippy told me Solly's pissed with you. What happened?"

"Girl, I got caught in a lie," I admitted.

She looked at me like I said I slept with Solomon's brother. "I know you sure hate it. You know ballers don't trust *nobody*. You're gonna be workin' overtime tryin' to earn back his trust."

I took a sip of my pop, but didn't comment. I wasn't too worried about gaining Solomon's trust back. He needed to be worried about me giving him a second chance.

"What did you lie to him about?"

"Something that had to do with Jinx."

Her mouth dropped. "Why?"

I waved my hands. "I don't even wanna talk about it, Jai. At the time, I thought it was the right move to make."

"That's messed up."

"Whatever."

"You talked to him?"

"Nope, not since last week."

"Uhm, so you're on punishment, huh? I've been there before," she smiled. "He'll forgive you, eventually. When he gets tired of goin' without the booty, he'll forgive you."

"What's up with you and Tippy?" I asked changing the subject.

She smiled brightly. "Things are off the chain, as usual. I don't lie to my man."

"Forget you."

"Nah, for real, everything is cool."

"Are you still thinkin' about moving in with him?"

"Yep. I've been packin' for two weeks. I'm movin' in ten days."

"Say word." I started, then, caught myself. "Seriously?"

"Yep. You've been too busy with school and stuff for us to really talk. Otherwise, I woulda told you by now."

"Do you need any help movin'?"

"Are you offerin'? I could definitely use help. Thanks, Passion."

"That's what friends are for."

* * * * *

Ten days flew by. Before I knew it, it was the day of Jainelle's move. I got to her house at 11:20 on Sunday morning. Solomon pulled up right after me.

He had tried to make up with me a couple of times since our fight, but every time, I gave him my ass to kiss. Like he'd given me his. He needed to learn his lesson. I was teaching him that he couldn't just treat me any kind of way. I did miss having sex with him, though. It was almost two weeks since we had sex, and my body was starting to talk to me. I was dying to feel his touch. He walked up to my driver's side window. I looked over at him. He was so fine, I got hot and bothered from just looking at him. I slowly let the window down.

"What the deal, Shorty?"

"What's the deal with you, Solomon?"

"You still buggin'?"

"Nope. Are you?"

"I've been tryin' to squash the madness with you for a week. You're the one who keeps trippin'."

"Well, I didn't appreciate the way you dogged me the last time I was at your place."

"I ain't appreciate the fact that you lied to me about Jinx. Can we move on from that, or what?"

I was horny from just being so close to him. "Yeah, I guess so," I relented.

"Get out the truck and gimme a hug."

I got out of the truck. I wasn't dressed up, because I planned on doing manual labor. But I made sure that I looked cute, because I knew he would be there. He looked me up and down, taking in my Guess jeans, and fitted baby-tee. My hair was in a ponytail, covered by a bandana. He had never seen me dressed that way.

"Damn," he smiled. "Can I have some of what's in those jeans?"

I winked at him. "You know it."

"Yo, let's hurry up and get your girl moved. I ain't put my hands on you in a minute."

"You're damn right," I agreed.

He bent down, and kissed me on the lips. I felt my nipples harden. He felt it, too. He discreetly rubbed his fingertips across them. He put his mouth to my ear.

"Damn, I really want you, Shorty."

I looked up at him.

"Ay, don't look at me like that." He turned his head away.

"Like what?" I asked, innocently.

"Like you want me to hit it, right here, right now."

I licked my lips suggestively.

"See, you're about to make me stand your girl up," he warned. "She's gonna be trying to move without no help."

I didn't care if Jainelle got stood up or not. I

wanted some. She would have to understand.

He bent down, and kissed me again. This time, it was a real kiss. He placed his hands on the back of my head, and played with my ponytail.

I rubbed my hands up and down his back. I let the tips of my fingernails graze his back gently.

He kissed me more deeply.

"Good morning." A perky voice said.

Solomon and I broke away from each other. Jainelle was standing right beside us.

"Y'all ready? I gotta lot of boxes that need to go." She pointed towards her driveway.

"Yeah," Solomon said, and started walking towards her house.

I gave her the evil eye. "Blocker!"

CHAPTER TWENTY-ONE

The month of October came in cool, and wet. One Saturday night in the middle of the month, Solomon and I were chilling out at my place. I had my books, my folders, and test study guides scattered everywhere. I could tell he was pissed, even though he didn't say anything. My education was a major problem for him. We fought about it enough for me to know that. Instead of seeing school as a way for me to better myself, he saw it as the main thing that kept us apart. He constantly complained about how much time I was spending on homework and studying.

When he complained, I would do the fool and try to make him happy. I would blow off studying, and try to spend more time with him. But that just worked against me, because then, I would have to stay up late to work on what I should have been working on while I was with him.

"How much longer are you gonna be doin' that?" he asked.

He had been at my house for almost forty five minutes, and I wasn't paying him enough attention. Plus, he was horny. He kept touching me, and messing with my hair and stuff. I was horny, too, but I needed to get my work done. I never would've told him, but as good as his loving was it couldn't compete with my desire to succeed in school.

"Sweetie, I have to study. I got mid-terms next week."

"I'm goin' outta town," he blankly announced.

"What?" I asked, looking up from my history book.

"I'm goin' outta town. I've been needin' to make a run, and I've been puttin' it off. Since you're so involved with school and whatnot. You got mid-terms and stuff. I figure I might as well do it now."

"Where are you goin'?"

"St. Louis. Tippy gotta connect down there. He's been tryin' to link me up with this cat for a minute. So, I'ma go down there, see what this dude is talkin' about."

"When?" I was concerned. Road trips could be deadly for a baller. In a lot of cities, out-of-towners weren't welcomed.

"Thursday. We should be back by Monday."

I stared at him.

"What the deal, Shorty? You look spooked."

"I don't really dig the thought of out of town moves too much. Too many cats come home in body bags. I don't want nothin' to happen to you."

He smiled. "Nothing's gonna happen to me."

The expression on my face didn't change.

"Don't worry, Shorty," he said, more sincerely. "I'll be straight."

"You know, Lorenzo was murdered. I'm not tryin' to put you in the ground, too."

"Come here."

I went into his open arms. He held me, and stroked my hair.

"You ain't gotta worry about that. I wouldn't put you through nothin' like that."

"You can't make a promise like that, Solomon. You don't know what might happen."

"I'ma be straight."

I let him hold me for a few seconds. But it really didn't make me feel any better about him going out of town.

"Would you please put those books away for a minute? I want some attention," he demanded, after a while.

He said it so sweet like, that I couldn't deny him.

"Yeah. You've been real patient. I'ma give you some attention."

"Thank you."

"What can I do for Solomon?" I teased. "What can I do to please my man tonight? Let me cater to you, like Destiny's Child."

"Say word," he said, grinning at me. Then he leaned over, and whispered his desire in my ear.

I listened, pulled away from him and made a face. His request was outrageous. He knew I wasn't down for anything like that, but we played with each other that way.

"Uhn Solomon, you nasty," I teased.

He had whispered something about a whole different kind of back-shot. I wasn't down with that type of doggy-style.

"You dig it."

I nodded in agreement. "Yeah, but I can't make nothin' like that happen."

"You're straight," he said easily, "Just come here." He pulled me to him, and kissed me passionately.

* * * * *

Jinx called my cell phone the day after Solomon

left for his out-of-town run.

I was leaving the salon. "What's up, Jinx?"

"How did your mid-terms go?" Unlike Solomon, Jinx was mad supportive of me going to school.

"They were cool. I'm just happy to be finished."

"You wanna go celebrate being finished, or what?"

I looked down at my Coach watch. It was 9:20. It wasn't too late.

"Yeah."

"You want me to scoop you from the salon?"

"Nah, I'm on my way home. Pick me up from there. I need to change," I acknowledged.

"Cool. I'll holla back around 10:00."

* * * * *

I dressed up to go out with Jinx. I put on a camel colored suede miniskirt, a matching suede jacket, and Dolce & Gabbana's lizard - embossed boots. I hit the ends of my hair with the curling iron, touched up my perfume, and refreshed my lipgloss. I was ready and waiting when he got to my crib.

He took me to a bar called, *Misty's*. The place was cracking. It was filled with refined ballers and their women. It had a nice atmosphere. The music was soft and mellow. The décor was easy on the eyes, pale pastel walls, and low lights. It was just nice. Jinx and I sat at a table, instead of sitting at the bar. He pulled out my chair for me. I grinned at him. He was the epitome of a polished thug in my opinion.

"I wasn't plannin' on bringin' you here, but you were lookin' so damn good, I wanted to show you off," he cheesed.

I laughed. "You're crazy."

"How did you get away? I know your boy likes to keep you on lockdown."

"He's out of town," I admitted.

Jinx watched me.

I wouldn't make eye contact with him. I knew he was trying to read me. I tried to close myself up, keep my emotions inside, but I was too late. He saw what he needed to see.

"Is he movin' work?"

I nodded.

"You worried about him?"

Jinx and I were too close for me to bother lying to him.

"Yeah. One of my biggest fears is havin' to put somebody else that I care about in that ground."

"He'll be straight. He knows what he's doin'. He's been around this game for a long time."

The waitress popped over and took our orders. He asked for a beer. I asked for a Pepsi.

"What's up with Ebonie?" I asked to make conversation.

"She's cool," he said, simply. "Where did you get the bracelet?"

He noticed everything.

My eyes flew down to my wrist. I had forgotten all about the platinum tennis bracelet that was resting comfortably at the end of my arm. It had three carats of diamonds, and was hard to miss.

"Solomon."

He looked at me. "Damn! Solly ain't playin' when it comes to keepin' a female iced up. First the big ass ring, now the flashy ass tennis bracelet."

"Yeah," I nodded.

I thought about all of the rings, necklaces, bracelets and ankle bracelets that Solomon got for me. That was his way of showing me that he cared. It would've been a hell of a lot cheaper for him to just tell me verbally. But that wasn't how he did things.

"What, does he think that's the only way he can hold on to you?"

I looked into Jinx's eyes. His tone let me know the comment was a dig.

I shrugged, "I think he just really likes to shower me with gifts." I knew that was a lie, even as it came out of my mouth.

"Yeah right," he said, "Solly's used to buying women's affection."

I knew there was some truth in that statement.

"What would you do if he never gave you another piece of jewelry, Passion?"

I felt like he was testing me.

"Get over it." I said, honestly. "I could buy all this same jewelry for myself. You know that."

We were both quiet for a minute. I sipped my Pepsi staring up at him.

"What?"

He shook his head, but I could tell he wanted to say something.

"What, Jinx?"

"What the hell are you doin' with dude?" He asked.

I almost choked on my pop. That wasn't what I expected him to say.

"Where did that question come from?"

"I just wanna know. I can't understand it. Explain it to me. What are you doin' with Solly? Why are you with him this long?"

I flipped it on him. "Why are you with Ebonie?"

"I'm usin' her as a distraction."

"Does she know she's just a distraction?"

He shrugged his shoulders. "I don't know what she knows. What are you doing with Solly?"

I knew there was no way for me to avoid the question. I didn't really know how to answer it, though. I dug Solomon, but I wasn't in love with him. I couldn't say that. So, I said the first thing that came outta my mouth.

"I'm comfortable with him."

"You're comfortable with him?" he repeated.

"Yeah."

He didn't ask me any more questions about him after that.

"Okay. What's up with school, then?"

I grinned. I never really got to talk about school. Solomon was not trying to hear about school.

"School is cool. It's different from what I thought it would be. Hell, it's harder than I thought it would be. I don't have time for myself no more. All I do is study."

"Uhm, your guy must *love* that."

"It bothers him," I admitted. "But it is what it is. My father expects me to take over his businesses one day. I need to know what the hell I'm doin'."

He nodded his understanding.

I looked over at Jinx. He had so much going for him. I liked the way his eyes shined whenever he smiled or laughed. I liked the way he was always real with me, no matter what. It seemed like now every time I saw him, he looked better than the time before. I wondered why I never noticed that.

We talked a little while longer. We ate two orders of hot wings and headed back to my place.

* * * * *

Jinx parked in front of my building, and walked me to my front door.

I turned around to thank him for showing me a good time, and realized he was right up on me. I took a step back, and bumped into the front door of my building.

"Jinx," I began.

Whatever I planned to say was lost in the kiss he gave me. He kissed me deeply. Passionately. I was shocked, but I didn't stop him. His breath was warm. His mouth tasted like wintergreen Certs.

He pulled away and watched me. Waited to see my reaction.

"Jinx," I started again.

"I've been waitin' to do that for a minute."

I looked up at him. My heart was pounding. I liked the kiss too much. I wanted him to hold me longer, kiss me longer.

"You have a girlfriend," I muttered, like he didn't know that.

"She ain't you, though."

"What about Solomon?"

"What about him? You aren't serious about that punk."

I didn't respond.

"I've wanted to get at you for a minute. I've been real patient...but I can't wait no more. There are some moves I'm ready to make, and I need you with me when I make them."

227

"Jinx," I repeated.

"From here on out, I'm through fuckin' around, Passion. I'm about to make you mine, and God ain't created the nigga that can stop me."

Butterflies went berserk inside of me.

"Solly can play his game. I'ma do Jinx. We'll see who comes out on top." He paused. "The only person who can stop me is you, Baby Girl. Tell me you don't want me and I'll leave you alone."

How could I tell him that I didn't want him? I loved him. He meant a lot to me. He was always checking up on me, and looking out for me. No matter how much I messed up, I knew Jinx would always be around to help me put the pieces back together. He was my security.

I wanted to get all into Jinx, but I couldn't. I had to think about Solomon. He was my man. I was his girl. I couldn't just go out like that on him.

"Jinx..."

He cut me off, again. "Ain't no, 'Jinx'. Tell me you don't want me, and I'll leave you alone. Just tell me you don't want me, Passion."

I buried my face in his muscular chest.

He put his hand under my chin, and lifted my head. When I looked up at him, he was smiling.

"You're about to be mine. I'm through bullshittin'."

He kissed me, again. And as much as I tried to fight it, I lost the battle. I kissed him back.

"The gloves are comin' off," he said. "Tell your weak ass boyfriend to bring his 'A' game."

I watched him walk away. Every woman wanted a man to want her like this.

How am I supposed to deal with this, and school, too?

I thought to myself.

He posed a challenge and it was hard for me not to accept it. Solly picked a fine time to go away.

* * * * *

Jinx wasn't playing with me when he said he was through bullshitting. He started turning up everywhere I did. He would be outside of the salon, waiting to take me to dinner when I got off. If he knew I was studying for a test, he would drop by my place with food and stuff. He would show up at my school. Sometimes he would leave flowers on the hood of my truck. Other times, he would wait beside it, until I came out of class. When I got there, he would kiss my lips tenderly, whisper sweet things in my ear, give me a hug, then leave. I would still be standing there bugging – all romanced.

The oddest thing was he never ran into Solomon while he was doing Jinx. Solomon was off somewhere, doing him.

* * * * *

One Wednesday night in early November, while Solomon was on yet another drug-run to St. Louis, my doorbell rang. I was lying on the couch in my family room studying. I got up, and answered the door.

It was Jinx. He looked upset.

"What's the matter?" I asked, as he stepped into my condo.

"I'm goin' out of town tomorrow mornin'. I needed to holla at you before I left."

"What are you goin' out of town for?"

It had been two weeks since we first kissed. I didn't want him to go anywhere.

"My mother, she's sick."

I didn't know his family. And as much time as him and I had spent together, he never really mentioned them. I just knew he was originally from Brooklyn, New York, and his family still lived there.

"Is she gonna be okay?" I asked, taking his hand and leading him to the living room couch.

"She has malignant cancer." He said, plopping down. "She's not doin' too well."

I hadn't seen him this upset since Lorenzo got killed.

"Jinx, no!"

"Yeah, I need to holla at Brooklyn. Take care of a few things. Wrap up all of her loose ends before anything goes down."

"I am so sorry."

He touched my cheek tenderly. "I just want you to know where I am. I don't want you to forget about me."

"I could never forget about you."

"I gotta go. I gotta lot of packin' to do. I don't know how long I'ma be there."

"Who's gonna watch your shop?"

"I got that taken care of. Don't worry about that. Are you gonna be straight?"

How was he thinking about me, when his mother was sick?

"I'll be cool. Are *you* gonna be straight?" I asked in return.

"Yeah, I'll be cool. You got my cell. You can hit me up any time you need me. I'll let you know when I get there. Give you the number to where I'm stayin' and everything."

"Okay."

"Don't look so sad." He said, winking at me. "I'll pop into town every now and then."

"I'm gonna miss you."

"Yeah, I know. Gimme a kiss."

I kissed him, and he held my face to his. He kissed me deep to let me know exactly how he felt about me.

"I'll holla," he said, as he left my condo.

When I was alone, I put an Earth, Wind & Fire CD into my CD player. I went to the track for *Love's Holiday*, and hit the repeat button. I climbed into bed while the brothas of Earth, Wind & Fire told me their story.

I didn't sleep at all that night. I was too worried about Jinx and his mom.

CHAPTER TWENTY-TWO

The following Friday afternoon when I walked into the salon, Kimberly was waiting for me.

"Hey, Passion. I have some mail for you."

I was tripping. The only mail I received at the salon was advertisement and hair magazines. "Okay. Let me put my stuff down."

I sat down my bags, and set up my station. Then I went back up to the reception desk. Kimberly handed me a large manila envelope. The envelope didn't have a return address, and my name and the address of the salon had been typed onto a label. The envelope was post marked by the post office closest to the salon, on 75th and Exchange. I was kind of suspicious about opening the letter. Finally, my curiosity got the best of me. I sat down in my chair and slowly opened the envelope. Inside, were four 8x10 pictures. I studied the first picture for a minute. It was a picture of a silver car. It took me a second to realize the car was Solomon's Infiniti. The second picture showed him and another person getting out the car. I studied the picture carefully. I made out the other person as a female. I quickly turned to the third picture. It clearly showed Solomon and the female in front of a house. I got a good look at the female. She had brown skin, a shade or two darker than Solomon. She had slanted eyes that made her look half-Asian or something. She was slimmer than me, and taller than me. She had small breasts, a small waist, but a huge ass. I looked closely at the picture. I didn't recognize the house or the block it was on. The fourth picture showed Solomon and the broad kissing in front of the house. It was a serious kiss. A nasty looking kiss. He was dressed in blue jeans, and a hoodie. I was with him when he bought that hoodie. Now, he was wearing it while he romanced some random hoe? That pissed me off. The female had on orange jogging pants, a white t-shirt and house slippers. Something about the girl caught my eye. I held the picture closer to my face, and looked at her wrist. I would've been damned if that hoe didn't have on a tennis bracelet identical to the one I was wearing. I sucked my teeth in disgust. I wondered if he got a discount for buying two bracelets.

I couldn't help thinking that the pictures looked like a professional job. They were done with a high-definition camera. I could tell. They weren't from any Joe-blow's camera phone. Somebody laid down some loot on those pictures. The quality was too good. I mean, I could make out old girl's tennis bracelet. The pictures had to be professional. Somebody really wanted me to know that Solomon was messing around on me. If Jinx did this, he'd lose points with me for being so desperate. But this didn't have Jinx's name on it. He wouldn't do something like this. He'd make me chose flat out!

"Hey Passion, girl," Summer greeted me, and scared the daylights out of me.

I jumped out of the styling chair, and held the pictures close to my chest.

"I'm sorry. I didn't mean to scare you."

I forced a smile. "You're straight. I was just deep in thought."

She looked at the pictures I was holding. "Uhm, what's on those pictures, girl? You and Solly naked?" She joked.

I forced another smile. "Nah, girl. I gotta study these pictures for a test I have comin' up on Monday." I lied.

"So, what's really hood?"

"Nothin'. What's good with you?" I asked, shoving the pictures into one of my drawers.

"Girl, it's been a lonely week. Rico's out of town," she lowered her voice, "on business."

I knew that meant he was on a drug run.

"I thought you said Rico stopped ballin'."

"He did for a minute. Then, I guess he started missin' that dough, cuz next thing I knew, he was back in the game."

Before I could speak, she continued.

"Passion girl, you are so lucky you don't have to worry about that type of stuff with Solly."

I hesitated for a millisecond. "Uhm." I didn't have a clue as to what she was talking about.

"You know his daddy got killed durin' an out of town run."

"Right," I agreed. "He was tellin' me about that. It happened in uh...uh."

I was lying my head off. I didn't know anything about Solomon's father even being dead. Let alone being killed during an out of town drug run. That was all news to me.

"St. Louis," she supplied.

"Yeah, St. Louis." Somebody could've knocked me over with a feather.

"Solly's so wild, an out of town run is about the only thing that boy won't do," she joked.

"I know." Inside, my head was spinning.

Summer ran off at the mouth for the rest of the time she was there, but I didn't hear another word she said. All I could think was that Solomon was cheating on me. The same way Lorenzo cheated on me. I slipped again. I was too pissed with myself! Solomon was cheating on me.

When I left the salon that night, I felt a lot of emotions. Surprise wasn't one of them. I knew I went from hitting Solomon off with the booty four to five times a week, to once a week or once every two weeks. Any man worth his weight wouldn't put up with that. So, I wasn't surprised there was another female. I was surprised at how far dude went to fool me, though. Making up trips to the place where his father was killed. That was some sick shit! I didn't want revenge on him or, to get back at him. Actually, I was glad he finally showed me his hand. That way, I could move on without feeling any regret. I just wanted him to know he wasn't slick. I went up to the nearest 24 hour Kinko's, and made three copies of the incriminating pictures. I bought a large mailing envelope, too.

As soon as I got home that night, I called Jinx.

"Yeah," he said, when he answered the telephone. He sounded so down. My heart went out to him.

"Hey, Jinx." I walked into my bedroom and kicked off my shoes. I put them neatly on the shoe rack in my walk-in closet.

"What's up, Baby Girl? What's goin' on?"

I didn't wanna lay my problems on him. He had enough on his mind. "Nothin'. I'm just concerned about you."

"I wanted to get up there this weekend, but I can't make it happen."

"Don't worry about it, Sweetie. How's your mom?"

He was quiet for a second. "Uhm, she's straight. Today was a good day. She was her old self today."

I smiled, and walked into my family room. I sat down on my sofa. "Good. How are you doin'? Are you takin' care of yourself?"

"I'm straight," he responded, but I could hear him sigh heavily. "I got a lot to do. I mean, my sister and her kids stay with my mom, and... I just got a lot to do."

I didn't even know he had a sister. There were a lot of things I didn't know about him. There were a lot of things I wanted to say to him. A lot of things I wanted to do. I wanted to be there with him, hold him and comfort him.

"Jinx."

"What's up, baby?"

"I love you. I love you and I miss you." I expressed with mixed emotions.

"Thanks. I needed to hear that. I miss you, too. I'm out here straight grindin'. There's so much stuff to do. My moms got a lot of stuff that needs to be sorted out, and my sister ain't done a damn thing. It's like everything is fallin' on me. Yo, it's stressin' me out, ma. The only positive thing I got goin' for me, is you," he confessed.

Butterflies began to flutter around in my stomach.

"Damn, I wish I could see you. I feel like I'm losin' my mind."

I didn't know exactly what he was going through, but I knew my experience was close. I remembered trying to sort through all of Lorenzo's stuff after he died. It was real traumatic.

"It's normal for you to feel like that. But you aren't losin' your mind. There's just a lot goin' on right now."

He sighed heavily again, and my heart went out to him. I could tell he was in pain.

"There's no way you can fly in even for a day?" I really wanted to see him. I wanted to make sure he was all right.

"If I could fly in for an hour, I would do it. But I can't make it happen. I got too much to do."

"I got you, Jinx. Whatever you need, just tell me." That was all I could say.

"Stay down for me."

My heart ached. How could he think I wouldn't stay down for him? "I will. You know that."

He yawned.

"It's late. I'ma let you go. Get some rest."

"Yeah, I'm tired. And I gotta gang of stuff to do tomorrow."

"Okay."

"I'll holla back tomorrow."

"Bye."

"Ay, Baby Girl…"

"Huh?"

"I love you, ma."

It was easy for Jinx to tell me that. Solly had never uttered the word love to me except, "When is the next time I'ma hit that." That was saying I love you to him.

CHAPTER TWENTY-THREE

I got up early the next morning. I put on a pair of Salon Care disposable latex gloves, so there wouldn't be any fingerprints. I carefully put a copy of all four pictures in the envelope I bought. Then, I typed up a mailing label with Solomon's address. Instead of driving straight to the salon, I took a little road trip. I hopped on Lake Shore Drive, and drove until I got tired of driving. When I came off of the Drive, I was on Fullerton Avenue, the north side of Chicago. I drove down Fullerton until I found a mailbox. I quickly double parked my truck, dropped the envelope in the mailbox and headed for the salon.

* * * * *

The following week, Solomon remembered he had a girlfriend. I figured the pictures reminded him that he was neglecting me.

Friday, he showed up at the salon while it was still cracking. It was about 7:15 p.m. He walked in carrying a beautifully decorated box. Every female in the salon had her eyes on him. He walked right to my station.

My last client was under the dryer, so I was at my station alone.

"What the deal, Shorty?" he asked, grinning at me.

I smiled back, frontin', "Hey, Solomon."

I gave him a hug. Making him feel like everything was cool between us. That was another trick my father taught me. Keep your enemies off guard. Always make them feel comfortable around you.

"I picked up a little something for you."

I looked into his handsome face. "Ooh, thank you."

"Yeah, you been so busy with school, and I've been makin' moves. We ain't spent too much time together in a minute."

"And we definitely need to spend some time together." I said giving him my patented, "sex me" look.

He fell for it, as usual. "Say word."

"Word, Sweetie."

I opened the present. Inside the box, was a large, brown teddy bear, but the bear wasn't the actual present. The present was what the teddy was holding. She was holding a Prada purse. It was almost as big as she was.

My mouth fell open. One thing I had to give the bastard, he knew how to apologize. I liked the purse, but I couldn't help wondering how long it would be before the girl with the slanted eyes was flaunting the exact same purse.

I gave him another hug. "You're too sweet."

He nodded, like he was the man or something. "What time are you gonna be through up here?"

"Uhm, I don't know. Why?"

"I wanna see you."

"Well, I'll hit you up when I get off. I need to go home first, anyway. I wanna change my clothes."

He looked me up and down. "You look good, Shorty. You don't need to change."

I leaned close to him, so only he could hear. "I'm on my period, Solomon. I need to go home and change."

That was a lie. I wasn't on my cycle. But there was no way in hell that I was having sex with his cheating ass.

He turned up his face. He hated hearing about anything that had to do with menstruation.

"Damn, just holla back," he grumbled in frustration.

No, "I love you," for him tonight!

* * * * *

I went home that night and changed into a, "hurt me," outfit. That was an outfit that would have every sista in the place wanting to hurt me, because her man couldn't control his staring. I wanted Solomon to want me so badly; he would go home with blue balls.

The outfit started with an animal-swirl wrap halter top by Baby Phat. It had a plunging neckline and made my breasts look like they were fighting for their freedom. They were sitting up proudly, just asking to be noticed. It was too cold outside for the shirt, but I was willing to risk pneumonia. Solly needed to know exactly who he was dealing with. I continued the outfit with a black leather skirt that came below the knees. The skirt was kinda long, but it had a split up the front that would shame some women. I gently pulled on black, shimmering Givenchy pantyhose. Then, I stepped into my black Christian LaCroix pumps. I sprayed myself with Chanel No. 5, put everything I needed into my brand new Prada purse, and waited for the cheater to show up.

* * * * *

He took me to The Cheesecake Factory. I was overdressed, but that was cool. I had it, so I was flaunting it. It was a busy night at the restaurant, too. When I took off my leather coat all eyes were on me, men, women, and children. I didn't care, as long as Solomon was looking and he was.

"Damn!" He said, all ignorant and loud. "Look at my Shorty, lookin' like a star up in here!"

"That's right, baby."

He kept staring, with his mouth all open. "Why are you lookin' so good, when I can't get me none?"

Exactly, you dumb bastard! I thought to myself. "I gotta go to the ladies room." I lied. I just wanted him to get the full effect of my ensemble. I took my time standing up. I made my leg hit the split of my skirt, so he could see the skin of my thigh. I picked up my purse.

"I'll be right back."

I switched slowly through the restaurant. Once I got to the ladies room, I touched up my hair, gave my breasts a little lift, and refreshed my lip gloss. When my lips were as shiny as possible, my breast at attention, I left the ladies room. I switched slowly back to the table. Even the waiters were checking me out. I pretended not to notice.

When I was sitting down, I noticed Solomon watching the split in my skirt.

"I'ma have to hurt somebody up in this joint, Shorty. All these cats up in here are starin' at you. Even the white boys!" He shook his head. "You look mad classy."

I smiled at him, but on the inside I was as hot as

hell. He was sitting there acting like I was what he wanted, but as soon as I turned my back; he was off creeping with the next female. "So, you like this outfit?"

"Hell yeah." He lowered his voice. "If you weren't on that 'thing, thing', I'd take you home and rock the hell outta you."

Once upon a time, I liked for him to talk freaky to me, but now it just made me sick to my stomach. I thought about Lorenzo, and the baby he had with the other broad. I was sick of trifling cats. Hoeing around every chance they got.

"Solomon, I know we haven't been spendin' as much time together as we did in the past. I know school kind of got in the way of that."

He nodded his agreement.

"I know we used to have sex like crazy." I continued, playing my position. I wanted him to think everything was the same with us. I wanted him to think he still had me fooled.

He smiled at the memory.

"But now we go for weeks at a time without seeing each other. I love you, though. And I don't want you to switch up on me. I don't want you to start seein' no other female. I don't want you to think you gotta get booty from somebody else."

"Shorty, I don't feel like that," he lied. "A brotha be too busy to think about another female. I stay in the grind. I ain't got time to try to romance nobody else."

"Say word."

"Word. Besides, you know you're my only Shorty. I told you, can't no other female out there touch you, Passion. You're classy, smart, beautiful, and you're sexy. You're like, the whole fuckin' package."

He was sitting there feeding me bull, thinking I was buying it. Ballers were a trip. One woman was never enough for them. No matter who they had at home, somebody else always looked just as interesting.

Solomon and I ate, then, walked back to his truck.

All night, he kept telling me how good I looked. Telling me how I was the only female for him; lying to my face. I just kept thinking about how Lorenzo played me, and how Solomon was trying to do the same damn thing. I kept thinking about that picture of him tonguing that slanty-eyed hoe down. I thought about the identical tennis bracelets. The fake ass out-of-town runs. I knew while he was feeding me dinner and feeding me lines, he was thinking about sexing his new broad. I got him all worked up with my outfit, and he was about to go by old girl's house later that night, and give his hard-on to her. He probably couldn't wait to drop me off. The whole situation had me pissed.

Yeah, I was digging Jinx, but I wasn't running around with him behind Solomon's back. I wasn't sexing Jinx. I wasn't on film tonguing him down.

I made a big deal of getting out of Solomon's Hummer that night. I acted like I had so much stuff with me. In actuality, all I had was my purse, my coat, and my left over food from dinner.

"Solomon, can you please carry my food for me?"

I made sure I was leaning over, with my breasts looking like they were about to fall outta my shirt, while I asked him. I knew he wouldn't refuse, and he didn't.

While he was getting out of the truck, I dropped copies of the pictures I was sent on the passenger's seat.

CHAPTER TWENTY-FOUR

The following Friday when I got to the salon, another envelope was waiting for me. I took it from Kimberly, and walked over to my station.

Jainelle came over to me. "Hey Passion, what's up?"

"Hey, Jai."

"Girl, we need to talk."

She had a serious look on her face.

"Okay," I agreed.

"You busy after work? Maybe we can do dinner."

"That's cool," I confirmed, even though my heart wasn't in it. I had too many things on my mind. I hadn't heard from Solomon since I left the pictures in his truck. Not that I expected to. I knew he was probably trying to think up a lie good enough to cover his sloppy tracks.

On top of the garbage with Solomon, I was real worried about Jinx. From the phone conversations we had, it seemed to me that things in New York couldn't really be any more jacked up. I really wanted to be with him, but my semester was winding down. I had to get ready for finals. I sat down in my styling chair. Summer was gonna arrive in a minute. I quickly, but carefully opened the envelope. I really didn't even want to see what was inside. I knew it was more pictures of Solomon and his hoe. I didn't even care any more. Any feelings I ever had for him were dying an ugly death. After the garbage Lorenzo pulled, with the pregnant "fiancé", my tolerance for cheating was at zero. I was through with Solomon. The last time he got some of this booty, was the last time with his sneaky. Just the thought of him made me nauseous.

There were six, high quality 8x10 pictures in the most recent envelope. The first picture gave me a close up of the house that was in the previous set of pictures. I could see the address, 7316. It was a well-manicured house, with red brick, and nice landscaping. It was a typical Chicago bungalow, on a typical looking block. The second picture showed street signs at the intersection of 73rd and South Hartwood. I chuckled and shook my head. Whoever was sending the pictures wanted me to know exactly where old girl stayed – 7316 South Hartwood. The third and fourth pictures showed Solomon with me at The Cheesecake Factory. In one picture, my breasts were sitting up at attention, and I was smiling. The other picture showed Solomon taking a sip of his beer. The pictures made me feel uncomfortable. Somebody was following Solomon, and they knew who I was. I didn't like that. It was cool that somebody was following him and his hoe. But I didn't want anybody following me, taking pictures and stuff. Now, it wasn't funny. If it was that damn Isis, I was gonna kill that girl! I guess she wanted me to know that I wasn't the only one.

My first thought was to call Jinx. He would know what I should do. I quickly pushed that thought from my mind. He had his own problems. My second thought was to call my father. I didn't know if I needed protection, or what. My mother got killed, because of association. I didn't wanna go out that way. Especially not because of association with Solomon's whack ass.

I pulled out my cell and called my dad.

He answered on the second ring. "Baby Girl, good morning."

"Good morning, Daddy."

He immediately picked up on the intonation of my voice. "What's the matter?"

"Daddy, I need to talk to you. Are you gonna be at the lounge later tonight?"

"What's the matter, Passion? Are you all right?"

"It's a long story. I just really need to talk to you."

"What time are you talking about?"

"About 11:00 tonight."

"Do you need to see me now? I can make time."

"No. I'll see you at 11:00."

"Okay. I love you."

"I love you, too."

I hung up my cell phone, and pulled the last two pictures from the envelope. Both pictures showed the female with the slanted eyes. In one picture, she was getting out of the driver's side of Solomon's Avalanche. So, he was letting her push his whip? I shook my head. That was basically a slap in the face to me. That was just plain disrespectful. What if I had seen her in his truck? What if one of my people had seen her in his truck? That would've left me looking like an idiot.

In the last picture, she and Solomon were walking through the mall. They were holding hands, and he was looking like a straight sucker. Deep down inside, I hoped that the slanty-eyed hoe took him for every penny she could get out of him.

* * * * *

Jainelle and I ended up at Leona's Restaurant over in Hyde Park. She ordered shrimp. I ordered lasagna, but I played over it. I wasn't really hungry. I had too much going on.

"When's the last time you seen Solomon, lately?"

"A while ago," I answered vaguely. I didn't tell her that Solomon and I were finished.

"I know you ain't been seein' too much of him."

"Uhm." I was seeing more of his ass than she thought I was, because he kept giving me his ass to kiss.

"Well, you ain't heard this from me, but..."

I perked up right away. I knew she was about to give me the biz.

"Solomon had some extra tickets to see R. Kelly and Jay-Z Wednesday night. So, he gave them to me and Tippy. When we got to the concert, I was expectin' to see you. But instead, he was there with some other broad!"

"What did she look like?"

She thought about it for a second. "She was tall, brown skin, Chinese eyes, skinny."

It was the same broad. The very same female from the pictures that Solomon was lying about taking road trips to spend time with.

"You remember her name?"

"Some weird, crazy name. Uhm...Leilani."

I turned that information over in my head storing it in my mental rolodex.

"I just wanted you to know, Passion. Tippy told me to stay out of it, but you're my girl. I can't know your man is actin' up and not tell you." She was truly upset.

"Thanks for tellin' me, Jai. I really appreciate it. I won't say nothin' to Solomon about you tellin' me."

She took a sip of pop. "You know we can find this hoe, and beat her ass."

"Nah, it's not her fault Solomon's a bastard. She might not even know about me." I looked down at my watch. It was 10:17. I needed to be at my father's lounge by 11:00.

"I gotta blow, Jainelle. I gotta meet up with my father at 11:00." I pulled enough money from my purse to pay for my meal, and give something towards the tip. "I'll see you tomorrow, and thanks for the information."

* * * * *

My father was in his office when I got to *Classified*. I tapped lightly on the door.

"Come on in, Baby Girl."

I walked into the room. He was sitting at his desk with a stack of papers in front of him. He had his tie unloosened, and the first two buttons of his shirt were undone. He still looked handsome to me.

"Hey, Daddy." I sat down across from him with a smile.

He smiled back. "What's up, precious? You sounded upset on the phone."

I took a deep breath.

"What's the matter, Passion?"

I pulled the envelope with the pictures in it from my bag, and slid them across the desk to him.

"What is this?"

"Pictures somebody keeps sendin' me these pictures."

He took the pictures from the envelope, and slowly went through them. "Do you know who the

249

broad is?"

"I think that's the girl Solomon is messin'
around with. I'm not concerned about her. I'm
concerned, because somebody is obviously following
Solomon, and they have pictures of me."

He studied the pictures. "How long ago was
this?"

"I went out with Solomon about a week ago."

"Was that the last time you were with him?"

I nodded, "yeah."

"You haven't seen him at all?"

"Not since last week."

He put the pictures down, and looked at me.
"Where did you get these pictures?"

"Somebody keeps sendin' them to me at the
salon." I told him.

"Do you know whose house this is?"

"I think its old girl's house."

"And somebody's giving you her address, and a
picture of the cross streets?"

I watched my father, the way he taught me to
watch people. I took in his body language, and his
facial movements. He seemed too relaxed. Something
wasn't right.

"I think somebody wants you to know where
this broad stays. That's why they gave you her address.
73rd and Hartwood, I know that area."

"Uhm," I studied him. "So, you don't think
anybody's gonna try to pull something on me?"

"From the look of these pictures, it seems like
somebody wants to fuck with Solomon. But I'll put my
ear to the ground to see what I can come up with."

He was talking slick. All of a sudden I knew
who sent the pictures. Him! He had connections, and

he had his hands in all kinds of hustles. It wasn't anything for him to get a private investigator to follow Solomon, and snap some incriminating pictures.

"So, somebody wanted me to know that Solomon was messin' around on me?"

"That's what it looks like to me."

"Who would want me to know that?" I pretended to think.

He was silent.

"Well, if you don't think that I have anything to worry about."

"Nah, Baby Girl. You're fine. But like I said, I'll keep my ear to the ground, and see what I can come up with. Let me ask you were the pictures your only problem? You still seem upset."

"I have a lot on my mind, that's all," I admitted.

He turned my face to his. "What's the matter?"

"It's Jinx. He's goin' through a lot. I'm worried about him."

"His mom's not doing too well, I know."

"Nope, and I can tell it's killin' him on the inside, but he won't talk to me about it."

"Real men don't put their problems on their women. Real men handle their own business."

I didn't respond. My father had a skewed view of what a real man was, to a certain extent. I didn't think it was weak for Jinx to be hurting. His mother was dying. Who wouldn't be hurting?

"Lynne and I are expecting you on Thursday."

Thursday was Thanksgiving Day.

"I'll be there."

He came out from behind the desk and hugged me tightly. "I love you, Passion."

"I love you, too, Daddy."

251

I walked to my truck wondering why my father's methods were always so extreme. Why couldn't he just sit me down and show me the pictures? Why did he have to send them to me all anonymously and scare the hell out of me? What part of the game was that?

Chapter Twenty-Five

Thanksgiving Day was cold, but sunny. Daddy and Lynne's house was cracking when I got there. My father flew in a couple of Lynne's family members; her mother, her grandmother, three of her aunts, two sisters, and two nieces. My maternal grandmother was there, too. So was my paternal grandfather, two of my aunts, two of my uncles, and a host of my younger cousins.

I really didn't feel like being bothered with all those people, but I put on my game face. I mixed and mingled for about an hour. When I thought nobody would miss me, I went up to my bedroom. Jinx had been on my mind nonstop. I didn't see how I could have a good time, while he was in Brooklyn suffering. The whole situation seemed unfair to me.

My grandmother tracked me down. She tapped lightly on my bedroom door.

"Come in." I called, hoping that it wasn't one of the rug rats.

My grandmother hobbled in. "Lord, this house is too big, child. I think I'ma hafta drop some bread crumbs on the floor to find my way back to the kitchen."

I chuckled. She said the same thing every time she came out to the house.

"Hey, Grandmother."

"Hey, Baby Girl," she said, sitting down next to me on the bed.

"How are you?"

She was seventy-eight years old, but still in good health.

"Don't change the subject," she scolded. We hadn't even been talking, but that's how she was. "I didn't come all the way up here to talk about me. I came up here to talk about you. Why are you lookin' so sad?"

I silently debated whether or not to tell her about my problems.

"Just tell me." She rubbed my back gently.

"I have this friend." I began.

"Uh huh."

"His mother is dyin' of cancer and he had to go back to New York to take care of her, and take care of her business. Every time I talk to him, he just sounds so sad," I sighed. "It's breakin' my heart."

"Is this the young man, Jinx, the one that your father and Lynne are so crazy about?"

"Yes."

Lynne peeked her head into the room. "I was wondering where you were, Passion."

"She's up here, worrying herself sick over that little boy, Jinx." My grandmother tattled.

A look of concern crossed Lynne's face. "What's wrong with Jinx?"

"You know what's going on with him, with his mother being sick and all. I miss him."

"Passion, the last couple of times you been over here, all you do is tell me how much you miss Jinx. Why are you here talking about how much you miss him, instead of being there with him?"

"I couldn't have said it better myself." My grandmother seconded.

"But I have school."

"Uh, I think you can take a break from studying long enough to check on Jinx. I mean, take your books with you and study on the plane. Do something. Work it out." Lynne winked at me. "Just quit whining about it."

A smile spread across my face. I *could* take a short trip to New York. It wouldn't hurt me to take a little time to support my closest friend. I had studied so much; I knew I was ready for my tests. I jumped up and went over to my computer.

"Oh, there she goes on that computer." My grandmother teased.

"I gotta find a plane ticket for tomorrow."

"I'm serving dinner in twenty minutes, Passion. Don't be late." Lynne announced.

She and my grandmother left the room, while I logged on to the Internet.

* * * * *

When I got back downstairs, my daddy caught my eye, and motioned for me to follow him. I did. We went into the empty den. He shut the door, and turned to me. "I hear you're making moves tomorrow. What are your plans?"

Lynne couldn't hold water. I only made the decision to go to New York twenty minutes earlier, and he already knew.

"I'm goin' to see Jinx."

"Good. He needs you right now. When are you leaving?"

"Tomorrow morning."

I gave my father all of the pertinent information, like my arrival time, the name of the hotel, and everything. Once he was satisfied, he smiled at me again.

"I guess big things are happening in both of our lives, Baby Girl."

I didn't know what he was talking about, but I hugged him anyway.

"Hey, Daddy," I calmly remarked, looking up at him.

"Yeah?"

"I know you sent the pictures."

He smiled guiltily. "I knew you would figure out it was me."

"Why did you do that? Why didn't you just tell me?"

"That's not my way, Passion. There are some things that people need to see for themselves. I wanted you to see who Solomon is. I didn't want you to get blind-sided, like you did with Lorenzo. You need to be aware of who and what you're dealing with."

I turned that over in my mind.

"Chad, Passion, we're ready!" I heard Lynne call.

Daddy and I joined the rest of the family at the dinner table. My grandmother blessed the food. Then, we each went around the table and told what we were thankful for. Lynne was last. When we got to her, she was real emotional.

"I know some of you have been worried about me, especially since the fainting episode back in August. Chad and I got some news then, and we're finally ready to share it. We're gonna have a baby!"

I looked at my father. His hazel eyes were dancing. He looked happier than I had seen him in a minute. Everybody started hugging Lynne. I went to my daddy.

"That's what you meant." I hugged him.

"You're gonna be a big sister, Baby Girl."

"After all these years."

"After all these years," he repeated.

"Congratulations, Daddy. I'm happy for you and Lynne. I'm gonna have a baby sister or brother to spoil...finally." I hugged my father tightly. Happiness was a long time coming for him. He deserved to enjoy every minute of it.

CHAPTER TWENTY-SIX

Nervous energy ate me up during my entire flight to New York. I couldn't wait to see Jinx. When my plane touched down at LaGuardia Airport, I grabbed my luggage, exited the aircraft, and headed for the cabstand. The cab dropped me off at my hotel at 7:35 p.m. I checked into the Ritz Carlton, Battery Park, and went up to my room. It was total luxury. It had beautiful views of the New York Harbor, the Statue of Liberty, and Battery Park. That was important to me when I booked the room, but now that I was in New York, all that mattered was that I was closer to Jinx. We were in the same state and the same time zone.

I unpacked my bag. After unpacking, I realized that I was starving so I ordered a quick dinner, cheeseburger and fries, from room service. Once I had eaten, I knew it was time to holla at Jinx.

He answered his cell on the first ring.

"Baby Girl, holla," he said, sounding delighted to hear from me.

"Hey, Jinx," I sang.

"What's the deal? You must have been readin' my mind. You must have known I needed to hear your voice."

"I must have," I flirted. "What's up? Are you straight today?"

"Hell nah. I'm stressed out."

"You need to get away?"

"Hell yeah."

"Cool, cuz I would love to see you."

"Damn, I would love to see you, too." I heard him sigh. "I know when I left Chicago, I said I would get back every weekend or so, but I can never seem to make it happen."

"Don't even worry about it, because I got you. I'm here."

"Here, where?"

"Here, in New York. And I'm all yours for the weekend…if you want me."

"Awe baby," he said and it was the cutest sound I ever heard from him.

"I can't believe you came all the way for me."

"You know there's nothin' I wouldn't do for you," I said honestly.

"Where are you?"

"The Ritz Carlton, Battery Park." I was proud of that fact.

He laughed. I could imagine him shaking his head even though I couldn't see him.

"Why am I not surprised? You would be staying at one of the most expensive hotels in Manhattan, with your high maintenance ass."

I laughed.

"Ay, hold tight, I'm on my way to see you. I'm leaving Brooklyn in five minutes."

"Okay."

Jinx knocked on the hotel door around 9:27. I opened it fast, frantic to put my eyes on him. I had barely released the doorknob, when he grabbed me into his arms. He gave me kiss after kiss on the mouth.

He let his tongue explore me deeply. He kissed me like he hadn't seen me in years.

I loved the taste of him. His mouth always tasted like he just finished eating breath mints. He went under my hoodie and ran his bare hands across my naked back. His hands were ice cold. I shivered against his strong body.

He released me. "I know I'm cold, my bad. I just needed to touch you."

"Yeah, and trust, I need you to touch me."

After almost a month of being in Brooklyn, his accent was stronger than I had ever heard it. I liked it. He sounded sexy as hell.

He put his face in my neck, and inhaled. "I missed you."

"I missed you, too."

"How long have you been here?"

"Uhm…" I said thinking about it.

"Long enough to get your nails done, I see. You get your toes done, too?"

"Actually, I got my nails done in Chicago." I responded sassily, but really I was tripping. Jinx noticed everything. He noticed new hairstyles, new jewelry. He even noticed fingernail polish. He paid really close attention to me that made me feel special. "I haven't been here that long. My plane landed around 6:40."

"Damn, I'm glad you came."

"I'm glad to be here."

"You don't hear me, P. You're like a little piece of sanity, something normal for me to hold on to."

I smiled at him shyly.

"Yo, you done copped a suite at the Ritz Carlton. Show me the spot," he suggested.

I showed him around the space. The tour ended in the bedroom of the suite.

Jinx sat down in the armchair. He didn't know I peeped him, but I noticed when he rolled his head around slowly and stretched his neck. I didn't miss it when he reached up and firmly rubbed his right shoulder, either.

I went and stood behind. I started giving him a gentle massage. "Dang, you are really tense." I commented when I noticed how locked up his shoulders were.

"I told you, ma. I'm stressed the hell out."

"You know the bathroom has a spa tub in it. I'll run you some bath water. You can soak for a minute and hopefully ease some of your stress. I even have some aromatherapy to put in there for you. Since you're always looking out for me, this time I want to look out for you."

"Hook it up, P. I need to decompress."

I ran the bath water nice and hot, and poured in equal amounts of bubble bath, and aromatherapy oil. When the water was ready, I called for Jinx.

He walked into the bathroom, immediately grabbed me by the waist and pulled me to him. "Thanks, Baby Girl. I really need this."

"I know you do." I removed myself from his grip, then handed him a towel and washcloth courtesy of Ritz.

As he took off his shirt, I left the bathroom, pulling the door closed behind me. I sat down on the bed, planning to chill while Jinx relaxed away in the tub. But no sooner than I picked up the television remote to find something to watch he called my name.

"Ay P, come keep me company!" he requested.

I walked back into the bathroom. I let the lid down on the toilet and took a seat.

"How do you feel?" I questioned. He looked more relaxed than I had seen him look in a while.

He moaned sexily. "Mmmm. Yo, I feel lifted like a mothafucka. I don't know what you put in this water, but it got me feelin' kinda right."

I chuckled to myself. Then, neither of us spoke for a while. His eyes were closed like he was asleep, and I was trying to order exactly what I wanted to say to him in my mind.

"What's on your brain, P?"

"I'm buggin'. Two years ago, I never would've imagined this; us chillin' in a suite in the Ritz Carlton in New York. All this time, you've been like a big brother to me: my best friend. I never thought I would develop feelings for you." Jinx didn't open his eyes, but I knew he was listening to me. I could tell by his relaxed body language. "Jinx, you've been so good to me. After the way Lorenzo played me out, I never thought I would trust another man, but I trust you with everything I own. I trust you with my life." He didn't look surprised by anything that was coming out of my mouth. So, I kept talking. "I never expected my feelings for you to switch up. I didn't plan this. All I know is one day, I looked at you differently. It was the day I had that barbeque when Ebonie was with you. Before that day, it never bothered me that you always kept a female. But that day, I felt a little jealously towards Ebonie. She had who I wanted. She was at *my* barbeque, with *my* man." I had finally revealed my feelings for him.

262

Instead of saying something sweet, or romantic, when he spoke his voice held no emotion. "I'm ready to get outta this tub, P. You might want to leave the room."

That was not the response I had hoped for. I stood up slowly, waiting for him to speak again, because I figured that he was playing with me. Additional words never came, so I left the bathroom, and once again shut the door behind myself.

Jinx exited the bathroom with nothing but a bright white towel wrapped around his waist. I had an unobstructed view from my position on the bed. *Damn, Jinx is buff!* I thought to myself, as I tried not to stare.

He walked over to the bag he brought with him and retrieved a CD. His silence was killing me. I watched his every step. He placed the CD inside the CD player the hotel provided. While he was occupied with it, I stood up from the bed and made my way to the complimentary bottle of champagne and plate of strawberries that the hotel provided.

I picked up a strawberry, ate it, and then chased it with the champagne. I wasn't a big strawberry fan, but the champagne made the taste of the fruit pop in my mouth. I liked the sensation. Jinx found the track he was searching for, and let the music play softly. I popped another strawberry into my mouth, and chewed it. Once I swallowed, I immediately took a huge gulp of champagne. I barely had time to swallow the champagne before Jinx stood up and forcefully kissed me. He slowly savored the taste of strawberries and champagne coming off of my tongue. He drank me, sucked my tongue and then held my face to his. I wanted to melt. Then, he slowly put each one of my fingers in his mouth and sucked softly. The sensation nearly drove me crazy. I had no idea my fingers were a turn-on until Jinx put them in his warm mouth. I moaned quietly. I felt my nipples start to swell. They always gave me away. I had the most sensitive nipples in the world. He reached behind me, helped me take off my shirt and unhooked my bra. He set my breasts free. He put his fingers in the waistband parts and pulled them down. I slid my thongs down and stepped out of them and left it on the floor. Then, he attached himself to my left breast. His hands rubbed all over me. They were big and rough, but his touch was tender.

"Ooh," I moaned as he sucked and nibbled on my nipples. "Ooh."

He was sucking my breasts and caressing me. His hands were between my legs, gently massaging my candy. Sensations were going off all through my body. He wasn't in a hurry. He was taking his time. Slowly bringing me to where he wanted me, lower on the bed.

"Jinx," I moaned.

He put his mouth to my skin and I shook. He trailed wet kisses down and then up my body. Our tongues came together and he kissed me like he couldn't wait to get his hands on me. He put his hand between my legs again, made sure I was wet. Made sure I was ready. Then, dropped his towel and spread my legs, entering me gently. I let out a faint sound closing my eyes as I felt him. Shooting stars and fireworks exploded behind my eyelids. He felt too good. He just felt right so I grinded my pelvis up to his. Every stroke he gave me, I gave it back to him. He had me climbing the walls. I was hitting all kinds of notes singing any melody, giving a concert. I called his name over and over.

"Jinx! Jinx! Oh, Jinx!" I moaned and told him how good he was pleasuring me. "Jinx, I love how you feel."

He encouraged me to talk to him even urged me to express myself while he deeply pumped me.

"Tell me again, P. You sound so sexy moaning."

"Jinx," I moaned again.

This time, he covered my mouth with sweet kisses. I wrapped my legs around his waist and held him closer to me. He plunged deeper and deeper. I was crying real tears and screeching with pleasure. Then he took my legs and put them over his shoulders. Rocked me, dug me out giving me strokes that talked to my candy. It felt so good that I couldn't even make out anymore words and I wanted to. I wanted to tell him exactly how good he had me feeling. Then, he went deeper inside of me. I dug my nails into his flesh. He sucked my bottom lip and pulled my hair. I trembled. My legs shook. I ran my hands across his brick hard chest and held on to his strong arms. I felt him growing inside me. He pushed my legs back, opened me up even wider. My body invited him to go deeper. He did. He was digging in virgin territory. No dude had ever been so deep inside me. He whispered to me. Told me how he felt about me. How he wanted me for so long. When I started to moan louder, he increased his tempo. He started rocking me harder. I yelled his name. He had me open on a whole new level. He had me feeling like bottle rockets was going off inside my body. Then, he held my arms down, pinned me to the bed. I was his sexual prisoner. He hit it rough for a few minutes and made me cum. While I was doing my thing, I felt him do his. My tunnel was flooded with his warm liquid – his liquid. After he came, he gripped me tight. Little by little we came down off of our love induced high. Slowly, he rolled off of me and lay beside me. I tried to slow my breathing down. I tried to regain my composure. Finally, I looked over at him. His eyes were closed. He looked so sweet, lying there like that. I leaned over and kissed his lips. He didn't move. I figured he was asleep. He had been through a lot lately. He probably needed some sleep. I laid my head on his chest.

"Baby girl," he whispered, surprising me.

I sat up. "Huh?"

"I love you. That's my word."

Another warm sensation filled my body. I put my head back on his chest and smiled to myself before responding, "I love you too. That's my word."

* * * * *

Moonlight coming in through the open curtains woke me up hours later. I opened my eyes slowly. I was alone in the bed.

I looked over towards the offending stream of light. I saw his silhouette. He was sitting by the window. He was watching me.

"Hey," I whispered.

"What's up?"

"Why are you over there and I'm over here?"

"I couldn't sleep." He walked back over to the bed, and climbed in next to me. He rubbed his hand over my exposed thigh. "Damn, your skin is so soft."

"I'm a woman. I'm supposed to have soft skin," I teased. "Why couldn't you sleep?"

"I got a lot on my mind."

"What kind of cancer does your mother have, Jinx?" I inquired since he hadn't shared.

"Lung cancer. She's had it for six years, now. She knew the whole time, and never told me." He played in my hair with his fingers.

"Maybe that was her way of protecting you," I offered.

"I don't know. I still think it's fucked up."

I agreed, but didn't comment. "Where's your dad?"

"He stays uptown, in Harlem. We don't holla at each other too much. They've been divorced for fifteen years. He never really came around after that. Never really seen no loot from him."

"That's messed up."

"It is what it is. Everybody can't have an old man like Pretty Hill."

"True," I admitted. I knew for a fact that my daddy was one of a kind.

"You told me before that you have a sister. Is she the only sibling you have?"

"Nah, I gotta younger brother, too. I'm the oldest."

"You seem like you would be the oldest."

"What does that mean?"

"I don't know. You seem used to takin' care of people."

"I don't take care of my brother and sister. They're too damn hardheaded... both of them. They don't listen. That's why my sister has three kids by three different dudes, and why my brother's doin' a seven year bid up at Riker's."

"How come you never told me about your family before?"

"You never asked."

"Do you mind me bein' all in your business, now?" I had to ask, because I was a private person. I didn't want to be all in his stuff if he didn't want me to be.

"Nah, you're straight."

I snuggled up to him, and put one of my bare legs across his. "So, I'm the first person you ever had to take care of?"

"Pretty much," he confessed. "When Lay-Law died, you were so... so needy. You were lost. I could tell your old man wanted to be down for you, but I think a lot of stuff about Lay-Law's death reminded him too much of how your mother died. I think he started reliving the whole situation and it was too much for him. I felt like if I didn't do something, I was gonna end up watching you drown."

I thought about it. He was right. I probably would have drowned in my sorrow.

"When Lorenzo died, it was like somebody snatched the rug out from under me... again," I looked up at the ceiling. "You seemed like the only one who understood what I was going through."

"I understood your situation. You lost your guy. You were in pain." He ran his hand along my arm.

"Yeah."

"I worried about you a lot around that time. I didn't wanna see you link up with the wrong kind of dude trying to medicate your pain."

"So you weren't diggin' me all along?" I teased flirtatiously.

"I know you're playin', Baby Girl, but I can't let no garbage like that ride even as a joke. Lay-Law was my closest dawg. We were like blood. I never wanted *any* female that belonged to him. Not even you. Money over bitches – death before dishonor – that's the way we rode. I thought you were fly. You looked good, but I ain't want you. Besides, when you were with him, you were too young-minded."

"Young minded? I can't believe you said that."

"You were on something. All you cared about was doe, shopping, and getting your nails done, but Lay-Law liked your style, that was what mattered. I didn't start diggin' you until you grew up some – when you embraced womanhood. The first time you told me you would never mess with another baller was the first time you looked sexy to me. I was pissed at you when you first started kickin it with Solly."

"Really?" I asked even though I wasn't surprised.

"Yeah, I felt like you betrayed me."

That shocked me. I wasn't expecting him to say that. "Why?"

"Because you kept screamin' you weren't gonna holla at no more ballers. Then, as soon as another baller showed up, you hollered at him. That had me thinking, that you were fake. Made me wonder if you were still the same chic that used to mess with Lay-Law. Made me think you were still young-minded."

I didn't have a response.

"But after a minute, I realized you were just passing time with Solly. You weren't serious about him."

"How did you figure that out?"

"You showed me."

"What are you talkin about?"

"When Lynne was in the hospital---" he stopped.

269

"Yeah?"

"You sent your guy away to talk privately with me."

I thought about it. I did do that.

"I don't know why I did that. Tension I guess."

"You know why you did it."

"I guess I didn't feel like dealing with Solomon's jealousy or being bothered with him." I didn't tell Jinx that my father pulled Solomon's card and held it up to my face. I didn't tell him that all I could see at that time was Solomon's weakness and it turned me off.

"But you felt like being bothered with me?"

"You don't get on my nerves like other guys. You never bothered me."

He ran his hand through my hair. "That's because I understand you and they don't."

I silently agreed. He did understand me. He always seemed to know exactly what I needed.

"On the day of your barbecue..." he continued. "When I pulled up, you were standing there with Jainelle. You had on pink - pink shorts and a pink and white striped shirt."

Firecrackers went off inside of my stomach. I couldn't believe he remembered the outfit I wore three months earlier.

"You were standin' there with your girl, Jainelle, when Ebonie and I walked up. I peeped the whole shit, Passion. And you knew I peeped you. You couldn't even look at me."

I knew exactly what he was talking about. Since I was straight busted, I didn't say anything. I remembered watching him approach and thinking that he was fine. Like, I was seeing him for the first time.

He kept talking. "That was the day that my

feelings for you started to switch up. I noticed that we had a connection – a different kinda connection. Ebonie must have picked up the vibe we were puttin' down that day, too. Her ass argued with me all the way to the crib. She kept bitchin' about me wantin' to get with you."

"What did you say?"

"I told her nothin was goin on, but she didn't believe me."

"Solomon didn't believe me either. How funny is that? What made you decide to pursue me?"

"You. I kept going back and forth with myself about whether or not to mess with you. I kept tellin' myself to leave you alone. You weren't ready for me. Then the day I brought your truck up to the salon, you let me know you were ready."

"Huh?"

"You heard me. The day I brought your truck up to the salon, you called me that night."

I smiled at the recollection.

"We sat on the phone and listened to Floetry together," he recalled. "I ain't never done nothin like that."

"Me either."

"That was some different type stuff. That seemed like..." he searched for the word he wanted to use.

"Romantic?" I provided.

"Nah, like Thug's Passion. I was feelin' that and you that night."

"*Awe.*"

Jinx had the floor, so he kept talking. "The day I took you out after your mid-terms..."

I remembered that day, that was the first time he

kissed me. "Yeah..."

"You dressed up for me."

My mouth fell open. I shut it real quick. He knew me too well. He was pulling all my cards the same way my daddy did Solomon.

"Uh uhn," I lied shaking my head.

"You know you did. It was a trip 'cause you always look nice. Don't get me wrong. You got your little fashion-plate thing happening, but that day, you went all out. You did a little something special. I noticed."

I didn't say anything, but I was thinking that he noticed *EVERYTHING*!

"When I kissed you in front of your building," he continued, "you gave it back to me. Your body language, the way you looked at me, the things you said...all that let me know you wanted me to snatch you."

"Is that what you did? You snatched me from Solomon?" I teased.

"I was destined to snatch you from dude. He was insecure, cuz he knew you were outta his league. He knew there was no way in hell he could hold on to somebody like you. That's why he broke his neck to keep you draped in whatever little blinged-out trinket he thought would impress you the most. That's what weak motherfuckas do."

"So, you snatched me from Solomon."

"Hell yeah. You're here with me, aren't you?"

He was right about that. I was definitely with him. Naked, and laying in the bed of a $500.00 a night hotel room.

"Go to sleep. We have a lot to do tomorrow."

"A lot like what?"

"First of all, I'm checkin' you outta this expensive ass hotel room in the morning. I'm kinda pissed anyway that you copped a hotel room. You thought you would come all the way to New York and I wouldn't look out? I got a place for you to stay. I'm takin' you to Brooklyn." Brooklyn was where he stayed.

"But before we head to my spot, I'ma take you to meet your future in-laws."

"My future in-laws?"

"Yeah, you wanna meet 'em before we get married, don't you?"

"When are we getting married, Jinx?" I asked playing along.

"I don't know yet, ma, but soon. I have to run it pass your father first."

Even though I didn't know if he was serious or not, I felt the flurry of butterflies inside my stomach. "You would wanna marry me?"

"I couldn't imagine myself wife'n nobody else but you, P."

* * * * *

The next day, Jinx woke me up to breakfast in bed. He had room service deliver Belgium waffles, and orange juice. Then, he treated me to another love making session. Once we showered and dressed, he took me out to Brooklyn to meet his family.

The house looked sort of scruffy on the outside, but the lawn was manicured and landscaped nicely. I was surprised by the house's interior. The entire joint had been refurbished from top to bottom. Everything was brand spanking new. The paint on the walls looked bright and fresh. The hard wood floors were gleaming. The curtains on the windows were crisp and bright. The furniture looked like it was delivered earlier that day. Every inch of the spot had Jinx's touch on it.

. I took off my leather jacket, and handed it to him. He hung it in the closet.

"Ma!" He yelled loudly. "Ma! Where you at?"

"Stop yelling. I'm in the kitchen." She called back.

"Come on."

I followed him down a long hallway, through the formal dining room, and into the large kitchen. His mother was at the sink. Her back was to us.

"What's good, gorgeous?" He teased, going behind her, and giving her a hug.

She giggled. "You're a mess, Jason. Stop it."

I smiled at his mother calling him by his given name. Sometimes, I forgot that his real name wasn't Jinx.

"You love it," he teased her. "Ay, I want you to meet my girl."

She picked up a towel, dried her hands and turned around.

Jinx's mom was an attractive woman. She was fair, like him and had the same laughing eyes. She looked good to be battling cancer. I figured she had to be a fighter. Figured she was where Jinx got his fight.

"This is Passion." He introduced us.

"Hi, Mrs. Waters. How are you doing?"

"So, you're Passion." She was looking at me like she had a secret. "Jason's told me a lot about you."

"Jason!" I heard a female voice call loudly.

Mrs. Waters cringed. "I don't know what's wrong with that girl."

"That's my sister," Jinx announced and then said, "I'll be right back," before leaving me alone with his mother for about ten minutes.

"Have a seat." She gestured towards her granite island.

I sat down on one of the bar stools. She sat down across from me.

"I'm glad to get a chance to meet you. I've been wondering about you, Miss Passion." She said it in a teasing way. I didn't take any offense.

"Really?"

"Yes, ma'am. Since Jason's been here, his mind has been a million miles away." She stopped and corrected herself. "No, actually, his mind has been on you. The only conversations we have revolved around my doctor's appointments, my medications… and you. He told me that he's never met anybody like you."

"To be honest with you Mrs. Waters, I've never met anybody like him, either."

She looked proud. "That's because there is nobody like him. When God made Jason, He broke the mold."

She wasn't lying about that. Jinx was definitely a new breed.

"Jason is my first born. He's my very first gift from God. I've always been a little over protective of him. I've always wanted the best for him."

I nodded my head. I was sure my father felt the exact same way about me.

"And he's always made me proud. He has a good head on his shoulders. He's self-sufficient. He stays on the right side of the law. Never brought me home no grandbabies to raise. He's upright and honest."

275

I agreed with everything she was saying.

"You must be pretty special for him to have bought you over here for me to meet."

"Jinx is my best friend. We've been through so much together. His friendship means a lot to me. He means a lot to me."

She stood up. "I'm going to get something to drink. Do you want something?"

"No, thank you."

She walked over to her side-by-side refrigerator. When her back was to me, she spoke again. "Do you love him, Passion?"

I didn't hesitate. "Yes, I love him."

"Good, then be there for him. When the Lord calls me home it will really hurt him. He wants to save the world, so it bothers him that he can't even save me. Help him not to drown in his sorrow." She sat back down at the island with her glass of orange juice. "Jason is strong. Sometimes, that makes people think that he doesn't need them." She sighed. "Young girls today, they want their men to be rough at all times. They want to date supermen; men who kill without emotion – men who'll love without emotion. I know my daughter is that way. Don't be like that Passion. Let him be soft with you. Don't take it as a weakness. If he needs to cry after I'm gone, let him cry. Love him." Her eyes were pinned on me. "Okay?"

"Okay," I agreed.

"I think he's in love with you."

"I think so, too."

"He's definitely a good catch. He's responsible, trustworthy, and soooo handsome."

I wanted to tell her that she didn't need to sell Jinx to me. I knew what type of man he was. Besides that, I was already in love with him.

"He tells me that you're in college." She seemed pleased.

"I am."

"What are you studying?"

"Finance."

"Good for you. I knew my child would do all right for himself. He has an excellent head on his shoulders. I don't know about those other two, but Jason is all right."

*****

We spent the rest of the day at Mrs. Waters' house. It gave me an opportunity to see Jinx in his element. I laid in the cut and watched him. I watched him prepare his mother's treatment. I saw the concern on his face every time he looked at her. I watched him feed baby food to his eighth month old niece. I watched him wrestle with his two nephews in the middle of the living room floor. I watched as he agreed to put the kids to sleep for his sister, Faith, so she could get dressed up and go trick off with her girlfriends. I shook my head and tried not to laugh when I saw him slip her a fist full of dough. Even though he insisted to his mother that he wouldn't give Faith any loot.

The more I watched him with his people, the more familiar he became to me. Then I realized that was because he reminded me so much of my daddy. Jinx and Pretty Hill had a lot in common. They were both hard working, loyal men who loved their families.

No wonder I'm in love with him. I thought to myself.

* * * * *

We left his mother's house in Park Slope around

10:30 that night and drove to Jinx's brownstone in Brownsville. The place was a shoe box. His place could have fit inside of my condo two times. I had to give credit where credit was due, though. Jinx had it hooked up really nicely, so, I didn't comment on the size of the apartment.

At least not until he showed me to his guest bedroom. It was barely bigger than a jail cell. The only furniture in the room was a twin sized bed, and a small dresser.

"Damn!" I said before I could catch myself.

He laughed his ass off. "Ay, baby Girl, what can I say? It's New York, ma. Space is at a premium."

"But I thought that was the point of livin' in the boroughs. I thought you at least got more space when you moved outta Manhattan."

"You do."

"You know this is really makin' me appreciate Chicago, right?"

"I know with your high maintenance ass."

I followed him out of the guest room and back into the living room. We sat down on the sofa side by side.

"Your mother is mad cool." I expressed to him.

"That she is."

"You know you're her pride and joy, right?"

"Hell, that ain't hard to believe, look at her other two kids."

"That doesn't have anything to do with it. She's real proud of you."

He blew me off with a wave of his hand. "Moms are like that. They're damn near proud of anything their kid does."

He closed his eyes. We sat there in silence for a

few minutes. Finally I spoke.

"Boo, if you're sleepy, why don't you go to bed?" Concern laced my tone.

"I couldn't sleep right now if I tried. I feel like my shit is in overdrive. I feel like I haven't slowed down since I been in New York."

"Not even last night?" I teased.

He looked over at me then licked his kissable lips. "I can't even lie, P. Last night was the first time I felt relaxed in I don't know how long. You're the only one who can ease the tension, Baby Girl."

"I wish I could move here and help you out for a minute. Look out for you, the way you always look out for me."

"That's a sweet thing for you to say, P. But if I encouraged you to move to Brooklyn, your old man would have the syndicate lookin' for me."

I laughed. "Forget you."

"You know it's the truth."

"Yeah, if I moved here, how much you wanna bet that him and Lynne would be movin' here the very next week?"

"Nothin'. I wouldn't take that bet. You know he ain't about to let you move 900 miles away from him. Your old man is bananas about you, Baby Girl."

I didn't respond. Instead, I pulled my right foot into my lap and began to lightly rub my toes.

"Your foot hurt?"

"Yeah, I think I should've gone up a half-size on those boots," I admitted.

"Gimme your foot."

I gently placed my foot in his lap. My sock might as well have not existed for the barrier it provided against the stimulation of the touch of his hand. A bolt of electricity went through my body and landed right in my sweet spot. I shifted myself on the sofa a little bit. I pretended like I was trying to find a comfortable position, but really, I was trying to stop the tingling in my panties.

"Am I hurtin' you?"

"Not at all," I replied truthfully.

"Ay, how long do I have you for?"

"Until tomorrow. My plane leaves at 3:05." I hated that I had to leave the next day, but I was starting finals on Monday.

"That's right, you got school and everything. Gimme your other foot."

I lifted my left leg, and he took my foot in his hand.

"Damn, I wish you could stay 'til Monday. Floetry is gonna be at The House of Blues. If you were stayin', I would cop us some tickets."

"Man, I would love to see them."

"It would be cool to actually be able to *touch* you while we listen to that song you dig."

The way he was massaging my foot, and the words that were coming out of his mouth had me feeling just right. I removed my foot from his grasp, and slid across the sofa towards him. When I was close enough to make contact, I pressed my lips against his and kissed him softly. He pulled me closer. I was almost in his lap. We kissed again and again. My body was completely pressed up against his. That was how I felt his cell when it started to vibrate. It tickled me. I pulled away from him.

"My bad." He snatched the phone from his waistband and checked the number. He eased away from me. "I gotta take this."

I watched as he walked out of the living room with the cell phone to his ear. I sat in the room by myself for about four minutes.

"I gotta ride back over to my mother's spot." He announced reentering the room.

"Why? What's wrong?"

"Every now again her treatments make her sick. That was DeVaughn on the phone saying that she keeps throwin' up and he's scared for her." DeVaughn was his five year old nephew.

I started putting my boots back on.

"Nah, P. You're straight." He started moving towards the front door.

"Jinx!"

He turned around.

"I'm going with you."

We stood there having a staring contest for about a minute. Finally, he relented.

"Hurry up then, Baby Girl. I need to blow."

* * *

At Mrs. Waters' spot, Jinx took care of his mother, while I went in the bedroom with his niece and nephews and put them back to sleep. He wasn't trying to leave Mrs. Waters there alone, so we sat at the dining room table and waited for Faith to get home. Jinx tried calling her about 50 times, but she refused to answer her cell. She strutted into the crib around 2:00 a.m. She almost bugged out when she saw Jinx and me.

"What are you still doin' here?"

"We're not 'still here'," he informed her. "We left. We had to come back. What the fuck is the purpose of you havin' a cell phone if you ain't gone answer it, Faith?"

She looked surprised by Jinx's tone. "I forgot to charge it today," she stammered. "Is something wrong with mommy?"

"If somethin' was wrong, what could you do? It is three damn hours later, Faith. If somethin' had gone down, what could you do at this point? How are you gonna leave your kids with your sick mother and not call to check on the spot? I know the rats you run with have cell phones you could've used." He stood up from the table.

"I'm sorry, Jason. Damn, I slipped. I'm sorry."

"You slip too often, Shorty." He scolded her. "Let's ride, Baby Girl."

I stood up from the table, and pushed my chair in. As we started to walk away, Faith spoke again.

"Hell, I said I was sorry. I ain't perfect like you, Jason. I know you never drop the fuckin' ball. You live and breathe for mommy's ass. Well, mommy and her damn disease ain't my every fuckin' thought."

"Maybe it should be. This ain't no damn game. Mommy ain't gone be here forever."

"You think I don't know that?" She was getting pissed. Her voice was getting louder and louder. "Who the hell do you think took care of her while you were off playin' footsies with this bitch in Chicago?"

She gestured toward me. And I had to catch myself. I couldn't believe she had the balls to call me a bitch like that, when she didn't know a damn thing about me.

Jinx didn't bother to address the fact that she called me out of my name. Maybe he was too pissed to go there. "Faith, walk away right now. Go check on your seeds. Do somethin'. Walk away right now."

From the tone of his voice, it was obvious that he was dealing with barely controlled anger. Had I been Faith, I would've *run* away. But she was a rider. She stood her ground.

"Fuck you, Jason. You don't run nothin' up in here. You don't like how I run mines, then, bounce the hell out. If you weren't such a fuckin' suck-up..."

Mrs. Waters entering the room cut her off. "Jason, go home. It's late. I'm fine. You can go home. Faith, go to bed." Her voice was filled with disgust and weariness.

"Go to bed?" Faith questioned, "I'm a grown woman. How are you—"

"Take your ass to bed, Faith!" She shouted.

The loud noise set Faith's daughter off, and the house was filled with the sound of the baby's shrieks.

"I can't deal with all of the nonsense!" Mrs. Waters put her hand to her head.

Faith left the room.

"Ay, mom--," Jinx began.

"Tomorrow, Jason. We'll talk about it tomorrow. Go home. It's late."

He wanted to say more. I could tell by the look on his face. But the look on his mother's face was saying that she didn't want to hear anymore. She wanted to be left alone.

Out of respect for her authority in her own house, Jinx and I blew the spot.

* * * * *

He was quiet on the drive back to his place. I left him alone, because I understood the types of thought that were probably running through his mind. I knew he was pissed with Faith. And I knew he was bugging about his mother's illness and the toll it was taking on her.

Back at his spot, he hung my coat in the closet, turned to me and finally spoke.

"Ay Ma, I'm about to call it a night."

"You want me to keep you company?" I offered.

"Ma, I'm dyin' for you to keep me company, but not tonight. I got too much shit on my brain. I wouldn't be no good."

"Okay." Reluctance filled my words. "Good night."

He gave me a hug. Squeezed me tightly, and kissed my lips. "Good night."

I went into the jail cell of a guest bedroom by myself. I stripped out of my clothes and slipped into Victoria Secret shorty pajamas. I climbed in bed, and closed my eyes. I don't know how long I had laid there, but right when I was drifting off, I heard a voice.

"Ay, P."

I opened my eyes slowly. "What's up?"

"I ain't really tryin' to be alone right now. Come keep me company."

In Jinx's bed, I was laying on my left side. He was posted up behind me, with his arm wrapped around me. He lightly ran his hand across my back.

"Your sister called me a bitch."

"I know. I heard that shit. I'm sorry she went out like that. Faith is...a trip. She's different. I can't really describe her. And I know this doesn't make it any better, but trust me, it wasn't personal. It wasn't even about you. She was tryin' to use you to get to me. Faith is the type that'll say anything to win a fight. She's always been like that." He sighed. "The more you're around her, the better you'll get to know her."

"I don't mean to say anything foul about your family, but I don't wanna get to know Faith. I don't wanna spend no time around her."

"I can understand that P, but y'all are gonna have to find some way to be cordial towards each other after we're married."

That was the second time he mentioned something about marrying me. I was starting to think that maybe he *was* serious. "Stop playin'. You're crazy."

"I'm serious. I'm dead serious."

I let his words sink in while I laid there in silence for what seemed like minutes, but was actually probably only seconds. "When do you wanna me marry, Jinx?"

"I ain't sure. I told you, I gotta get the 'go ahead' from your old man. Once he says he's cool with it, I'll let you put it together. You can work out the details."

I was still tripping. I turned around and faced him. I needed to look at him. I needed to see his facial expression. "And you're serious?"

"I'm more serious than you can probably comprehend." He pulled me closer to him. I placed my head on his rock hard chest. The firm and steady beating of his heart started lulling me to sleep.

"Damn!" I heard him say.

That brought me back from the brink of sleep. The pain and the anguish in that one word ripped my heart to shreds.

"Baby, what's wrong?" I asked him.

"My moms, Shorty. All of this..."

He wasn't crying, but the pain was right beneath the surface. I couldn't imagine where his head was. I couldn't imagine what it was like for him to watch his mother slowly perish. I didn't get that opportunity. My own mother was viciously and unexpectedly snatched from me. I wrapped myself around him. I held him as tightly as my arms would allow.

"I'm under too much fuckin' pressure." He whispered.

I rubbed and caressed him. I dropped light kisses all over his face, and never loosened the grip I had on him. I remembered that when my mother died, all I wanted was for my daddy to hold me and never let me go.

While I was recalling my own pain, Jinx took my breasts in his hands and held them, caressed them. He tenderly massaged my nipples. We laid there like that for a minute. Then he put his face in my neck, and started to lightly run his tongue along my skin. Goose bumps popped up all over me. My nipples threatened to explode. He licked my neck, again. I started getting wet.

"Passion, I need you, baby."

"I need you, too, Jinx."

He helped me pull off my top, then, I relieved myself of my pajama bottoms and panties. Jinx climbed down my body. He spread my legs, and put his head inside. A soft moan escaped from my lips. His tongue was soft. I put my hands on his head and enjoyed the feelings he was giving me. Jinx increased the pressure of his tongue. I arched my back, pressed my pelvis forward. I moaned long and low. It felt too good. Jinx put my legs in the air. He put his palms on my feet, pushed my legs back, and exposed all of my candy to his mouth. While he licked, sucked, and nibbled, I tried not to wake up everybody in the brownstone. I was screaming and calling his name all loud, begging for mercy and everything, but he didn't show me any. He nibbled and sucked, until I shook and came hard.

Then, I laid there, and tried to catch my breath. Tried not to let him get me sprung.

Once I came back down to earth, he flipped me over and gave it to me doggy-style. He pulled me back on him with every stroke.

"Ooh," I moaned.

Then, he started pulling my hair. I loved it. He stroked me harder, faster; hammering me. I was hanging like a champ. But I was loud. I was loud to my own self, so I knew I was loud. I leaned over and put my face in the pillow trying to muffle my own screams.

Jinx was touching me everywhere. His hands

were on my breasts, my hips, my thighs, and my face. He was kissing me on my spine. He was doing all kinds of new things to me.

He rolled over on his back. I got on top of him, and bounced up and down. I leaned over, and kissed his mouth. He put his hands on my waist to help me ride. I called his name like it was my own personal cheer.

Finally, relief came in like a flood. I felt his well burst. The familiar sensation erupted inside me. I bucked harder for a few seconds then joined him.

I crashed down on his chest.

"Damn, Baby Girl, it's like that? You just right." he motioned, still trying to catch his breath.

I couldn't even respond. I was exhausted. But in my mind, I was thinking, "Hell yeah!"

CHAPTER TWENTY-SEVEN

I got back to Chicago on Sunday morning. My plane touched down at Midway Airport at 9:32 am. My cell had been blowing up all morning. I knew it was Solomon, because I didn't answer any of his calls while I was in New York. Sure enough, I had 15 missed calls all from Solomon's cell.

I retrieved my truck from long-term parking. Once I was away from the traffic of the airport, I took my phone from my purse and called him.

"What's up?" I asked, when he answered.

"Where have you been all weekend, Shorty? I've been callin' you since Friday."

"Uhm, I was out of town."

"Out of town?" He repeated loudly. "When did you leave?"

"Why?"

Apparently he didn't realize we weren't a couple anymore.

"Why?" He repeated again, sounding like a parrot.

"Yeah, why?"

"What are you sayin'? I'm not supposed to ask my girl where she's been all weekend?"

"Your girl?" I repeated. "Solomon, I ain't your

289

girl. Didn't you get those pictures I left in your truck?"

He was silent. I silently gloated.

"So, you're the one that's been sendin' me those pictures?" He asked coldly.

"No," I lied. "Somebody's been sendin' pictures of you and the female with the slanted eyes, up to the salon. She's your girl, right?"

"Naw, she ain't my girl."

"Didn't you take her to the R. Kelly concert?"

"I know that bitch, Jainelle told you that."

"Why is Jainelle a bitch, cuz you messed up? You didn't have to take that slanty-eyed hoe to the concert. Anyway, Jainelle didn't have to tell me. I have pictures of you with her at the concert." I lied, again.

"I need to talk to you, in person."

"For what? You know good and well you don't wanna be with me. You wanna be with old girl." I said. "I got pictures of you all hugged up with her. I got pictures of y'all kissin' and whatnot. I got pictures of her gettin' out of your Avalanche."

"I ain't comfortable talkin' over these cell phones, Shorty. You never know whose listenin'."

"I don't care whose listenin'. I don't have nothin' else to say." I hung up on him.

* * * * *

I saw the Avalanche as soon as I turned on to my block. Instead of parking and going upstairs, I drove right past him. I didn't feel like being bothered.

He called my cell phone.

"What do you want?" I asked him.

"Where you goin'?"

"To my father's house," I lied. "If you wanna

talk to me, come on. We can talk out there."

He was silent. I knew he wouldn't follow me out to Frankfort. He was too spooked of my dad to do something like that.

"I don't feel like drivin' all the way out there just to talk to you. I'll get at you another day."

"Why don't you get at Leilani?"

Again, he was silent. He didn't expect me to know her name.

"Who?" He asked, trying to play it off.

"You know, Leilani, your girl, the one who lives at 7316 South Hartwood." I could almost see him peeing on himself. I was enjoying it.

"What you know about that?"

"Let me tell you what I know, Solomon. I know you're messin' with this girl. And I know you've been lyin' about makin' out of town runs. When you were supposed to be in St. Louis, you were with her."

Again, silence.

"On the real, I don't have hard feelings against you for gettin' with her," I continued. "It is what it is. Live your life. Do your thing. Just leave me the hell alone."

"Leave you alone?"

I almost choked. "Yeah. Leave me the hell alone!"

"Shorty," he said. His voice was pleading with me.

"What?" I didn't have any sympathy for him. I knew he would land on his feet. Grimy bastards always did.

"I know things ain't been right between us. I'm tryin' to work things out."

I sighed heavily. "Why are you talkin' slick?

291

Who in the hell do you think you're bullshittin'?
Things between us are over. There's nothin' left to be
worked out. I'm about to hang up."

"Shorty, we need to talk."

"About what? You wanna have both of us, me
and the slanty-eyed hoe?"

"That ain't it. And I ain't with that girl."

"Stop lying. I'm too tired to play with you. I
gotta go." I hung up my cell.

I put my mind on Jinx. Thought about how it
felt to have his hands on my body. That made me smile
and forget all about Solomon.

* * * * *

The Friday after finals, Solomon showed up at
the salon. He walked in and came directly to my
station. I was organizing my work counter trying to
determine if I needed to make a run to the beauty
supply store.

"Shorty," he said, softly.

I looked up at him. It was the first time I had
seen him since we went to The Cheesecake Factory
together. His full-length leather coat was open. I could
see what he was wearing. He was dressed like he just
came from court. He had on slacks and a sweater. What
used to look so good to me didn't have the same affect.

"What's up, Solomon?" I asked easily. I didn't
want to argue with him.

"Yo, you got a customer or something?"

He was acting really humble. He wasn't acting
arrogant, like I would have expected.

I shook my head, "nope."

"Can I holla at you outside for a minute?"

My next client wasn't due for another twenty minutes. I agreed.

The two of us exited the salon, then, stood off to the west of the building, where prying eyes and ears wouldn't be all in our conversation.

"Yo, you're lookin' good. You look real happy."

I smiled, "Thanks. I am happy."

"So, your new guy put a little pep in your step, huh? Gave it to you good, huh?"

I stared at him. If he wanted to have a civil conversation with me that was the wrong way for him to start it off.

"I wanted to come up here and holla at you. I mean, things went straight down hill with us. We used to be so good together. Then, everything got fucked up."

A part of me wanted to tell him that the girl with the slanted eyes was what messed up our relationship, but I knew that wasn't true. She just gave me a "guilt-free" out.

"You know we always wanted different things out of life, Solomon."

"Yeah, I guess."

"I promised myself that I wasn't messin' with no more ballers. Then you came along and I broke that promise to myself. We never had no business tryin' to mess with each other no way. We're too different. You ain't ready to stop ballin', and I can't have that around me no more."

"Nah, I could never choose no female over the hustle, Shorty. Not even you."

At least he was real enough to admit it to my face.

"You know I know you're with Jinx, now."

I tried not to let surprise show on my face.

"Your girl, Jainelle told Tippy, and you know it got back to me. At first, I was hot as hell."

"I know how you felt. I was pissed when I got those pictures of you and Leilani."

"That's different and you know it. Anyway, I thought about wildin' out on Jinx. I thought about doing some real foul shit to him. But when I calmed down, I realized that you were where you needed to be."

I let that comment ride, because I knew that was straight bullshit.

"Are you happy with Leilani?"

"Yeah, she's cool. She ain't nothin' like you, though."

"Is that a good thing, or a bad thing?"

"Sometimes it's a good thing. Sometimes, I kinda miss your ways."

I smirked at him.

"Nah, she's just different. She got the street in her veins. She can help a don out in the grind. She knows how to measure, bag it up. She ain't scared to carry it in her purse and whatnot. I never would've asked you to do nothin' like that. You weren't right for the part." He winked at me. "You were my uppity-Shorty; my Princess Shorty and a thug's passion."

I smiled. I liked the sound of that – A Princess Shorty that's a thug's passion.

"Solomon, can I ask you a question?"

"Yeah, what's up?"

"Why did you lie to me? Why did you tell me you were makin' out of town runs to St. Louis, when you knew that wasn't true?"

"What was I gonna do, Shorty? Tell you that I

was messin' with somebody else?"

"Nah, that's not what I'm talkin' about. Summer told me your father got killed doin' a drug run through St. Louis. Why would you use St. Louis in your lie? That was kind of crazy."

"Yeah," he shook his head, "I guess it was kinda messed up of me to use that location. On the real, that was the first place that came to my mind."

"I guess you wanted some of Leilani's big ass so bad, you would've told me just about anything to be free to get some, huh?"

"Aw Shorty, you know you don't care about that. Your pride is just bruised. I still think you wanted to get with Jinx all along. Me messin' with Leilani gave you the perfect opportunity."

"That's not the point. I was down for you, and you cheated on me. I saw pictures of you kissin' that broad. Do you know how, that made me feel? And you were lettin' her drive your whip. You don't think that was disrespectful?"

"I guess it was messed up. I wasn't tryin' to do you dirty, Shorty. I had beef with you for the way you were runnin' your shit. I felt like school took priority over me in your life. I wanted to find a female who would put me first."

I didn't reply, but I thought that was a typical baller response. I wasn't stroking his ego enough, so he replaced me with a female who would swing from his balls.

"Did you find everything you need in this new hoe?" I asked sarcastically.

"Quit trippin'. You don't wanna go there."

I rolled my eyes at him.

"I guess we can try to be friends. I don't know,

though. I'm not Jinx. I ain't never really been friends with a female unless I was sexin' her."

"Well, you know that's a no-go." I told him.

"Anyway, like I said, I wanted to holla at you for a minute. Let you know that I wasn't trippin' off of us not being together, seriously."

He tried not to make it obvious, but I knew the only reason he showed up, was because of who my father was. He wanted to make sure we ended on good terms, so he wouldn't be dealt with by Pretty Hill.

"Kickin' it with you was interestin', Shorty. I never met nobody like you."

"I never met nobody like you, either, Solomon."

"I never met nobody who had me checkin' for them, the way I was checkin' for you," he admitted. "It will never happen again. That was a first and the last."

We stood there staring at each other for a few seconds. I was thinking about some of the good times I had with him. I was thinking about some of the times that he made me laugh, how he how would have me wilding over the way he laid it down in the bedroom, and about how he held me when I was upset about my truck and the fact that Lynne was in the hospital.

"I gotta blow, Shorty. Give me one last hug."

I hugged him, and kissed his smooth caramel colored cheek. "Solomon, be careful out there."

"Don't worry about me. I'm that nigga."

"All right, then." That was classic Solomon, cocky until the bitter end.

He turned and walked out of my life, and into Leilani's open arms.

CHAPTER TWENTY-EIGHT

Right before Christmas, Jinx came back to Chicago for good. He flew to New York every weekend to check on his mom. I went with him as much as possible. On Christmas Eve, the two of us were at his house. We finished making love, and were lying next to each other in his bed. The news was on the television, but the sound was on mute. Neither of us was watching TV. We were looking at vacation brochures. I had them spread all across his bed. We were trying to decide where to go.

"I've never been to Hawaii." I said looking at the brochure. "The Kahala Mandarin Oriental in Oahu looks nice."

"Yo, Hawaii is like an eight hour flight, Baby Girl." He responded, spanking me lightly on the butt. "The Caribbean is closer. What about Ochos Rios or Aruba?"

"Uhm, what about Ixtapa, Mexico?" I picked up the brochure for Mexico.

"Ay P, check it out." Jinx grabbed the remote for the stereo and killed the music. Then he turned up the television.

This house, along with four others on the city's

South Side was raided today. The reporter was saying.

"I know that house," I muttered.

It was a red brick Chicago bungalow.

Suddenly, police officers were bringing two people out of the house in handcuffs. The two people were trying to cover their faces, but I could still see them.

Jinx started to laugh. "Is that your boy, Solly?"

I stared at the television blankly. There was Solomon and his girlfriend, Leilani being escorted away by the police.

"Dumb ass," I whispered.

The reporter was still talking, but I didn't hear anything she said. I was just watching her lips move.

"A street value of over seven hundred thousand dollars?" Jinx repeated.

I snapped out of my trance. That was a hell of a lot of drugs.

Jinx looked over at me. "You straight?"

"Yeah. The last time I talked to Solomon, he told me that he loved the hustle. My father used to say, the hustle don't love nobody. I guess he had to learn that lesson the hard way."

"Damn, I hope homey can afford a good lawyer."

"He'll do what he needs to do." I was confident that Solomon would land on his feet. Grimy bastards usually did. I snuggled up to Jinx.

"Anyway, I've been to Jamaica. I wanna go somewhere I've never been," I said, going back to the travel brochures.

After all, Solomon was the one going to jail. I was free; free in love, and happy. It was the first time in a long time.

PTE Order Form

QTY	TITLE	PRICE
	Around The Way Girls 2 by KaShamba Williams, LaJill Hunt & Thomas Long	$14.95
	At The Courts Mercy by KaShamba Williams	$14.95
	Dirty Dawg by Unique J. Shannon	$14.95
	Doe Boy by G. Rell	$14.95
	DRIVEN by KaShamba Williams	$14.95
	Girls From Da Hood 2 by K. Williams, Nikki Turner & Joy	$14.95
	Girls From Da Hood 3 by K.Williams, Mark Anthony, Madam K	$14.95
	Hittin' Numbers by Unique J. Shannon	$14.95
	In My Peace I Trust by Brittney Davis	$14.95
	Latin Heat by BP Love	$14.95
	One Love 'Til I Die by Tony Trusell	$14.95
	Mind Games by KaShamba Williams	$14.95
	Stiletto 101 by Lenaise Meyeil	$14.95
	The Tommy Good Story by Leondrei Prince	$14.95
	Thug's Passion by Tracy Gray	$14.95
	Victim of The Ghetto by Joel Rhodes	$14.95
	Platinum Teen Series	
	Dymond In The Rough	$6.99
	The AB-solute Truth	$6.99
	Runaway	$6.99
	Best Kept Secret	$6.99
	Total:	

Please include shipping and handling fee of $2.50.
Forms of payment accepted – money orders, credit card,
Paypal, debit cards, postal stamps and Institutional checks.
Please allow 7-10 business days for books to arrive.

Precioustymes Entertainment
229 Governors Place, #138
Bear, DE 19701

PTE Order Form

QTY	TITLE	PRICE
	Around The Way Girls 2 by KaShamba Williams, LaJill Hunt & Thomas Long	$14.95
	At The Courts Mercy by KaShamba Williams	$14.95
	Dirty Dawg by Unique J. Shannon	$14.95
	Doe Boy by G. Rell	$14.95
	DRIVEN by KaShamba Williams	$14.95
	Girls From Da Hood 2 by K. Williams, Nikki Turner & Joy	$14.95
	Girls From Da Hood 3 by K.Williams, Mark Anthony, Madam K	$14.95
	Hittin' Numbers by Unique J. Shannon	$14.95
	In My Peace I Trust by Brittney Davis	$14.95
	Latin Heat by BP Love	$14.95
	One Love 'Til I Die by Tony Trusell	$14.95
	Mind Games by KaShamba Williams	$14.95
	Stiletto 101 by Lenaise Meyeil	$14.95
	The Tommy Good Story by Leondrei Prince	$14.95
	Thug's Passion by Tracy Gray	$14.95
	Victim of The Ghetto by Joel Rhodes	$14.95
	Platinum Teen Series	
	Dymond In The Rough	$6.99
	The AB-solute Truth	$6.99
	Runaway	$6.99
	Best Kept Secret	$6.99
	Total:	

Please include shipping and handling fee of $2.50.
Forms of payment accepted – money orders, credit card,
Paypal, debit cards, postal stamps and Institutional checks.
Please allow 7-10 business days for books to arrive.

Precioustymes Entertainment
229 Governors Place, #138
Bear, DE 19701

Searching for "safe" Urban Fiction books for your
10-15 year olds to read?
Try the Platinum Teen Series.
No explicit language or explicit content.

PTE is the 1st Urban Fiction Publishing
Company to delivery a teen series of this kind!!

Coming Soon!

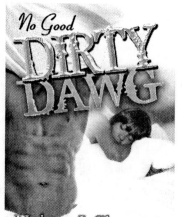

September 2007

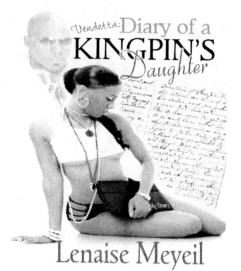

Another Author representin' Chi-town!

REVENGE IS A DISH BEST SERVED COLD... Shantae is sexy, spoiled, and one of the most ruthless females of her time. Down on her luck since the death of her mother, Shantae has had it with people using her for their personal gain - molestation, prostitution, being an eye witness to senseless bloodshed and the brutal victimization that caused her to lose her first baby - all before she turns 25. After years of silent grief, the pain is still present and Shantae begins to slowly transform. Never again will she allow someone to cause her pain. Not as long as she has her man Rio, a thoroughbred hustler, her best friend Neeko, another down chic and the piece that she carries in the tuck, out of eyes view. Armed with game and a strong desire for revenge she decides it's about time for peace in her life and if that means taking someone else's to protect herself and her family, she will. This is one urban tale you won't soon forget!

www.precioustymes.com

Black & Nobel Books
&
Distribution

1411 W. Erie Avenue
Philadelphia, PA

(215) 965-1559

www.myspace.com/blackandnobelbooks
www.blackandnobel.com